Maggie's Revenge

JB WINSOR

BOULDER DIGITAL PUBLISHING, LLC
Boulder, Colorado USA

Maggie's Revenge
by John B Winsor

Copyright © 2020 John B Winsor

All rights reserved.

For permission requests, contact:
Boulder Digital Publishing
568 Marine Street
Boulder, CO 80302

Cover & Interior Design by NZ Graphics
Maps by Caroline Borst

ISBN-13: 978-0-9829194-7-7 (paperback)
ISBN-13: 978-0-9829194-6-0 (e-book)

Library of Congress Cataloging-in-Publication Data

First Edition 2020

Printed in the United States of America

Other titles by JB Winsor

NOVELS

RIVER STONE
LOVE OF THE HUNT
THE PUNISHMENTS
MAGGIE'S REVENGE

SHORT STORIES

THE LOVER
FINDING SUGAH MAMA
DUTCH TREAT
THE WOLF
CHAPMAN BENCH
FIRE BEAR
SENIOR PROM
MEMORIES

To Tish
As Always

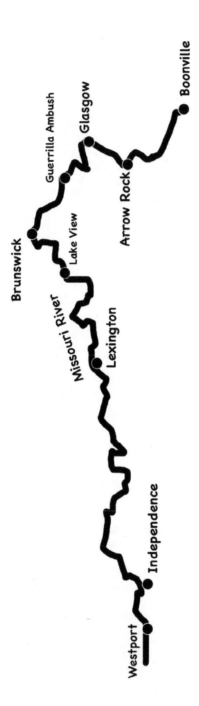

MAGGIE'S RIVER JOURNEY

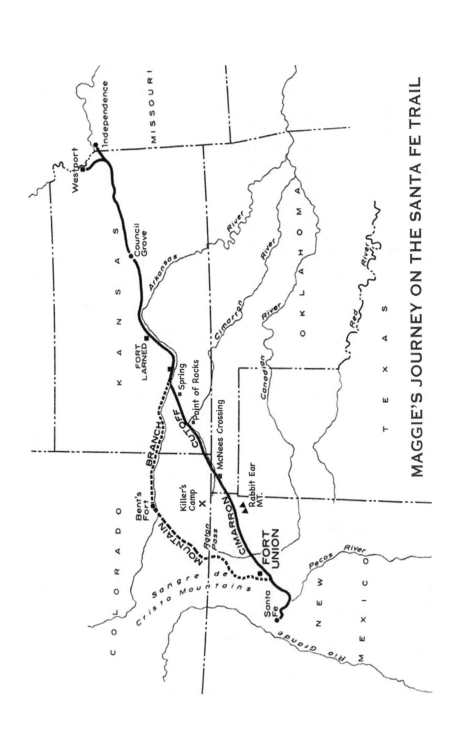

MAGGIE'S JOURNEY ON THE SANTA FE TRAIL

Chapter 1

―――――――

March 1864

Boonville, Missouri

Mrs. Margaret Hartstone, owner of *White Haven* Plantation, social and cultural maven of the Civil War frontier town of Boonville, frustrated by the law's inability to deliver justice, and ignoring all considered advice, decided to take matters into her own hands.

She snatched a wool bonnet from the four-poster wedding bed George had made from the walnut trees on their land. She'd trimmed the edge of the hat with brown cotton tape and added a long one-inch wide matching ribbon. Careful not to disturb the shining black braids coiled tight around each ear, she settled the bonnet on her head.

She shouted, "Come get my trunk, Sam. We're going to be late."

Turning in an impatient circle, she tied and retied the ribbon into a large bow. It complimented broad stripes that ran down the light gray dress and sleeves.

George appeared, leaning against to her armoire, but now was not the time to talk.

She heard footsteps running up the stairs. Sam appeared and knocked on the doorframe.

"Don't just stand there and stare, Sam. Take my trunk to the carriage."

"You looks mighty pretty today, Miz Maggie."

George nodded.

"You like this gray dress better than black?"

"Yes ma'am," Sam said, walking to her trunk. He began to pick it up but straightened and looked at her with tight lips that covered his usual bright smile.

"What?"

"I want to go with you."

"You can't."

"Is somebody else going with?"

"No."

"Not safe for a beautiful lady to travel alone."

George, standing behind Sam, nodded with vigor.

"I'll be with other people," Maggie said.

"There is bad people out there. Scallywags. I need to come to keep you safe."

"You would be a big help, Sam, but I need you to stay here to take care of the place."

"When is you coming back, Miz Maggie?"

"Sometimes, you are impertinent, Sam. Go on now."

"Yes ma'am." He picked up the trunk, walked toward the door, then stopped and turned to her.

"Is that good or bad?"

She spun toward him, swatting her skirt as if swatting a pesky fly. "Is what good or bad?"

"That word – impertinent."

"It means you ask too many questions, Sam."

"Un-huh." He disappeared through the door.

She smiled. She'd miss Sam.

She turned to talk with George, but he had vanished.

Holding her parasol in one hand, the railing with the other, she hurried down the curving stairway. She avoided the gaze of portraits of their ancestors that lined the walls. Their faces were solemn, eyes critical and disapproving of her decision.

She'd sewn greenbacks into the dress lining, before hemming up the front, so she wouldn't trip walking upstairs or down a gangplank. She'd also shortened the skirt so it wouldn't drag in the mud.

She felt matronly. Replacing the whalebone stays in her corset with gold coins added weight and bulk, destroying her still-girlish figure. That was good; she'd look less attractive and draw less attention from scallywags.

She stopped at the bottom of the stairs, standing in the wide entrance hallway, and broke her vow not to look in the parlor at her beloved Erhard piano. Its front leg had snapped in half. The keyboard, missing several teeth, dug into the hardwood floor. White and black keys had scattered across the floor. A part of Maggie's soul perished with the piano that night.

She shook her head and walked past the chest in the foyer where Captain Eppstein discovered the cockade that George had worn before the war to show his support for the Southern cause. That's when freedom of speech was the law of the land.

She turned and strode out the front door where her housemaid Sally and cook Cissy waited to say farewell. She thanked them and gave each a gold coin. They were speechless. It was more money than they could have expected to see in their lifetime. Their loyalty had earned the bonus. But with all that money would they, like several slaves on neighboring plantations, make a run to freedom in Kansas?

Sam walked Maggie through two-story porch columns and down the steps toward the open carriage. The mule brayed.

"Would you like the top covered, Miz Maggie?"

"No. I'd like fresh air."

He steadied her when she climbed into the tufted leather back seat. He placed a dust cover over her lap. She gripped the edge and pulled it high while he climbed into the driver's seat.

"You ready to go, Miz Maggie?"

She fought the impulse to scream no. Any rational person would not go. She should listen to the people she respected who warned her against going, saying, "You'll end up killing yourself."

"I can't be late. Let's go, Sam".

He slapped the reins against the mule's haunches. It raised its tail, passed gas, and then stepped out in a slow walk down the lane toward the Rocheport Road leading to Boonville.

The plantation house looked sad and worn, yet when she saw the table and chairs on the side porch, her spirits lifted. The porch had been one of their favorite summer places. Each morning, after George rode back from inspecting the fields, they would sit in its cool shade. Sally would bring them hot tea and sweets. They would talk and laugh, and there were beautiful times they would retire to the bedroom for some pre-noon intimacy.

"Can't you get that darned mule to go faster, Sam? I don't want the boat to leave without me."

"Yes ma'am." He flicked the reins against the mule's butt until it picked up the pace.

She glanced back at the house. George and Jenny stood on the second-floor portico, and he held Jenny's waist with his good arm. Maggie waved. They seemed indistinct, as if she was looking at them through a mourning veil. Would she ever see them again?

She turned and picked up her favorite possession, other than the piano, of course. It had been the very best birthday gift from her father.

The parasol.

She slid it from its cover and opened it, once again admiring its brilliant colors and tiny bells on the fringes that jingled to the rhythm of the buggy. She spun it and watched a kaleidoscope of red and yellow and blue reflect the sunlight. She held the parasol over her left shoulder and listened to the music of the bells sing counterpoint to the sound of the mule's hoof-beats.

No matter how difficult one's life, one's appearance shaped perception, and perception spoke louder than fact.

Soon after turning right on the Rocheport Road, she saw Tracy's old schoolhouse, used as a hospital after the first battle of Boonville.

"I hope I didn't embarrass you there, Mother."

Maggie spun at the sound of Jenny's voice. Her daughter sat next to her.

"I can't stand the sight of that dress. Can't you appear in something else?" Maggie asked.

"I am what you remember."

Maggie didn't want to remember.

"You took me to help at the hospital. The smell of burned flesh and the flies and the moans made me sick."

"You were a big help, especially with Jeff McCutchen."

"I'll never forget his final words."

"It was the Reverend Painter's fault."

Sam turned in his driver's seat. "Is you talking to me, Miz Maggie?"

"You never mind. I'm just talking to myself."

"Lately, you've been talking to yourself more and more. Think maybe you should put off the trip?"

"It's none of your business, Sam."

"Surely is," he muttered as he turned back toward the road, slapped the reins hard against the mule's butt, slumped his shoulders and shook his head.

Later, in front of Boonville's Thespian Hall, a long caravan of ox driven wagons blocked the intersection.

Sam reined in and set the brake. "Looks like we'll be here a while, Miz Maggie.

"Pull ahead a few more feet so those drivers can see we need to cut through. Someone will let us through." She looked at the four story high Greek revival building built by the Thespian Society.

How many posters had she posted on its columns to announce upcoming arts performances? Maggie missed being the driving force to make Boonville the cultural heart of Little Dixie.

Now Thespian Hall served as a Union hospital, its basement used as stables for officer's horses. And now, with the war, all her efforts to create a civilized society on the frontier had been destroyed, along with everything and everyone else she had loved.

"Sam, we have to cut through that line of wagons, or we'll be late."

"Yes ma'am."

"Well, do something."

Sam stood and waved to an oncoming wagon driver. He waved back.

Maggie looked at the Presbyterian Church across the street and remembered the times when Reverend Painter tried to squelch her rage at God for allowing the killings.

The Reverend's counseling of forgiveness changed after his beloved relatives died at the Battle of Vicksburg. Still, his insistence the Good Book contained the solution to her bitterness caused her to pack her family Bible, even though she found nothing in it to ease her anger. In fact, she now questioned if God existed.

Sam watched the wagon driver pass without allowing them to pass. "Not enough space between the wagons. Guess we'll have to wait."

The entire wagon train came to a halt with the sounds of creaking leather, the clanking of chains, and hee-hawing of mules. Maggie was blocked.

"We will not wait." Maggie threw off the dust cover and stood up and shouted at the oncoming wagon driver. "Please halt and let us through."

"Army business, lady. You'll have to wait."

"I'll miss my boat."

"Union business first."

Maggie folded her parasol and stepped down from the carriage. She walked toward the driver's lead mule and stood next to its nose. She waited.

"What'da doing, woman?"

The wagon in front jerked and rolled forward.

Before the driver could move his mule team, Maggie shoved her parasol in front of the lead mule's nose. She snapped it open in a flare of color and tinkling of bells. The frightened mule shied away from the umbrella. Rearing and kicking, its legs tangled in the chains of traces of its mates. One mule lost its balance and toppled, leaning against the other. The wagon couldn't move.

The wagon in front continued forward, creating space between them.

"What the hell?" the driver shouted.

She waved Sam through the open space and then turned to the driver. "Don't you dare use foul language in front of a lady!"

"You're not a lady – you're a bitch."

She hurried to the carriage and climbed in as the swearing wagon driver climbed down to untangle his mules from the traces.

As they drove past the wagon driver, Maggie said, "You wouldn't know a lady if she sat in your lap."

Chapter 2

Sam urged his mule to hurry away from the conflict with the Union wagon driver. He twisted and looked at her with a big grin. "That was sure something, Miz Maggie."

She concentrated on calming her breathing as they drove past two-story brick commercial buildings toward the river. They hurried down the dirt main street crowded with wagon trains, freighters and buggies. People scurried across, jumping mud puddles and animal dung. Her nose wrinkled from the stench.

Wounded veterans wearing ragged clothes sat on the wooden sidewalk or leaned on homemade wooden crutches. The bare stumps of legs and arms evidence of the horrors of war. The wounded begged for money or food or other kindnesses from the same people they had terrorized.

Maggie avoided eye contact. The injured needed help, but there were so many of them and she was only one woman. What could she do, other than hate the politicians who started the war and destroyed the lives of thousands?

Near the river bluff, they passed the Trigg building. Maggie wished George had been as smart as Dr. Trigg, who closed the bank he'd started in 1847 and moved his family to New York to escape the ravages of the war.

Sam reined the mule to a slow walk as the buggy reached the end of Main Street at the edge of the bluff. He stopped as the street plunged down to the river's edge.

Maggie saw the north edge of the river brown with silt and on the far side plowed fields and beyond them the timbered bluffs where the guerrilla, Quantrill, was rumored to hide out during the winter.

"You ready, Miz Maggie?"

She braced her leather walking boots against the facing seat. "I'm ready now."

"Hold on tight, hear?" Sam urged the mule over the edge.

The iron buggy wheels screeched and sparked against cobblestones as Sam maneuvered it down the steep road toward the steamship. The odor of rotten fish, damp earth, decay, and stench both human and animal enveloped her. Heaving and sweating Negro slaves loaded the ship, chanting monotonous river melodies.

Her fingers tightened on her parasol when she spotted that blockhead Union Captain Eppstein, who had threatened to imprison her. He waited next to the gangplank. Two blue-coated soldiers stood at attention by his side.

Would he arrest her? On what grounds? Treason? Had one of her friends informed on her?

She'd openly criticized the latest Union martial law order to shoot armed civilians on sight. It would have been easier to have lied and supported the rule. Still, she hated liars and had been open about her opinion.

One had to be honest. Of course she had voiced her view about the stupidity of the law to shoot armed civilians. How else could innocent people protect themselves from roaming gangs of robbers and murderers?

There was no way to board the ship without confronting Captain Eppstein. She pushed her Colt Pocket revolver deeper into the concealed pocket of her dress. She looked down, hoping the gun did not produce a noticeable bulge.

Three years ago, Eppstein, a German immigrant, now dressed in Union blue, had ordered his troops to search her home for firearms and proof of Confederate support. He'd found George's cockade, the blue ribbon worn before the war to show support for the Southern cause.

Evidence of treason, Captain Eppstein had gloated. She'd claimed it had been left unnoticed by one of their guests. He couldn't prove otherwise.

She moved her parasol to her left shoulder to hide her face, and then pulled her bonnet tight. She felt the lace around her throat and touched the locket George had given her.

"Miz Maggie? Captain Eppstein is standing near the boat."

"I see him. Keep going."

Eppstein would love to find an excuse to get rid of her.

Had someone told him she was leaving? Was it someone jealous of her unofficial position as the cultural leader of Boonville and Little Dixie, and wanting to cause her trouble?

She'd learned making enemies was the curse of achievement.

What had the world come to if you couldn't trust your friends?

Halfway down to the landing, Sam stopped the mule to allow it to catch its breath. She heard wagon masters' shouts and the bellowing of oxen.

Should she risk arrest or turn back to the safety of the world she'd grown to hate?

Captain Eppstein turned and shaded his eyes with his hand to better see the buggy. Waiting for her? Did he recognize her? What proof did he have to arrest her?

Well, she carried proof. Under martial law, she thought again, any citizen caught bearing firearms were to be immediately executed. She checked her revolver. Should she try to hide it by jamming it between the seat and back cushion? She shook her head, pushed the gun further into the folds of her dress.

Sam said, "I can turn around as soon as we gets to the landing. Let's go home."

"Keep going." She opened her valise and retrieved her Bible.

There were so many ox-drawn wagons and livestock and people on the landing that Captain Eppstein might not notice them. Yet why did he look up at her buggy?

They neared the landing, and she inhaled deeply to calm her mind. The safest thing would be to flee.

She had to stop looking at Captain Eppstein, or he'd notice her.

Concentrate on the steamboat.

Captain Kinney's *Cora II* looked like a giant three-tiered wedding cake adorned by two black smokestack candles. The anchored stern-wheeler faced upstream. There was no dock, just the large cobblestone landing. Two large gangplanks swung from the bow to the shore, to allow cargo and passengers to transfer.

The ship's sizeable main deck was filled with cargo: firewood for the boilers; cotton bales; barrels of whiskey; boxes of retail goods; farm implements; cattle; mules; and chickens. Many passengers, who for the price of several dollars plus help with gathering firewood for the ship's boilers, would endure the trip in the open.

Captain Eppstein looked over the crowd at the empty road above her. He turned to the two blue-coated soldiers and said something. Then he pulled out a pocket watch, stared at it, and once again looked at the road.

Was he waiting for someone else?

Oh, God, she hoped so.

She forced herself to study the ship.

On the main deck, passengers scrambled for space near the warmth of the boilers and undercover from inclement weather, where they would sleep and eat whatever food they had brought with them.

The second deck contained the first-class cabins, a dining area, and a salon. The third – and highest, and the smallest – layer of the cake held the pilothouse.

The buggy arrived at the foot of the road.

"I'll turn us around and go home," Sam said.

"Drive the buggy between Captain Eppstein and the gangplank."

"You sure, Miz Maggie?"

"Just do it."

Sam nodded and jockeyed the buggy toward the bow of the ship through a swarm of wagons, swearing drivers, slaves hauling cargo, passengers, and well-wishers. Excited children shouted and scrambled through the crowd.

Sam ignored curses from other wagon drivers and parked the buggy near the gangplank. He pulled the brake handle to lock the wheels and jumped down to open the door for Maggie. She threw off the dust cover, handed the parasol to Sam, who held it above her as she stepped onto the cobblestones.

"Mrs. Hartstone! One word, please." Captain Eppstein strode toward her.

No escape. Maggie turned towards him, holding her Bible like a shield against her chest, right hand in her pocket, fingers wrapped around the handle of her revolver.

Chapter 3

The Captain tipped his broad felt hat in greeting. He was well built, with a large head and blond hair showing below his hat. He looked at her with bright blue eyes.

He stopped uncomfortably close. Maggie took a step back, her fingers closed on the handle of her revolver. Sam stood by her side and held her parasol high to provide shade. Would Sam be stupid and try to protect her if Eppstein were to arrest her? She prayed he'd stay out of this. It was a hanging offense for a slave to interfere in white people's business.

Captain Eppstein's penetrating eyes studied her, glanced at her Bible and his hand touched the trunk strapped to the back of her buggy.

"Going somewhere, Mrs. Hartstone?"

She had expected a hostile tone in his voice. "Surely you don't object to me leaving on a trip upriver, Captain?"

His smile unnerved her. "Of course not, Mrs. Hartstone. I think it's a grand idea."

She hated people who lied. "Really?" Her fingers loosened on the gun's handle.

"Our lives will be much more pleasant if you do not return until after the war."

She blinked. Whose lives? His? Hers? "I see. I cannot promise you I'll be gone that long, but I will let you know the minute I return."

"I hope we could become friends after the peace like we were before the war."

How naïve, she wanted to say. They hadn't been friends before the war. He had been a merchant. She had been as pleasant to him as to anyone else in town when she shopped. How could he relate common courteousness with friendship? Especially after he had invaded her home and threatened her with treason?

Captain Eppstein noticed a buggy driving toward the landing. He turned back to her. "Here are the officers I need to greet. Please excuse me, Mrs. Hartstone. Have a pleasant trip." He tipped his hat, turned on his heels, and walked away to meet his guests.

Maggie exhaled and slumped. Sam held her elbow to steady her.

"I thinks he has designs on you, Miz Maggie."

"Don't be ridiculous, Sam. He's only interested in a widow with a large plantation. I should talk to Captain Kinney about boarding."

Sam stood next to the buggy to guard her trunk.

She turned toward the ship and smiled when she saw Ephraim Johnson standing near the gangplank, stroking his long white beard down toward a potbelly.

He was shorter than Maggie, and brown eyes watched her from under a well-worn wide-brimmed felt hat. His smile revealed tobacco-stained, crooked teeth. He leaned heavily on his right leg due to a limp he acquired in the Mexican War. A widower, he must have been twenty years older than Maggie.

"What a pleasant surprise!" she said. "What are you doing here?" She could not have asked for a better neighbor and more reliable friend; she had reached an agreement for him to manage White Haven while she was gone.

"Came to see you off, Maggie." He ordered his buggy driver to help Sam carry her trunk.

She wondered if Ephraim wanted to back out of their business deal or renegotiate it at the last minute when she had no choice.

Captain Kinney greeted them at the foot of the gangplank and introduced them to Andrew Jackson Spahr, a towering, powerfully built young man with sandy hair. His brown eyes locked tight on hers. He seemed to resist any urge to look at the rest of her.

He shook her hand. "Please call me Bud."

"Aren't you David's son?"

"Yes, ma'am. Captain Kinney asked me to look after you during the trip."

The Captain had not wanted to sell her a ticket. It was, in his experience, too dangerous for a beautiful woman to travel alone. So this had ended up being his compromise.

"Why aren't you working with your brothers at your family's tobacco plant?" she asked.

His forehead furrowed.

Sibling problems?

"I've loved the river since I was a little boy. Captain Kinney agreed to teach me to be a captain, so someday I can have my own boat."

Captain Kinney stepped forward. "This is your last chance, Mrs. Hartstone. Still set on going?"

"Nothing will change my mind," she cut a glance to Captain Eppstein. "When will we be leaving?"

"At dawn," Captain Kinney said.

"Oh, I thought we'd depart this afternoon."

"The Missouri River always changes its course. It is too dangerous to travel at night. We need daylight to navigate with safety."

"Oh. I misunderstood."

"Bud will show you to your cabin, where you can unpack your things. A steward's bell will announce dinner at six. We depart at dawn. I'll be piloting this trip. Welcome aboard, Mrs. Hartstone."

She stepped onto the gangplank and touched the Captain's elbow. "Thank you for making this possible, Captain."

She actually pried a smile out of him.

They followed Bud across the main deck, up a set of stairs to the cabin level. The large salon area contained tables and comfortable lounge chairs. She paused and looked at the upright piano, its black and white keys. She shook memories from her head. Several passengers gave her curious looks as she walked through the salon into the hall toward the cabins.

Bud opened a door at the end of the hall. "I hope you find this satisfactory, Mrs. Hartstone."

She stepped into a lovely compartment and touched the double bed and trailed her fingers across the down comforter. A large oak armoire was more than adequate for her clothes. A chair and combination desk-dressing table and mirror occupied the far wall. Sunlight poured through a window. She would be able to read and write in private.

As she turned to put her Bible on the table, she overheard Sam whispering to Ephraim, something about her talking to herself.

"Sam, you may place my trunk next to the wardrobe." She was glad she hadn't brought Sally; she was perfectly able to unpack her own clothes.

Bud excused himself, and Ephraim ordered his driver to wait at his buggy. Sam and Ephraim looked at each other and then watched her.

"You may return to the plantation now, Sam," she said.

He shuffled from foot to foot and cut a swift glance at Ephraim before lowering his head.

"What is it, Sam?" she asked.

"Well, I was just a-thinking."

"That can be dangerous."

"Im-pert-t-nut?"

"Close enough."

Ephraim stroked his beard as he watched them.

"It's not too late," Sam said.

"Too late?" she asked.

"I'll go with you. To look over you."

Ephraim nodded. "I agree with Sam."

"I know. You offered to send your nephew to babysit me." She regretted the edge to her voice.

Sam nodded furiously. "Yes, ma'am. I'll get some food from the store and live down on the main deck, but I'll be here for you. I hear it don't cost but a dollar or two for a soul to travel on the first deck."

"I can't take you away from your family, Sam."

"They'll get along just fine without me. Besides, we're coming back pretty soon, isn't we?"

She walked to him, put her hands on his shoulders, and pecked his cheek, something she'd never done before. Sam's eyes widened and he touched his face. He looked at Ephraim for guidance.

Ephraim shook his head.

Maggie said, "Take the buggy back home. Ephraim will need your help keeping up the place while I'm gone."

Sam's face deflated. "You're making a mistake, Miz Maggie."

She turned toward the dresser and caught their reflection in the mirror. Sam leaned close, whispering something she couldn't hear to Ephraim, who nodded and then glanced at her.

Sam walked out of the cabin.

Ephraim said, "He says you're talking with imaginary people. Worried you're not fit to go."

She turned toward Ephraim. "Take care of him while I'm gone."

Ephraim nodded. "A little bold, but I wish they were all that good."

"It's time for me to unpack. Thank you for coming to see me off, Ephraim."

"Plenty of time, Maggie. You can unpack later. Join me in the salon before I go."

So he did have something on his mind.

Chapter 4

Maggie locked her cabin door and they walked to the salon, where several passengers lounged. A newspaper hid the face of a tall man sitting cross-legged in a tufted-leather chair.

Another passenger – a portly, short, curly-bearded man – read a book through thick spectacles. He wore a crumpled old suit, and his white shirt had lost its starch long ago. His tie was askew; it looked like a child had tried to tie the knot. He looked at them with a harmless, dimpled smile. Ephraim nodded at him. She ignored the man. They selected a table far enough away so as not to be overheard.

The steward asked for their order.

"Your best bourbon for me," Ephraim said.

"Of course,'" the waiter said. "Mixed with water?"

"Straight, in a shot glass. A glass of water on the side."

The steward turned to Maggie.

"I'll have the same," she said.

The steward's eyebrows rose. He looked at Ephraim.

Ephraim gave him a slight nod.

Anger flared in her belly. Men never thought she was capable. Did it just happen to her, or to all women? Men hovered, acting like gentlemen, but it seemed to her they were grasping for power. Where was their respect? She could make her own decisions.

The steward brought their drinks, and set down her whiskey with a look of disapproval on his face.

Ephraim raised his shot glass and said, "Here's to a successful trip."

She swallowed the bourbon, thumped down the shot glass, and savored the burning sensation slide down her throat.

"I was concerned Captain Eppstein was here to stop you," Ephraim said.

"The majority of St. Louis' population is made up of blockheads like Eppstein, who believe in universal freedom. Without those German immigrants, General Price could have taken the state for the Southern cause."

"And we'd control the Mississippi and Missouri Rivers. But the reality is that it didn't happen," Ephraim said.

"I hate the reality of this war – the torn relationships, suspicion, polarization, fear, mistrust. I hate the 'if you aren't on my side, you are my enemy' attitude. I hate the contempt each side displays toward the other. How can family members get so hot-blooded that they shoot one another? Why can't people respect each other's differences?"

Ephraim took a sip of whiskey. "It's called war, Maggie. It's been like this since Cain and Abel."

"Well, I don't like what the world has become. And I wonder; when one side eventually wins the war, will the wounds mend? Will we return to a peaceful, civilized society?"

They sat in silence for a few moments. The tall man reading the newspaper turned a page. Then he looked up and gave her a brazen examination that began at her feet and drifted over her body to her eyes.

Heat rose to her cheeks. Thankfully, the gold coins hidden in her corset made her look dumpy and less attractive – he was obviously not a gentleman.

A far cry from the portly gentleman, his suit looked custom-made, his shirt starched, his tie perfect. His mustache was as fair as his hair. A long scar that stretched from his left ear to his chin marred his stunning good looks. At the same time, it made him look dangerously handsome. He smiled at her with brilliant white teeth.

Ephraim caught her glancing at the man. "Sam's right, you know. You shouldn't be traveling alone. In fact, you shouldn't be going at all. Nothing good can come of this. There's still time for me to drive you back to White Haven, where you belong."

"I've said all there is to say about my plans."

The steward returned, and they ordered another round.

"And there's one other thing that bothers me," she said, wanting to let it all out.

"What's that?" Ephraim leaned back, hands resting on his belly.

"No one bothers to ask a woman what she really thinks, what she really believes. Men make assumptions about what they see. They believe what they perceive without bothering to ask for the truth."

"Like what?"

"Like Captain Eppstein. He's fighting for the Union, yet he owns a slave. Hasn't given her freedom. And he sees me at *White Haven* with all our slaves, and his perception is that I'm pro-slavery."

Ephraim lurched back in surprise. "I thought you stood for the Southern Cause."

"In spite of the Bible approving slavery, I'm against it. I believe all men should be free . . ."

Ephraim slapped his palm on the table. "I can't believe this."

The handsome scallywag lowered his newspaper to look at them.

"You never asked what I believe. George and I argued all the time about slavery. I understand freeing the slaves will ruin the plantations. I understand we need people to plant and harvest the crops. But I asked him why don't the politicians and Lincoln come up with a plan to buy all the slaves from owners and then set them free? That would give owners enough money to pay wages to the slaves so all the economics balance? It would be cheaper than this stupid war."

"You just don't understand . . ."

"That's what George said. Then you come up with a better plan."

"Well . . ."

"The point is that you, like Captain Eppstein, thought I was pro-slavery, but I'm not. I should have freed them before I left."

Ephraim shook his head and glanced at the ceiling.

"And here's another surprise," Maggie said. "Had women the right to vote, I would have voted for Lincoln."

"Oh, dear God. One never knows what's in the mind of a woman."

Maggie chuckled. "Just ask her."

The steward delivered their drinks. Ephraim looked relieved. Maggie picked up her shot glass and smelled the bourbon's scent: warm caramel and toasted vanilla.

Ephraim raised his shot glass as a toast. "You are quite a woman, Maggie, but don't overestimate yourself. Sam is right. You shouldn't be going on this quest."

"I . . ."

He cut her off. "Let me finish. You've turned into a hell of a shot, but what you are doing is a lot different than shooting squirrels and rabbits. Bad guys shoot back. Or do you have something else in mind?"

"They stole George's horse. I'm going to bring Traveler home."

"You can't bring George and Jenny back, Maggie."

She sat in silence and glanced at the passenger with the scar on his cheek. He smiled at her.

Ephraim coughed into his fist and then stroked his beard. "There's something else."

She turned her gaze from the scallywag. "What?"

"Sam's worried you're not of right mind."

She shook her head in surprise. "He what?"

He stared out the window and then turned to look directly into her eyes. "He told me you have been talking to yourself."

"He should keep his thoughts to himself."

"He worries about you, Maggie. Is it true?"

"How long ago did your Emma die?"

"Eight years ago. What does that have to do with it?"

"Have you ever talked to her since then?"

He sat back in the chair. "Talk to my wife after she died? Never heard of such a crazy thing." He shook his head. "Nope. Never heard from her, thank the good Lord."

"Why thank the Lord?" she asked.

"Cuz toward the end of our marriage whatever words came to her mind flowed directly out of her mouth. Words, words, words. Came out like a river current. Not that I didn't love her dearly."

She sipped the bourbon. There was no use to try to explain her conversations with Jenny and George. Talking to ghosts wasn't something one talked about in civilized society. Ephraim thought she was going nutty. Maybe she was crazy.

"I agree with Sam," Ephraim continued. "I don't believe you're thinking straight. Maybe it would be better to let me drive you home, give you time to ponder over things a little better."

She raised her glass. "Here's to both of us, Ephraim. Thank you for teaching me how to shoot and agreeing to manage my place while

I'm gone. To our success."

Ephraim stood, said goodbye, and limped toward the door, past the tall man. Each nodded to the other. Their gestures seemed to her to be an acknowledgment, respect, and challenge at the same time.

She stared at her empty whiskey shot glass, hoping she hadn't alienated Ephraim, but she wasn't crazy. Not by a long shot.

"Hello." The handsome man stood in front of her table. "My name is . . ."

"I'm certain that before the end of the trip we will be properly introduced. If you will excuse me, I must unpack." She stood up, brushed past him and walked across the salon toward her cabin.

Chapter 5

Maggie returned to her cabin and unpacked her trunk. She hung her fashionable travel dresses, three cotton camp dresses for the trail, and skirts in the armoire. Her shirts, bodices, chemises, crotchless pantaloons, cotton stockings, and lace fingerless mitts fit on the top shelf of the armoire.

Unpacked, she wondered what had attracted that scallywag's interest. The man's attention was annoying yet, at the same time, a bit of a pleasant shock: she'd believed she was beyond titillation. She sat at the dressing table, unwound her braids, picked up a hairbrush, and looked in the mirror. Even though her gold coin filled corset hid her figure, she still looked younger than her thirty-five years. Long eyelashes set off intense almond eyes, arched eyebrows, a cream-smooth face, petite nose, and full lips. Her neck was long and sensuous.

"You're making a mistake, Maggie."

She spun to see George leaning against the wall next to the armoire, tall and handsome. He scratched the stump of his right arm.

"I hate it when you do that."

"What, surprise you?"

"Scratch it."

"My fingers itch."

"You don't have any fingers."

"Crazy, isn't it? They still itch. But you can't leave, and you can't undo the past, Maggie. Get off the boat and go home while you still can."

She shook the brush at him. "Don't you talk to me about mistakes, George Hartstone. Not after running off to join General Price and getting your arm shot off."

"That's not fair, Maggie."

"Fair? I haven't said it before, George, but I'll say it now: You came home half a man. Your laziness killed our daughter and yourself, and I'm good as dead. So don't you dare talk to me about my decision! Justice must be done."

"You're as stubborn as an old Missouri mule."

"Learned it from you." She slammed the brush on the table.

"And another thing. You don't know how to ride a horse."

"I've told you, ladies don't ride horses."

"Betty Nothingham is an excellent horseman."

"I wonder . . ."

"What?"

"Did you ever . . . ride with Betty Notingham?"

He slowly faded into the wall.

"Come back here. We need to talk this out." But he didn't reappear.

She wondered what sparked her question about George's infidelity. It was the first time in their marriage she'd questioned his admiration for the slut. George's avoiding the issue was all she needed to know.

She should have kept quiet.

Her hands trembled, and she stared into the mirror. The face that stared back hid the gray loneliness in her heart.

"You're more beautiful than when I married you."

George now sat on the end of the bed. Could she will him back whenever she wanted?

"I wanted to tell you that I've never felt so lonely."

"That's natural. You've only been a widow for a year and a half."

"I've always felt lonely, even when I was young. The only time I didn't feel gray was when I was with you. Or when I played the piano." She smiled sadly. "Sometimes, I even feel alone when I'm among other people."

"Why didn't you tell me this when I was alive?"

"I wonder if my mother felt lonely, too? I doubt if my father did."

"I don't know, Maggie."

"I never asked them. I don't know much about their relationship. Now there are so many things I'd like to know about them."

"You should have talked with them when they were alive. It's too late now."

There was a knock on her door and a voice. "Dinner is served in thirty minutes, Mrs. Hartstone."

When she looked back into the mirror, George had disappeared. She brushed her shining black hair, parted her hair in the middle, wove two braids, and then curled each over an ear.

She picked out a full white-cuffed shirt with full sleeves and a dark gathered skirt and wrapped a broad white sash around her waist.

Maggie thought about leaving her revolver in the cabin but decided she should get used to carrying it, no matter the circumstances. So she hid it in her waist sash and walked with as much regal poise as she could muster, listening to her skirt swish as she walked into the salon.

Four Union army officers sat at one table. Captain Kinney rose from the Captain's table and invited her to sit with him and several other travelers.

He introduced her to the men at his table. Mr. William Beckly was the portly and kindly book reader; Mr. Henry Herndon, the scarred scallywag; and a man she'd not yet met, Mr. David Williams.

Williams was slight but well built, with an intelligent-looking head and enormous bushy eyebrows. Muttonchops curled to the corner of his thin lips, and he had penetrating black eyes and a gravelly, sophisticated voice.

Captain Kinney pulled out the chair on his right for her, and she smiled at the men. She hung her purse on the back of her chair, gathered her skirt, and sat down.

Captain Kinney raised his wine glass and offered a toast. "Here's to a safe and prosperous trip."

Maggie asked, "Is there reason to believe our trip might not be safe, Captain?"

"There's nothing to be alarmed about, Mrs. Hartstone. We've made many trips without incident."

Mr. Herndon smiled with his flashing white teeth. "What the Captain is reluctant to say in these uncertain times, Mrs. Hartstone, is that Quantrill's guerrillas freely roam the country through which we will be traveling."

The Captain's eyes hardened.

Mr. Beckly's rotund face paled, eyes flashing nervously. He took off his glasses and wiped them with the napkin that he'd tucked into his shirt collar.

Mr. Herndon continued, "They have been known to shoot at steamboats and rob the passengers."

"While that's true, Mr. Herndon," the Captain said, giving Maggie a reassuring smile, "we have not yet experienced those problems, and we do not expect to."

The waiter arrived with the soup course, a creamy potato leek.

She decided to redirect the conversation. "What is the purpose of your trip, Mr. Beckly?"

Mr. Beckly coughed into his fist. "I am a salesman of agricultural goods. And yours, Mrs. Hartstone?"

She pretended not to have heard and asked the rogue, Mr. Herndon, about the purpose of his trip.

His mocking eyes locked with hers. "I'm traveling west to seek fame and fortune."

That was undoubtedly dishonest. There had to be more to that story. Maggie concentrated on her soup, hoping they would not ask about her business. She shouldn't have brought up the subject. She didn't want them to know her real business, but she wouldn't lie.

Mr. Herndon turned his smile on Mr. Williams, "And you?"

Mr. Williams put his soupspoon down and looked at each of them as if preparing a vital proclamation. Bright eyes betrayed the excitement his voice sought to hide. "I come from Boston to examine property I purchased in a newly developed town, Lake View. Perhaps you've heard of it?"

Captain Kinney nodded. "I saw a new sign for Lake View on my last trip, but could not see the town for the river bluff. I have heard nothing about it. There is no dock there, so we'll have to improvise to drop you off."

"Lake View is a new concept in development," Mr. Williams explained. "We've kept its promotion quiet because we want to control the kinds of people who live there. We will accept only the cultured best. I intend to settle there to take advantage of its growth."

Captain Kinney raised his wine glass. "We wish you the best of luck, Mr. Williams."

The waiter removed the soup dishes and brought the main course: braised beef and potatoes.

"Who are the Union officers, Captain?" Maggie asked.

"They've been assigned to Fort Leavenworth. The tall one will be in charge of building Fort Zarah, about 150 miles west of Leavenworth."

"Unusual name, Zarah," Williams observed.

The Captain said, "Quantrill's Raiders disguised themselves by wearing Union blue jackets and rode into a Union detachment. They massacred over 100 men. Young Major Henry Zarah Curtis and a man by the name of Johnny Fry, the first westbound rider of the Pony Express, were among those killed. General Curtis named the new fort after his son."

Mr. Williams spoke up. "The eastern newspapers paint Quantrill and his gang as ruthless killers, not bound by the rules of war. Is that true?"

Mr. Beckly pulled the napkin off his stomach, revealing soup spots on either side of his suit coat. "Newspapers exaggerate everything to sell copies."

"It's certainly no exaggeration," said Mr. Herndon. "Quantrill killed every man and boy in Lawrence – more than 150 overall."

"But they did not kill the women, girls, or babies of either sex," Mr. Beckly said. "Besides, the Lawrence raid was in retaliation for the Union's murder of women relatives of Quantrill's men. The Union couldn't catch Quantrill, so they arrested his men's wives and sisters and jailed them in Kansas City. The jail collapsed. The women were maimed or killed. Quantrill's raid on Lawrence was an eye-for-eye retaliation."

"What about his cold-blood shooting twenty unarmed Union soldiers taken off the train in Carthage?" Williams asked.

Maggie stood up, picked up her purse, and said, "Thank you for a wonderful dinner, Captain. It's time for me to retire." The men stood, and she walked past the piano toward her cabin.

At the entrance to the hall, she glanced back at the table. All of the men - except Mr. Herndon – were talking. He caught her eye, nodded, and flashed his smile.

She turned toward her cabin, torn between being insulted or pleased.

Chapter 6

The next day, the boat stopped at Arrow Rock. Standing on the hurricane deck under the shade of her parasol, Maggie watched passengers and freight unload and load.

She heard footsteps approach behind her. Mr. Herndon stopped and stood next to her. "What a beautiful parasol. I've never seen one with bells on the umbrella."

She couldn't help but spin the parasol, to hear the bells ring.

"The colors are so unusually bright," Herndon continued. "Where did you get it?"

"My father brought it as a gift from Paris. Now, if you'll excuse me, I must go below to catch up on some reading." She walked down into the salon and discovered the room was empty. Everyone must be in town or watching the activities.

She walked to the upright piano, looked at the keys. Her fingers spread, hand reaching for the keyboard, but she stopped an instant before touching the keys. She turned her back to the piano and returned to her cabin.

Later, deciding her cabin was too lonely, she returned to the still-empty salon. She found a comfortable chair and read her Bible, which also provided a shield from unwanted conversations. However, reading the *Good Book* did not help her understand her relationship with God – if He existed. How did they know He was a male? Why not a woman god? Obviously a female supreme being would not allow wars and hate and suffering. In fact, there where times she wondered if there was a god at all, that people simply needed a myth to explain what is not knowable.

Yes, when overwhelmed and desperate, she prayed to God for help, and later felt she was a hypocrite to call on Him only when she needed support. She envied people who had unshakable faith, yet she noticed many of those used their absolute certainty to justify greed and cruelty. Besides, the Bible was full of contradictions like its conflicting directives for revenge and forgiveness.

During dinner with the others, Mr. Herndon asked about the purpose of her trip.

"I travel west to attend to private business matters," she said, hoping they wouldn't pry.

And indeed, all Mr. Herndon said was, "I see."

The group fell silent as if they were aware that they stood on the edge of a forbidden boundary. Several minutes later, Mr. Herndon suggested the men play cards to pass the time after dinner.

Maggie returned to her cabin, undressed, sat on the edge of the bed and willed George to return. Nothing happened.

Jenny had appeared several times at *White Haven*. If she could see George here again, she might be able to call forth her daughter. Oh, God, how she missed Jenny. Missed them both.

She failed to conjure them, so she blew out the oil lamp and crawled under the quilt.

There was so much she didn't know about the journey ahead, mainly about the Santa Fe and Oregon Trails. Sam had taught her how to harness the mule and drive the buggy. But what else did she need to know about traveling on the prairie and avoiding its dangers? She needed help from someone experienced.

Mr. Beckly didn't seem experienced, nor did Mr. Williams, the man from back east. Captain Kinney's experience was obviously on the river. That left Mr. Henry Herndon. She didn't know enough about his background to see if he could be helpful. She'd have to find out.

Later the next afternoon, the *Cora II* pulled in next to a wooded shore, anchored, and lowered her gangplanks. The crew and first deck passengers departed to cut firewood for the ship's boilers.

At supper, the Captain suggested that Maggie join him, at her convenience, in the pilothouse the following day. "You might be interested in watching how we control the ship. At the very least, it would provide a refreshing view."

So, midafternoon the next day, Maggie sat at the desk in her cabin, looking in the mirror to check her face. She'd realized long ago that her loop-around-the-ears hairstyle was perfect for framing her oval face and ivory skin. The only other style she used for informal activities was brushing her hair down and tying it in back with a ribbon.

She touched her cheek. It was smooth, untouched by the sun; it wouldn't do for a lady to be sunburned. The walk to the pilothouse was short, so she wouldn't need to wear a bonnet or take her parasol.

She walked through the salon, pausing to listen to a Union officer play the piano. She returned Mr. Herndon's gaudy smile with a mildly pleasant expression. She'd learn about his experiences later.

Bud Spahr passed her on the stairwell to the pilothouse. "I'm sorry I haven't checked on you, Mrs. Hartstone, but Captain Kinney keeps me informed. Once again, please don't hesitate to call if you need anything."

"Thank you," she said, before continuing up the stairs.

She thought about knocking on the pilothouse door to announce her presence. Still, she had come at the Captain's invitation, after all. She opened the door and peeked inside.

They hadn't heard her open the door. Captain Kinney stood at the ship's steering wheel, hands spinning the spokes, turning the ship's bow toward the far shore.

Portly Mr. Beckly stood close behind the Captain – close – too familiar. Then she saw the derringer Beckly pointed at the back of the Captain's head.

She sucked in a deep breath and pushed the door partway closed and held on to the handle. She feared Beckly might hear her panting through the crack in the door.

Maggie shook her head, peeked inside.

Mr. Beckly pressed the pistol muzzle against the Captain's neck. "There! Land the boat there." He pointed to horsemen waiting, partly concealed by the cottonwoods on the shore 300 yards ahead.

"It's too shallow. I can't land there." The Captain made no attempt to steer toward shore.

Mr. Beckly shoved the derringer hard against his neck. "Don't take me for a fool! We've tested the depth of the water. Land there now!"

The Captain spun the wheel, and the bow swung further toward the guerrillas' hiding place.

"Quantrill?" the Captain asked.

"And Bloody Bill Anderson," Mr. Beckly chuckled.

She couldn't let this happen. Shouting for help would only alert Beckly. He might pull the trigger, kill the Captain, lock the door, and take over the steering wheel. She slipped the Colt revolver from her waist sash, tiptoed into the wheelhouse, and crept close behind the men.

"You can't do this, Beckly, they'll kill innocent people," the Captain said.

"That's the fortunes of war. Besides, we need supplies."

Maggie smelled Beckley's sour scent. She raised her revolver and pointed the muzzle an inch from the back of Beckly's neck. She pulled the hammer back. The metallic click of the cylinder locking into place made Mr. Beckly freeze.

"Mr. Beckly will not be shooting anyone, Captain. Steer back to the middle of the river."

The Captain spun the wheel to the left. He rang the bell three times, then three times again. Agonizing seconds later, the bow began a slow turn toward the middle of the river. The ship was close to the shore.

"You're a woman. You won't shoot me!"

Maggie forced herself to laugh. "That's what the last man I killed said before I pulled the trigger. Place your left hand on the muzzle of your gun and hand it to me over your shoulder."

"I don't believe you," Beckly said.

"Hand it over."

"Shoot me then. Captain, steer back toward land."

Maggie's hand shook as she pushed the muzzle against his earlobe. Her finger closed on the trigger. "Give me your gun. Now."

"Fuck off, bitch! You'll never pull the trigger." He swung toward her.

The Captain swung his elbow and hit Beckley in the back. Beckley staggered into Maggie. She stepped back, pointed her revolver at his leg, and pulled the trigger.

Beckley howled. The derringer fell from his hand and clattered against the floor. He lurched into her. She stepped back and swung her revolver against his face. He collapsed into a fetal position on the floor, holding his leg and moaning. Blood spurted from his nose.

Maggie stood over him, pointing her pistol at him. "That will teach you not to swear in front of a lady."

The Captain picked up Beckley's derringer, and slipped it into his pocket.

She glanced at the shore. The guerrillas ran to the edge of the riverbank and began shooting at them. A bullet crashed through the window, spewing shards of glass into the cabin. Maggie's cheek stung. She felt warm blood course down her neck.

The door flew open; Bud Spahr rushed in, pistol in hand.

Captain Kinney shouted, "He's a spy for the Quantrill gang. Get him out of here and tie him up."

Spahr lifted Mr. Beckly up and helped the groaning man limp through the door.

"Are you hurt, Mrs. Hartstone?"

"Just a cut on my cheek. What will happen to him?"

"We'll turn him over to the Union officers for execution."

"Execution?" Maggie slid her revolver in her waist sash and pressed a handkerchief against her cheek to slow the bleeding.

"Union orders. All guerrillas are to be shot on sight."

Another bullet smashed through a window and buried itself in the wood ceiling with a loud thump. Too late, they ducked.

Some on the main deck returned shots at the Quantrill bunch.

She stood next to the Captain while the ship steamed out of rifle range. She couldn't stop her left leg from shaking. Her foot tapped against the floor, making a rhythmic sound she hoped the Captain didn't hear. She pressed her hand against her thigh to slow the nervous foot.

She said, "You were right about things being more interesting in the pilothouse."

The Captain smiled for the second time.

"I should thank you, Mrs. Hartstone. We would all have been killed without your intervention. Now, would you please go below and let Bud look at your cheek?"

"Please don't tell others that I carry a pistol."

"Of course." The Captain nodded. "I do have one question before you go: did you really kill a man?"

She grinned. "Why, of course not, Captain. I'm a lady."

"Thought so. Now get below and have Bud take care of that cut."

Once below, she found Bud locking Mr. Beckly's cabin door.

"I've dressed his wound, tied him up, and locked him inside. He'll do us no harm," Bud said. "Let's look at your cheek."

She sat on a dining room table chair while Bud probed the gash with his fingers. "It's a clean wound. That's good. There's no glass inside. Put pressure on it until I come back."

She waited, closed her eyes, and felt as though a giant wave washed over her. It was as if her very life drained into a mass of smothering gray nothingness, alone, drowning in the knowledge that nothing mattered, life was all for nothing. All she wanted to do was climb into bed and pull the covers over her head.

Bud returned with hot water, clean cloth, a needle, and black thread. He cleaned the cut. It hurt.

"It needs to be sewn up, Mrs. Hartstone."

"I'll heal quite well without stitches."

"Just a minute." He returned with a small mirror.

She looked and agreed the cut needed to be sutured – it did her face no favors. "Who will do it?"

Bud smiled. "I've sewn up a lot of horses, and several men." He threaded a large needle.

"I need a drink, then. Bourbon, if you please."

He brought her a glass, and she gulped the whiskey down, hoping it would take effect before Bud touched her with the needle. It didn't.

"Don't you have anything but black thread?" she asked.

"Don't worry. The stitches will come out, Mrs. Hartstone."

Tears fell as he poked the needle through her skin and drew the thread tight. She moaned, trying to stifle screams of pain as she counted eleven stitches, gripping the edge of the table in an attempt to fight dizziness and nausea.

"That's enough!" she said through clenched teeth.

"A few more. I'm sorry to hurt you."

"I'll never forgive you," she hissed. The scar would ruin her looks.

After he finished, he said, "I have a roll of adhesive plaster I'll cut as a bandage."

"I'll wait to see how badly I bleed before using the bandage."

He shook his head and cut several squares of cloth for her to use to stop the bleeding.

Several minutes later, after some of the pain had decreased, she said, "I'm sorry for snapping at you, Bud. I appreciate your help."

He gave her a small jar of honey to apply to the cut. "This will keep your cut moist as it heals."

She thanked him and shuffled back to her cabin. Before she climbed into bed, she had to look at her face in the mirror. She sucked in her breath. The black stitches puckered her cheek. The thread also pulled the skin away from the bottom corner of her eye, making the white enormous. Her eye bulged.

Moisture flooded her eyes. She watched the fluid pool in her sagging eyelid. Tears ran down her cheek, and then plunged to splatter on top of her dressing table.

Chapter 7

Bud offered her adhesive plaster as a bandage, but Maggie couldn't stand the thought of having something stuck on her face. She should make a mask to hide the scar until the ship landed at a town where she could purchase a proper mourning veil. Why did she leave hers at White Haven?

She found a handkerchief and folded it into a triangle, pinning each side to the braids around her ears. The woman looking back from the mirror looked like a crazed droopy-eyed bank robber.

She pulled the revolver from her waist sash, pointed the muzzle at the mirror, and shouted, "This is a holdup!" She giggled and dropped the gun on the desk, and then sobbed.

Later, while Bud steered the ship, the captain called a meeting of all passengers on the main deck. Maggie felt ridiculous wearing her mask. Captain Kinney explained that Maggie had saved them from certain death by her sudden appearance in the wheelhouse. He kept his promise and said nothing about her pistol.

The Union officers held Mr. Beckly by the arms. Apparently, her shot had only been a flesh wound, because he could walk with a limp. An officer informed the crowd that, under martial law, a spy was to be put to death immediately. The crowd cheered and then fell silent.

The crew lowered the gangplank two feet off the rushing water – the ship was going full throttle. Two Union officers hosted Mr. Beckly onto the plank and pushed him toward the end. The officers walked a few paces back and drew their weapons.

The engine shafts pounded, and the sound of water curling from the ship's bow broke the silence. Someone coughed.

Two shots.

The ship rocked as everyone rushed to the railing to watch Mr. Beckly's body float away on the surface of the muddy river.

Maggie ran to the opposite side of the boat, leaned over the side, lifted her veil, and vomited. She hated the reality of war.

She returned to her cabin to replace her stained mask. She washed her face and looked in the mirror at her disfigured face and flung the washcloth at her image.

She recalled a s story about a dance hall girl working in a Colorado mining camp who wore a mask to conceal her face. She also wore silver dancing shoes, earning her the nickname of "Silverheels." When a smallpox epidemic swept through the camp, she had used her own money to bring doctors to the camp to treat the miners and their families. Eventually, Silverheels caught the disease, which left her face pockmarked, but she survived.

Later, the miners collected a bundle of cash to show their appreciation. Still, when they went to her cabin, she had disappeared, never to be seen again. No one ever knew her real name or had ever seen her face. They named the camp and the nearby mountain "Silverheels".

Noble, to be sure, but how happy had the woman's life been beyond her good deeds? Did Maggie want to spend the rest of her life hiding behind a mask?

If she had no future without George and Jenny, why in the world should she care now how she looked? She wouldn't hide like Silverheels.

She would adopt no nickname, no false identity. She refused to hide behind a mask.

They docked at Brunswick that afternoon. Maggie was toasted many times during dinner. Yet, she noticed the men secretly glanced at her scar, eyes darting away when she caught them staring. Everyone looked away except Mr. Herndon, whose eyes all but caressed her stitches. The man had no respect.

Mr. Williams complained about how much money he'd lost playing cards to Mr. Herndon, who smiled and said, "I must admit that I had the luck of the draw last night. Perhaps you will recoup tonight, Mr. Williams."

After supper, Maggie walked toward her cabin. Mr. Herndon walked out of a nearby room and blocked her way.

"Thank you again for saving us, Maggie. May I call you Maggie?"

"I prefer Mrs. Hartstone."

His smile broadened. "As you prefer, Mrs. Hartstone. No one told us how you managed to save us in the pilothouse."

"I simply used my feminine wiles, Mr. Herndon."

He stepped closer. Maggie backed up, reached behind her, and touched the wall. She felt light-headed.

"I'm interested in the details," he said.

"A woman must maintain her secrets, Mr. Herndon."

His eyes searched hers. Maggie pressed deeper against the wall.

Someone coughed. "May I pass?" Mr. Williams had approached unnoticed.

"Of course," Mr. Herndon said, brushing against her as the man passed.

Mr. Williams walked to his cabin, entered it, and shut the door. Maggie pushed Mr. Herndon back, though not as far as she'd intended.

"A gentleman would have stood to the side."

He smiled. "I don't pretend to be a gentleman."

She wanted to say something biting and witty, something about ladies and scallywags. She felt her blood pulsing through her scar. His musky scent overpowered all other smells: the food and cigar smoke from the lounge, the walnut wall against her back, the pungent smell of the river sliding below them.

He laughed. "In any case, Mrs. Hartstone, we now have something in common."

"Oh?"

"We both carry the scars of war on our cheeks. You now look even more beautiful and intriguing. Perhaps we can find more things in common before the end of our journey."

"I doubt it, Mr. Herndon. I'm exhausted. Good luck with your card game." She waited for him to move.

He didn't.

She brushed past him and returned to her cabin, locked the door, and leaned against it. Later, in bed, she closed her eyes and felt Mr. Herndon's presence again. Swept by guilt and feeling the presence of George, she opened her eyes and discovered, once again, she was in a gray world and utterly alone.

Chapter 8

The next day, the *Cora II* pulled to the riverbank. While everyone was ashore gathering firewood for the ship's boilers, Maggie sat alone in the salon with the Bible open in her lap. The conflict between the commands to forgive your enemy, and take an eye for an eye continued to bother her.

Why couldn't the Bible be consistent? If God commanded 'Thou shalt not kill', why a thousand years later, were people killing each other? Yes, Cain killed Abel, but why was God unable to stop killings? She stared at the upright piano until her eyes lost focus.

Her mind drifted back to her parlor at *White Haven* and her beloved Erhard piano. Playing it every day gave her solace from loneliness. Music dissolved that gray cloud, which would form in unexpected moments, smothering her like a transparent shroud.

Maggie leaned back and shut her eyes. She remembered how they would retire to the parlor after supper. She played the piano while Jenny stood barefoot on top of George's shoes as he taught her dance steps. Sometimes Jenny would play while George waltzed her around and around the parlor. What joy.

Jenny had thought Maggie had been mean when she refused to allow her to take dancing lessons with her classmates. Maggie had said "no" from fear Jenny could become enamored with being in a boy's arms, and what that could lead to. Now she wished she'd let the girl go. It was too late now.

Opening her eyes in the ship's salon, Maggie wondered if she'd ever see her daughter again. Maggie pressed her head back against the chair. You can't go back. She felt guilt and anger ignite in her heart, rising until the flames would consume her body, and she burned to nothing more than ashes, to be blown away in the wind.

How she missed Jenny and George and her beloved Erhard piano.

She remembered the evening when a guerrilla gang, wearing Union blue jackets over Confederate gray trousers, forced their way into her house. They had demanded to know her loyalty.

She couldn't tell if they were Confederate or Union sympathizers. If she picked the wrong side, she'd be shot. She claimed she was neutral.

That made the guerrillas mad, but at least they didn't shoot her. They demanded food, searched the house for valuables to steal, and finally forced her to play her piano.

"Play the *Bonnie Blue Flag!*" The men clapped and cheered.

She played.

The men joined in the chorus:

> *Hurrah! Hurrah!*
> *For Southern rights hurrah!*
> *Hurrah for the Bonnie Blue Flag*
> *That bears a single star.*

A man shouted, "*Play Dixie!*"

The men took up the chant. "*Dixie! Dixie! Dixie!*"

So she played again. The men linked arms and swung around and around, faster and faster, until someone knocked over a table. The glass lamp crashed against the hardwood floor. Coal oil spread, flames rose. One of the men used his coat to stamp out the fire. In the embarrassed silence, they looked at her.

"Out!" she screamed. "Out! Get out!"

A short thug had stolen her best chemise from her bedroom dresser and slipped it on over his filthy clothes. He belted on his revolver, and said, "You gotta be on one side or the other. You can't be neutral. Bet you're a damn Union liar."

He kicked the piano leg with fury; it snapped. The piano lurched toward Maggie. She toppled from the bench. The keyboard crashed on the floor just inches from making her a cripple. Keys broke loose and clattered across the floor. The piano's hammers bounced against the strings, filling the room with lingering dissonance.

The men stomped out.

She refused to fix the piano. She would never again touch a keyboard. It had been her only relief from loneliness, and now thinking about the piano brought back memories of parties, and dancing, and laughing with Jenny and George.

Gone forever.

She woke from her memories when she heard the ship's engines start. The passengers would soon be returning. She had no desire to talk to Mr. Herndon. It was time to retire to her cabin.

Several hours later, Maggie heard the engines slow. They would be dropping off Mr. Williams at Lake View, then.

She put on a bonnet and checked her face in the mirror, picked up her parasol and walked to the bow of the hurricane deck to watch his departure.

The Captain maneuvered the ship upstream and slowed the engines. The boat drifted closer to shore near to the Lake View billboard; the gentle slope of the lower bank made a safe landing spot. He rang the bell to alert the crew to drop anchor and lower the right gangplank for Mr. William's departure.

Bud Spahr took the wheel while the Captain hurried down to see Mr. Williams off.

Mr. Williams turned to the Captain. "See here, I expect my belongings to be carried to town."

The Captain raised one eyebrow. "The contract you signed stated I deliver you and your belongings to the dock or shore. They are your responsibility from that point on."

"But—"

The Captain interrupted. "I'm certain you can hire someone from Lake View to retrieve your goods."

"Very well, then." Mr. Williams huffed away without saying thank you or goodbye and walked across the plank. Maggie watched as he hurried up a trail and disappeared over the top of the steep bank.

The Captain ordered the crew to raise the gangplank and returned to the pilothouse.

Maggie heard screams and looked up the grassy slope.

"Help! Wait! Stop!" Mr. Williams ran back down the embankment frantically waving his arms.

"Wait! Help!" He fell and tumbled and rolled head over heels down the hill until he splashed on his back into the water. Union officers pulled their guns and aimed them at the top of the ridge, expecting to see Quantrill's men or attacking Indians.

Three men pulled Mr. Williams back onto the deck. He gulped for breath and then began to cry.

"Guerrillas?" Bud Spahr asked.

"No," Mr. Williams spluttered.

"Indians?"

"It was a fraud! There is no town. I've been duped! I'm bankrupt!"

Bud ordered the crew to lower the plank again and retrieve Mr. Williams' trunks. The shaken man rose, leaned his elbows against a cotton bale, and buried his head in his hands. He sobbed as water dripped off his suit and pooled at his feet.

Maggie looked at Mr. Herndon and shook her head. He raised his palms as if to say, "What now?"

Late that afternoon, the ship stopped south of Brunswick. During supper, Maggie noticed a new passenger, a respectfully quiet Union officer who sat with the others.

The man was small and stoop-shouldered. Almost a head shorter than her, he couldn't have been over five feet tall. He was squarely built, and his arms and legs looked too short for his body, though his head was large, with receding brown hair that fell to his shoulders. He had high cheekbones, a straight nose, and deep-set blue eyes.

The Captain told her he was the famous Kit Carson, now a Union Brevet Brigadier General, bound for a new posting as commander of Fort Garland in Colorado.

She looked at the famous frontiersman and decided, quite quickly, that he would be her teacher.

Chapter 9

Kit Carson didn't acknowledge her for several days. After they steamed away from Lexington, she found him leaning on the hurricane deck's rail, staring at the white foam bow-wake curling into the muddy river. She introduced herself.

"I understand you saved the ship from Quantrill's raiders, Mrs. Hartstone." His words flowed slow and soft and gentle as a woman's. She was surprised – she had imagined a voice hardened by violence.

"We were lucky, General Carson. I do not want to seem forward, but I have begun a journey far beyond my experience. It would mean a great deal if I might seek your counsel."

"I'm not at all certain my advice would be helpful."

"I'm tracking down the murderers of my daughter and husband."

His mild blue eyes turned cold and hard, reminding her of a rattlesnake. "I'm sorry," he said. "Tell me about it."

They walked into the lounge, found a quiet corner table, and ordered tea.

She told him the story: about returning from a luncheon and finding Jenny raped and dead in the arms of the dying George; the theft of her daughter's silver cross; and of Traveler, their distinctive black head and necked, white-mane Tennessee Walker. One of the killers had bright red hair and beard, and the other a grotesquely misshaped mouth.

"The authorities have been no help, but someone spotted a red-headed man on Traveler in Independence. The best guess was that the killers are planning to head west on either the Oregon or Santa Fe Trail, to seek a fortune in the new goldfields or homestead. Perhaps they were also trying to escape punishment for their crimes."

Carson listened carefully. "And you plan to find them?"

"Yes."

"And then what?"

The waiter brought her tea and she used her hanky to pat the cut on her cheek – damp, but not bleeding.

When the tea arrived, she stirred two teaspoons of sugar into the cup.

Carson again asked, "What do you intend to do if you find them?"

She shook her head. "I don't know. The Bible preaches forgiveness."

"I've never read it, but I understand it also says to take an eye for an eye."

"The *Good Book* seems as conflicted as I feel. I have a difficult time with forgiveness. What do you think, General Carson?"

"I believe in taking swift revenge against wrongdoers. But I have the skills to do so."

"Skills?"

"Pardon my saying so, but you are a woman, without experience in gun fighting. You would hesitate before pulling a trigger. Those men are hardened killers who would not. If you go after them, you'll be killed."

"I've become an excellent shot with my pistol," Maggie said. "I can bark a running squirrel out of a tree."

"Different than facing down a killer," Carson observed.

"What you don't understand, General Carson is that I, too, died when they killed my loved ones. I have nothing to lose."

"That's easy to say here, sitting in the first-class lounge of a steamship, Mrs. Hartstone, but life suddenly becomes precious when a killer has a pistol pointed at you."

"I had one pointed at me yesterday."

"Yes. The captain said you handled yourself well."

"Will you help me?"

"I would if I weren't in the army with a responsibility to command Fort Garland."

"I need nothing but to hear from you about what I should know."

"If your killers go down the lower cutoff on the Santa Fe Trail, do not follow them. The desert will do the work for you. It's called the Cimarron Cutoff, but the Mexicans call it *La Jornada de Muerto*."

"The journey of death? What makes it so dangerous?"

"Beyond Fort Larned, the Santa Fe Trail splits into the mountain trail, which is dangerous enough, and the *Jornada de Muerto*. There's no water through the first ninety miles of that desert. It's flat, with few landmarks. People follow mirages that look like water but lead nowhere. It's difficult to know which trails lead to water and which to death. If you make it through the first part alive, the lower trail splits Kiowa and Comanche lands. News of the Sand Creek Massacre stirred up those Indians. Both routes are more dangerous now than in the past."

"What's one to do?"

"Return home."

"You know that's impossible."

"In that case, join a large wagon train that has a military escort. Make certain the wagon master has made the trip many times. Even then, the trip is dangerous."

She turned back to Carson. "I'll need a buggy."

"Horse would be better."

"I don't ride."

He studied his teacup. "A regular buggy won't make it. Have one built for you by Hiram Young in Independence."

She shook her head. "If I wait too long, the trail will go cold."

"Let me think it over," Carson said.

Several days later, Maggie stood on the hurricane deck as the *Cora II* approached Westport Landing near Independence. Shabby looking frame and brick warehouses, dry goods stores, groceries, and saloons lined the waterfront.

The rugged bluff overlooking the buildings were covered with dead trees and brush that partially hid lean-tos and an occasional log cabin. There were a few women and children, mostly Negroes, sitting on their porch, watching the boat.

Prairie schooners, vast piles of Mexican freight, horses, mules, oxen roustabouts, Indians, Negroes, emigrants, hotel drummers, and a brass band crowded the dock. Human and animal sweat, dung, and an unknown rotten smell made her sniff a sprig of lavender clutched tightly in her hands.

Dockworkers shouted, mules brayed, horses whinnied, and iron wagon wheels screeched against a brick pavement assaulting her ears.

After docking, Captain Kinney and Bud Spahr stood next to the plank on the main deck, shouting instructions and directing traffic.

The crew carried Maggie's trunk across the plank and placed it on the dock. Kit Carson ordered a lieutenant to load her chest into a waiting military buggy.

Bud approached Maggie to say goodbye.

She touched the scar on her cheek. Her face was not as swollen, but she still hated the line of black the stitches. "Thank you for doctoring me, Bud."

"You were a brave patient."

"I hope I didn't make you uncomfortable when I cried."

"I think the scar makes you look even more beautiful than before." He blushed and disappeared before she could respond.

Captain Kinney greeted her next to the gangplank. He smiled at her – only the third smile since she'd booked her passage. He took her hand and kissed it like a medieval knight saying farewell to a princess.

Heat rushed to her cheeks, and she patted her scar with a handkerchief.

"I misjudged you, Mrs. Hartstone. I didn't think you had what it takes for the journey you intend. You proved me wrong. You saved my ship and my life. As a small token of my appreciation, when you return to Boonville, your passage will be free."

"When will you be returning, Captain?"

"In four months, depending on a great many things. In any event, we always telegraph our planned arrival. God bless your quest, Mrs. Hartstone. I look forward to seeing you again."

She kissed him on the cheek and opened her parasol as she walked across the plank to the dock. It was fun to see the Captain blush.

Kit Carson led her to his carriage. "We'll have an armed military escort take us to Hiram Young's wagon shop in Independence, where you can inquire about buying a plains buggy."

"I'm sorry to take you out of your way, General." She wondered why Carson was being so helpful. She remembered the widespread story about the capture of Mrs. White.

According to newspaper accounts, Carson had led a rescue party but was too late. He found her with an arrow through her heart. He later searched the Indian camp and found a book about him and his exploits rescuing people from Indians. Mrs. White must have been reading it, praying for him to save her. Perhaps he carried guilt from that tragedy.

Carson said, "It's not out of my way. I'm meeting Mr. McCoy, Hiram Young's business manager, with a contract to build 300 wagons for the army."

"Where is Mr. Young?" she asked.

"An interesting story. Mr. McCoy had been mayor of Independence, and Mr. Young hired him. As you might know, Young is a freed black slave who came out here, started his wagon and yoke business, and is now one of the wealthiest men in these parts. He moved up to Fort Leavenworth during the war for the safety of his family. However, much of his business is still conducted here."

"A black man hires a white former mayor as his business manager?'"

"The world's a-changing."

"For the better, I hope."

Mr. McCoy greeted them at the Hiram Young and Company offices. Dark eyes stared from under bushy overhanging eyebrows; a bulbous nose protruded over a barbwire beard that hid his lips.

The office had the musty stench of old paper and wood shavings. Maggie tried to hide her discomfort as they sat at a large oak table.

"We're most eager to start work on your order, General Carson. We will start as soon as after we sign the contract today."

Carson smiled and said, in his gentle, slow voice, "Before we do our business, Mr. McCoy, I need to know how soon you can build a Dearborn wagon for Mrs. Hartstone. She needs to traverse the Santa Fe or Oregon Trail. It is an emergency."

"This is a bit unusual. What do you have in mind?" asked Mr. McCoy, who leaned back in his chair and looked at his pocket watch.

"A light-weight, sturdy wagon to haul only Mrs. Hartstone and her personal provisions: just a trunk, saddle, bedding and blankets, and horse feed, nothing heavy. She needs a small, fast wagon that can be easily pulled by a mule or horse, and with a weather cover and two fifty-gallon water barrels. It should be just long enough for her to sleep dry in the wagon bed along with her trunk, food, and cooking utensils."

Mr. McCoy rolled out a large piece of paper and began sketching out the wagon dimensions as Carson spoke. They discussed the issue concerning the axle length. Should the axles be the same length as those of regular prairie schooners, so they could fit into the ruts made by previous wagons? Or should the shafts be shorter, for a bumpier but faster ride? Maggie chose short axles.

"I would like to request one more thing, Mr. McCoy," Maggie said. "Would you build me a hidden shelf under the spring seat to keep my valuables, like my parasol?"

Mr. McCoy spent several minutes figuring the costs. He looked at Maggie and said he could build her buggy in a month.

"I can't wait a month, Mr. McCoy."

"It normally takes three months for us to deliver a regular wagon based on our standard patterns. What you propose is custom work."

General Carson pulled the army contract from his jacket and placed it on the table. "I would hope you could make this a special case."

"Yes. Well . . ."

Maggie interrupted Mr. McCoy. "I'll pay additional if it's finished in one week."

"Two weeks," McCoy said.

"A fifty dollar bonus if you deliver it to me this time next week. Greenbacks. Half now. Half upon delivery," Maggie said.

The men looked at each other, and then her. Mr. McCoy frowned.

Carson picked up the contract and dropped it on the table with a light tap.

"Very well, Mrs. Hartstone, we'll rush your order."

Maggie picked up her purse. "Draw up a contract, Mr. McCoy, and I'll pay the first half when I return." She locked herself in the washroom and, retrieving a small pair of scissors shaped like a swan from her purse, cut out the necessary greenbacks from the hem of her skirt.

She returned, read, and signed the contract, and gave Mr. McCoy the down payment. She asked him to put his signature next to the contracted amount.

After Carson conducted his business, they returned to the waiting buggy and military escort.

"You are a good businesswoman, Mrs. Hartstone," Carson said.

"Thank you," she replied, "and thank you for convincing Mr. McCoy to build my buggy faster."

"You'll need a place to stay while you wait. I believe you'll be comfortable and safe at Watson's boarding house."

Mrs. Watson indeed had a room available, with breakfast, dinner, and supper provided to boarders. The upstairs room was clean, with a bed, a desk, an armoire, a chamber pot, washbasin, and towels. Carson ordered his soldiers to carry Maggie's trunk to her room.

"You'll need to buy a horse or mule for your buggy."

"I've never bought a horse. I wouldn't know where to begin, or how to judge an animal, or where to find one."

"I have a friend who might help us if he's in town. I'll check and let you know."

Maggie said goodbye and walked through the lounge toward the stairs to the bedrooms. A tall man sat in a leather chair reading a newspaper, which he put it down upon her arrival. He flashed a smile. "What a surprise, Mrs. Hartstone."

"What a coincidence, Mr. Herndon. Good night." She walked upstairs, wondering if his being here was really a coincidence or something else – it was as if he was following her.

Maggie locked her door and put her Colt revolver under her pillow and turned off the light. She lay on the bed, fully dressed, staring through the dark at the ceiling, listening for footsteps. She pictured his charming smile and thought how strange it was that they had cheek scars in common.

Chapter 10

Footsteps in the hall woke Maggie from a disturbing dream. The steps paused. She rose on her elbow, reached for her revolver, pulled back the hammer and pointed it at the door. She listened for the creak of the door handle being twisted. The footsteps continued down the hall, and then she heard a door opened and shut.

Her heart hammered in her eardrums. If someone listened at her door, they could hear her labored breathing. She sucked in a lungful of air, held her breath, and then released it slowly.

She listened. Whoever had been in the hallway had stopped at her door, but was gone. She lowered the revolver's hammer and spun the cylinder to the empty chamber for safety.

Why had she been frightened? Henry Herndon was aggressive, but he wouldn't cause her physical harm. Or would he? Had all the warnings about chasing the killers made her jumpy?

Falling back upon the pillows, she tried to recall the nightmare that had upset her. Patching disjointed pieces together was like catching tendrils of smoke. Slowly, scene-by-scene, the picture cleared – she had been making passionate love to Mr. Henry Herndon.

She shook her head. He was so dangerously attractive. Was it possible she was beginning to have feelings for him?

How could she have such thoughts while she was in mourning for George? She tried to put words to swirling emotions. It was simply too much to think about.

Maggie was the last to walk into breakfast. The only empty chair was next to Mr. Herndon. She blushed, touched her scar and hesitated. Perhaps she should skip breakfast.

He wiped his mustache with a napkin, stood, and pulled out her chair. Trapped, she thanked him and sat down.

Herndon leaned close and said, in a soft voice, "We were beginning to worry about you, Mrs. Hartstone. You look tired. I hope you are feeling all right."

"I'm just fine this morning. Please pass the toast and bacon, Mr. Herndon."

He paused, smiled, and reached across the table for the platter of bacon. He handed it to her. Their fingers touched.

She turned to the man on her left and engaged him in a somewhat forced conversation until Mr. Herndon excused himself.

Later, on her way to talk with the Sheriff, she walked through the rooming house lobby and onto its porch. Mr. Herndon sat in a rocker.

Men, women, and children walked along the street, dodging buggies and horsemen and oxcarts. The sounds were loud, the smells pungent.

She was alone on the porch with Mr. Herndon.

He touched the scar on his cheek. "Pardon me for asking, Mrs. Hartstone, but have I done something to offend you?"

She stopped at the top of the porch stairs, opened her parasol, and listened to its bells. She turned back toward Mr. Herndon and surprised herself by smiling. "No. I . . . I simply prefer to be alone."

He pulled on his mustache and nodded. "I'll honor your feelings, Mrs. Hartstone. However, this can be a dangerous town, particularly for a lady traveling alone. Many consider single women to be harlots . . ."

She touched her scar. "Are you suggesting I look like a harlot?"

He scrambled to his feet. "No, certainly not! I just thought you might not be aware of the dangers that could befall an innocent lady like yourself."

"Mr. Herndon, let me assure you that I'm quite capable of taking care of myself. Besides, Kit Carson will look out for me."

"Will he join you on the trail?"

"To which trail do you refer: Oregon, California, or Santa Fe?"

"Which one are you planning to take, Mrs. Hartstone?"

"That, sir, is none of your business. Good day."

She hated herself for treating him so roughly but nonetheless walked down the street and turned left toward the Sheriff's office, three blocks away.

Sheriff L.R. Clay sat at his office desk, writing on an official-looking document. He was tall, with a clean-shaven ruddy face under a sweat-stained hat that looked to be part of his head. He did not bother to take it off when he looked up with bright eyes.

She introduced herself and told him she was looking for a red-headed man who rode a spotted Tennessee Walker with a black head and neck, and a distinctive long white mane and tail. "Marshal McDearmon in Boonville said that you'd sent a telegram saying you saw him. Why didn't you arrest him for the murder of my daughter and husband?"

Sheriff Clay put up his hands. "Hold on a minute."

Maggie crossed her arms. "I'm listening."

"I didn't see any red-haired man. My deputy pulled him out of a bar. Red was drunk and had started a fight. He promised not to cause any more trouble and he climbed on the very horse you described and rode off. It wasn't until two days later when we got the wire from Marshal McDearmon. We never saw Red or the horse again."

"Why didn't you look for him?"

"Mrs. Hartstone, there's just the two of us trying to keep law and order in this town. He might have headed out. Might still be here. There are thousands of pilgrims milling around, waiting for the weather to harden the mud so the wagon trains can commence up the trails. If you spot him, let me know, and I'll arrest him for you."

"If I spot him?"

"I don't have time. I'm telling you what I can do. If I were to arrest everyone who's killed someone, half this town would be in this here jail. So let me know if you find your red-haired man, and I'll arrest him." He tugged down his hat brim, picked up his pen and concentrated on the paper on his desk. "Good day to you."

She didn't move.

He didn't look at her.

She didn't move.

He threw down the pen and looked at her with hard eyes that would have frightened a man with something to lose. "What?"

"If you were me, how and where would you go about looking for him?"

His body slumped into the chair. He plucked a tobacco pouch and cigarette paper from his shirt pocket. He shook a line of tobacco in the center of the paper, and then carefully rolled the paper around the tobacco, licked its edge, and stuck the cigarette into the corner of his mouth. His lips were chapped and cracked.

She didn't move.

He fished in his pockets for a match. Maggie picked one up and struck it on the desktop, held it out toward his face.

He leaned toward her and lit his cigarette. The chair squeaked as he settled back, and he blew smoke toward the ceiling. "Hate this damned paperwork."

"I understand, Sheriff. I hate chasing after murderers."

"Come back after dinner, and we'll look around."

"Will we walk?" she asked.

"We'll ride."

"I'll pick you up in a buggy right after dinner."

"I don't ride in buggies."

"You can tell people it's a date."

Smoke burst through his nostrils like a dragon. He laughed. "It's a date, then."

Maggie walked to the stables and found the owner, an oafish man with long tangled beard, mean eyes, and torn shirt. He pitched hay to horses inside stalls. "I would like to rent a buggy," she said.

He leaned on his pitchfork. "Gonna pull it yourself, or you want a Goddamned mule to go with it?"

"Don't swear in front of a lady."

"What?"

"I'll take a mule."

"Who's gonna drive?"

"I am."

"Women can't drive. You'd wreck it."

"I'm an excellent driver."

"Won't rent it if you plan to drive."

"So?"

"So, you gotta hire my boy up there." He pointed to the hayloft where a lanky man of about twenty stared down at her. His mouth drooled, and his left eye contemplated something on the ceiling of the barn.

After dinner, they pulled up in front of the Sheriff's office. She got impatient after a few minutes, got out, and stormed into his office.

"Time to go, Sheriff."

Clay shook his head, muttered something inaudible, walked with her to the buggy, and nodded at the driver.

"Hello, Jodi."

"Sheriff."

"I'm looking for someone for Mrs. Hartstone here. So do what I tell you."

"Sheriff." Bitterness tinged Jodi's voice.

They pulled up to a saloon. The Sheriff stepped out of the buggy, nearly slamming Maggie's hand in the door in the process.

"I'll go in with you, Sheriff."

"You'll stay here, Mrs. Hartstone. You don't want to be seen in these kinds of places."

Jodi watched the bar door swing shut behind the Sheriff and said, in a barely audible voice, as if thinking aloud, "Mighty embarrassed to be in a buggy with a lady."

"And why would he be embarrassed, Jodi?"

"Ain't manly. People will talk."

The Sheriff walked out, looked at Maggie, and shook his head. The next saloon was several doors down to the left. He walked.

"Guess we're to stay here." Jodi tugged a tattered straw hat over his eyes, leaned back, and put his boots up on the footrest. A bare toe peeked through a hole in the leather.

Maggie opened her parasol and waited under its shade.

A drunk staggered out of the saloon, tripped on the stairs and rolled onto the street. The Sheriff shook his head and walked into the bar.

She realized that the drunk was Mr. Williams, the passenger from the *Cora II*, who had been duped by land swindlers. She opened the buggy door and stepped out. Williams lay on his back in the dirt, trying to shade his eyes from the sun. She stood over him, shading his face with her parasol.

"Stand up, Mr. Williams! You're making a fool of yourself."

He blinked at her through bloodshot eyes. Vomit or food or liquor, or all three, stained his shirt and his filthy suit.

"I'm ruined," he slurred.

"Balderdash! You've felt sorry for yourself ever since you realized your mistake. You're not the only one during this war who has been forced to start over. You're smart and talented. So get up and start over."

"I don't have any money," he whined.

"Enough for a drink or three, it seems."

He raised himself to his elbows. "That was my last dollar. They threw me out."

"Stop bellyaching. You are at the crossroads of your life, Mr. Williams. The future is up to you." She reached into her purse, pulled out several greenbacks, and dropped them on his chest.

"That is enough for a bath and clean clothes. After you sober up, come see me at Mrs. Watson's boarding house. We will talk about your next steps."

He stared at the money as though it were strange and unusual. He stuffed them into his pocket and nodded, then rolled to his hands and knees, staggered upright, and weaved his way down the street.

Someone clapped. She looked toward the saloon. The Sheriff, standing next to the swinging doors, watched with several other people. Henry Herndon stood next to the Sheriff. He flashed her a bright smile and continued clapping. Standing close to him was a bar girl, hip cocked, her arm around his shoulder.

Maggie spun and returned to the buggy. Jodi jumped down from his driver's seat to open the door.

"That was something," he muttered as he held her elbow for the step-up.

The buggy rocked when the Sheriff returned and sat down next to Maggie. He ordered Jodi to drive to a saloon in the east part of town.

Several minutes of silence later, he looked at her. "You'd really help out that drunk?"

"If he doesn't drink up the money I gave him. If he cleans up and wants to change, I'll give him a stake, so he doesn't go hungry until he finds his next job. It's his choice."

"Huh." He pulled his hat down, trying to avoid stares from people he knew until they approached the Roust About Saloon. Two men, in the midst of an argument, burst through the door and out into the street.

The tall man was obviously drunk and screamed at the shorter man, "I knew you were a goddamned secesh from the moment I put eyes on you!"

The short man shouted, "You're drunk, Fred! We'll talk about this later."

"Like hell, we will. We'll have it out right here, right now." He put his hand on the handle of his pistol.

The short man held out his palms. "I'm not going to fight you. I'm going to turn around and walk away."

He'd taken about thirty steps when the Sheriff shouted, "Fred! Don't!"

Fred raised his pistol, aimed it at the short man's back, and pulled the trigger. The shot hit the street, throwing up dust.

The short man spun and raised his gun. "Stop it, Fred!"

Fred's second shot missed.

But the short man's didn't, hitting Fred squarely in the chest. Fred's last shot went wild as he staggered backward and fell face up.

"Jesus!" The Sheriff walked over to Fred's body, poked the fallen man's chest with the toe of his boot. "He's dead. You can put your gun away, Tom."

"I didn't want to shoot him, Sheriff. Didn't have no choice."

"Self-defense, Tom. Go on home." The Sheriff ordered someone to get the undertaker to pick up Fred's body, and then he pushed through the crowd into the saloon.

"Wonder if he's going to get a shot of red-eye?" Jodi asked.

"I would," Maggie said.

"Me, too."

"You're too young to drink."

"Drunk a lot."

The Sheriff walked to the buggy. "No news."

"I didn't mean to jump in your lap when the shooting started," Maggie said.

"I didn't mean to pull you over, Mrs. Hartstone, but bullets were flying. No way to tell where they'd hit."

"Are you getting in, Sheriff?"

"We'll wait here until the undertaker takes the body away."

"Did you know those men?"

"They were best of friends before the war. War split everyone up. Everybody's at each other's throats. The damned war between rich cotton-growers and rich factory owners, and we ain't either one or ever will be. Piss on the Virginia bigwigs, but piss on the Yankees twice as much."

"Amen," she said.

"Double amen," Jodi mumbled from the driver's seat.

"Sorry we're having trouble finding news about your horse, Mrs. Hartstone," the Sheriff said.

Jodi turned around. "What horse?" After Maggie described Traveler, he exclaimed, "I know that horse! One of the best I ever cared for."

They both stared at him.

"Why didn't you just ask me about him instead of going through all this rigmarole of renting me and Daddy's buggy and running all over town?"

Maggie's head snapped toward the Sheriff.

"We asked you about that horse weeks ago."

"Didn't neither," Jodi said in that same bitter tone.

"My deputy asked your father."

"Shoulda asked me. I do all the work."

Maggie snapped her parasol shut. "Who was riding him?"

"Guy with long red hair and beard. His partner was real scary."

"How so?" asked the Sheriff.

"He was so thin if he closed one eye he'd look like a needle. Besides, his mouth was all twisted to one side of his face."

"Those are the men, Sheriff!" Maggie exclaimed.

"Did you overhear anything?" the Sheriff asked.

"Like what?" Jodi asked.

"Like where they were going," Maggie said.

Jodi shrugged. "Sure."

Maggie stood up, looming over the driver. "Where?"

"Heard them saying about joining a wagon train going down the Santa Fe Trail. Something about like it was time to settle down, homestead a place now the war looks to be lost. I know they bought a couple pack horses for a trip."

"Anything else?" the Sheriff asked.

"Can't remember. But they're long gone. Wanted to catch the first wagon train out. They gotta be at least to Council Grove by now. You ain't gonna catch them."

"What do you think, Sheriff?" Maggie asked.

"Not unless they stop to homestead a place, but there's no law out there to notify."

Jodi dropped the Sheriff off at his office, and then stopped in front of Mrs. Watson's boarding house. Elated by the news, Maggie gave him a tip and held her skirts high as she ran up the stairs to the porch.

Mr. Henry Herndon sat on a rocker near the door, and she found herself giving him a big smile. He stood up to greet her.

"Have a good day with the Sheriff, Mrs. Hartstone?"

"It was a wonderful day, Mr. Herndon. Just wonderful!"

"I'm happy for you. I've had a wonderful day myself, discovered a most profitable poker game."

Maggie could hardly believe herself as the words tumbled out of her mouth. "Perhaps more profitable, but it could not have been more rewarding. However, if you are now flush with cash, how would you like to celebrate our wonderful day by taking me out to dinner?"

Chapter 11

Mr. Herndon walked Maggie through Independence Square and down Rock Street, toward the Noland Hotel for dinner. He took her arm to guide her past several piles of dung as they crossed the street. She squeezed his arm close to her body and then thought better of it and loosened her grip.

"I'm told the Noland serves the best food in town," Mr. Herndon said amiably.

"I'm certain it will be most satisfactory. In any event, I'm sure that nothing can spoil this day." She wore her fashionable blue dress.

Maggie noticed the grandeur of the Noland's lobby had lost a bit of its former glory. Paint peeled from several walls, and several lights were broken, but the room was still elegant.

She noted the high life and the babel of sounds – music from a piano and violinist, laughter, and conversations. Ladies of the house flitted about in white muslins, looking disengaged and unconcerned.

The tuxedoed maître d' met them at the entrance to the elegant dining room. He was tall and thin with black, slicked-back hair. A black goatee made his long face look mean.

Unlike the lobby, the dining room was quiet and intimate. Cut glass chandeliers hanging from a dark stamped tin ceiling gave the room a warm romantic hue. Fine linens, polished silverware, and candles adorned each table.

"Welcome, Mr. Herndon," the maître d' said. "I have reserved a special table for the two of you. Please, follow me."

Maggie raised an eyebrow. Herndon grinned.

Other diners stopped mid-conversation, giving them curious glances as they passed on their way to a secluded table. Maggie hid her scar with her handkerchief. The maître d' scowled when Mr. Herndon beat him to pull out Maggie's chair. She smiled, gathered her skirts, and sat down.

Mr. Herndon pulled out his own chair while the maître d' made a show of presenting a menu to her. He picked up her napkin, flicked it open, and gently positioned it on her lap.

"Would you like to start with a glass of wine?" Mr. Herndon asked.

"Certainly! We should celebrate our day."

Mr. Herndon turned to the maître d'. "We will have a bottle of your finest."

The maître d' bowed and walked away, shoulders back, nose high, and with a stride that made the back flaps of his coat wave.

"Have you been here before?" she asked.

"I came over while you were dressing to reserve a nice table."

"That was thoughtful, Mr. Herndon."

"Would it be possible for us to call each other by our first names?"

"It does seem that we've shared enough adventures to be a bit more familiar. Please call me Maggie."

"Maggie is a lovely name."

"My parents named and called me 'Margaret', but I never liked it because it sounded stuffy. I prefer to be called Maggie."

The maître d' returned with a bottle of red, made a show of explaining its virtues and pulled out the cork. He poured wine in each of their glasses and disappeared.

"I thought he'd let you taste it first," Maggie said.

Henry laughed. "So did I, but I suspect he figured there was no need since it was his selection. Here's to our successful day." He picked up his glass, clicked against hers, and swirled the wine to open up the aroma. Smelled it. Tasted it. Frowned.

Her wine smelled like dirty socks. She took a taste and coughed.

"It's turned to vinegar." He motioned to the maître d', who approached the table with a curious look.

"How is the wine?"

"I'd like you to taste it and tell me," Henry said.

The maître d' picked up a glass from an empty table and made a show of the tasting process. He held the glass high toward the light of a chandelier to examine the color. "Perfect deep hue," he said. He swirled it and sniffed. "A rich aroma." He raised the glass to his lips, tasted it. He held the glass in his right hand, raised his left hand, and rubbed his fingertips together. "This wine is the nectar of heaven. It is the very finest in our cellar."

Henry winked at her and then turned to the maître d'. "In that case, I would like to make you a gift of the bottle for your personal pleasure. Drink it soon, or it might spoil."

The smirk melted from the maître d's face.

"In the meantime, please bring me the wine menu and I'll select something more plebeian."

She watched the man sulk away. "You certainly handled that well."

"I didn't want to spoil our evening by punching him in the nose. In the meantime, perhaps we should look at the menu."

She laughed. "Let's not ask for a food recommendation."

He chuckled and looked into her eyes a moment longer than necessary.

The maître d' seemed a bit humbler when he returned with a wine menu, from which Henry selected a bottle of French red.

Maggie looked at the menu, pleasantly surprised by the quality and variety. Entrées included macedoine of wildfowl, vol-au-vent; buffalo tongue, sauce piquant; scalloped oysters, sauce Marin; pigs head, glace moutard.

"How in the world could they get oysters here without spoiling?" she asked.

"Packed in tins after they're shucked and washed," Henry said. "They can be shipped anywhere from the Chesapeake Bay."

"Interesting, but all the same, I think I'll order something else."

Henry laughed. "I agree."

"Look! They even have fourteen varieties of sweets and seven kinds of ice cream. It's hard to believe we're in a frontier town during the Civil War. This is amazing!"

The maître d' presented the bottle for Henry's inspection and approval.

"It's delicious," she said.

Maggie ordered the macedoine of wildfowl, while Henry asked for the buffalo tongue with sauce piquant.

They watched the waiter leave and then looked at each other, each waiting for the other to say something until the silence grew uncomfortable. They reached for their wine glass at the same moment and laughed again.

"Now that we're finally alone together, Henry, what should we talk about?"

He raised his glass. "The future."

"Yet we know nothing of each other's past. Shouldn't we start there?" Maggie asked.

"We could also reminisce about our trip on the *Cora II*. That would be discussing our near past."

"An excellent idea. You start, Henry."

"I would like to know why your attitude was so cold toward me, Maggie."

"I apologize. It wasn't just you. My daughter and husband were murdered last year, and I won't find peace until the men who killed them are brought to justice." Maggie gulped at her wine. "You are… a most attractive man, Henry, but you are a distraction from my goal."

Henry raised an eyebrow. "Shouldn't the law take care of them?"

"You saw me with the Sheriff today. I had to browbeat him into helping me get information about their whereabouts. The law doesn't help outside city limits."

"Then why was your day so good?"

"I discovered information about where to look for the killers."

"And?"

"I'm going to look for them."

"And if you find them?"

She averted her eyes and took another sip of wine. It was excellent, giving her a delightful buzz. "I'll turn them into the law."

"Bad idea."

"That's what everyone says."

"It would be too dangerous for anyone, even the Sheriff."

"I can take care of myself."

"Life is for the living, Maggie." He lifted his wine glass, and she followed suit in a toast.

"And what about you, Henry? Why have you shown such interest in me? Do you think I'm a widow in need?"

He laughed. "Good God, no! I was sitting in the lounge, reading a newspaper, and looked over to see you. I was transfixed. I wanted to know you better."

"Are you married?"

"I was." He looked down.

"And?"

"I own a small plantation near Holts Summit. In 1860, my wife and two children came back from a visit to her parents in Saint Louis on the Felix X. It hit a snag and sank near Hermann, Missouri. I searched for them for over a year. Their bodies were never found. I don't even have a gravesite to visit."

"I'm so sorry." She reached across the table and touched the top of his hand. Her fingers lingered. "What now, Henry?"

"I tried to sell the plantation but, with bushwhackers roaming the countryside, I couldn't find a buyer. So I leased it to a neighbor, scraped together all the cash I could, and decided to head west to start over."

"Where?"

"I hear good things about Denver City."

"You must be a good card player."

"There are many poor card players. Besides, one learns things in the army."

"Is that how you came by the scar?"

"A Union officer's saber cut me. Battle of Wilson's Creek."

"Oh! My husband lost his arm at Wilson's Creek."

"I'm sorry."

"He was captured and pardoned. After that, he wanted to stay home to protect us from guerrillas."

"I was captured and pardoned, also. The war changed everything."

"I was so naïve, I simply thought the politicians would never start a war. There had to be better solutions to the slave issue."

"You owned slaves?"

"Of course. How else could one work the land? Still, I was uncomfortable with slavery. I asked George why didn't the government simply pay the slaveholders for their slaves and set them free. Then the landowners would have enough money to pay them wages."

"Interesting idea. What did your husband think?"

"That I was a silly woman."

"Doesn't sound like a bad idea to me," Henry said.

Two waiters, carrying dinners covered by silver domes, arrived at their table, followed by the maître d'. The waiters set the plates down and waited for the maître d's signal to uncover the meals. He gave a curt nod, and the waiters theatrically lifted the silver covers, revealing the dinners.

Maggie looked at the buffalo tongue on her plate and the wildfowl on Henry's plate.

"Imbeciles! You set the wrong plates," the maître d' shouted. He threw his service napkin on the floor. "Cover the plates, exchange them, and uncover on my command!"

The waiters complied.

"Now!" The maître d' ordered with an upsweep of arms. "I do apologize, Mr. Herndon. It is just impossible to hire good help since the war began." He hurried away from the table.

Henry grinned and watched the man weave through tables toward his post. "A blowhard."

She giggled, "And highfalutin!"

"And hoity-toity!"

They toasted their judgments.

She felt strange - she was having fun!

They ate.

"The sauces are wonderful," Maggie said. "I never could teach Cissy, our cook, to make good sauces, other than gravy."

"Enjoy it now. You'll remember it with fondness if you go on the trail. By the way, which trail will you be taking?"

"Why do you want to know?"

"Hoping we'll be traveling together."

"Kit Carson is going to meet me in the morning. I'll decide after we talk."

"You can't go alone, Maggie."

"And why not?"

"You'll be putting your life in danger."

"That really doesn't matter to me at this point."

"I'll go with you."

"I've told you, Henry, I'm more than capable of taking care of myself."

"How?"

She stalled by taking yet another sip of wine. "I can protect myself."

"With what?"

"Do you carry a pistol, Henry?"

"Several: a Colt Navy .36 and a derringer. Don't tell me you carry a weapon?"

"A Colt Pocket .31."

Henry leaned back in his chair with a quizzical look on his face.

"I'm an excellent shot," she said, nodding her head for emphasis.

"I'll bet."

"Better than you." She shouldn't have said that. It was the wine speaking.

"I very much doubt that." He grinned.

"Are you a betting man, Henry?"

"Are you proposing a challenge?"

"Tomorrow," she said.

"And what are you willing to wager, Maggie?" he asked with a wicked grin.

"Why don't we think about what we'd like to win from the other and talk about it before our match . . . if you show up, that is."

He was speechless.

They ordered dessert. Henry's gazed at her as she ate her ice cream.

Maggie put her spoon in the saucer and looked at him. "What?"

"You used your pistol to save us on the boat from Quantrill's raiders, didn't you?"

She smiled. "It's all part of a woman's basket of charms."

"It seemed so unlikely that a lady like you . . ."

She interrupted him. "What a wonderful evening this has turned into. Thank you for bringing me to such an elegant place to celebrate our day."

"The celebration doesn't have to end now."

She tilted her head and gave him a quizzical look.

"They have a lovely suite upstairs."

"You didn't!"

He fished in his suit pocket and showed her a key to Suite #4. "I examined the rooms. It would be a lovely way to end a special evening."

Why wasn't she angry? "It's nice to know I haven't lost all my charms."

"Does that mean...?"

Maggie's forefinger traced her scar to the edge of her lips.

He leaned across the table. "Tell me you're not a lady, Maggie."

"I'm certainly not that saloon whore who had her hands all over you."

"Oh, her. That was just business. She was helpful with my card game. I gave her a big tip."

"I'll bet you did. And I'll bet that slut would love to use that suite with you tonight."

They walked into the lobby, where several attractive ladies of the house trolled. Henry slid the key across the counter to the clerk. "We don't need this room tonight."

The clerk grinned and looked at Maggie.

The musicians began playing a waltz.

Henry slipped an arm around Maggie's waist and danced her through the lobby toward the front door. He was light on his feet and graceful in his moves, a firm but a gentle leader.

Later, at Mrs. Watson's, they stopped in front of Maggie's door. There was a handwritten note tacked to her door. "Kit Carson will pick you up in the morning to look at mules."

She read the note and turned to Henry. "Thank you for a wonderful evening. Think about what you'd like to win if you can outshoot me tomorrow."

"Oh, I already know what I want." He tipped his hat, turned, and walked back to his room.

Chapter 12

Early the next morning, Kit Carson waited for Maggie on the street outside the boarding house. Wearing civilian clothes, he sat with another man in the back seat of a driven buggy. The driver opened the door, and Carson helped her step up into the carriage to sit opposite the stranger.

The man was over six feet tall, spare, and rawboned with a robust frame. He must have been in his early sixties, and kind gray eyes appraised her. He took off his wide-brimmed hat from abundant brown hair.

Carson said, "This is my old friend, Jim Bridger."

"Oh my god. I'm sitting with two legendary mountain men."

"Kit tells me he owes his life to you." Bridger's grip was firm and calloused.

"That's a bit of exaggeration, Mr. Bridger."

"Would appreciate it if you'd call me Jim."

She opened her parasol and put it over her shoulder to block the sun.

Bridger said, "Never seen an umbrella so bright, with little bells."

The driver hupped the mules, and the buggy started down the street toward the edge of town.

"Kit tells me you're heading down one of the trails and need to buy a horse or mule for your new buggy. I know a fellow who'll sell you whatever you're looking for. The trick is to pick out an animal that'll do the job, one with a good disposition. One you can handle."

Carson said, "She doesn't know which trail she'll take, so I sorta think she should buy both a mule and a horse. Both are strong, but a mule has more staying power. Better at crossing the dry country. They don't drink as much water, and besides, they can live on about a third of the feed a horse needs."

"Yep. Mule's smarter but slower and can be stubborn as anything. A horse is faster. Besides, if Maggie here needs to skedaddle, she can saddle the horse and ride out fast," Bridger said.

She regretted not letting George teach her how to ride.

"Think a mare would be best. Mules like mares. Be easier to catch," Carson said.

"Yep," Bridger said.

Thirty minutes later, they stood at the rancher's corral, looking at five mules that appeared to be identical. She listened to the men talk about the merits of each, details that escaped her.

"Let's take a closer look at them two," Bridger said, pointing at the ones he liked.

The rancher picked up halters, slipped through the gate. The mules walked away from him toward the opposite end of the corral.

"Aren't too friendly," Carson said, loud enough for the rancher to hear.

The mules kicked up dust as they avoided being caught. Finally, the rancher opened the gate to a smaller corral and forced them inside, kicking and braying. He haltered them and brought them back and tied them to the fence.

Bridger walked into the corral and examined the mules; hoofs, fetlocks, legs, teeth, ears, eyes, and muscular conformation. The rancher walked each mule in circles to check their gait.

Carson asked the rancher to put the two mules in separate pastures and take off their halters.

Bridger said, "Both look good to me."

"I agree, but this will be the test." He turned to Maggie, "We are going to see how easy they are to catch when free in a pasture."

Bridger grabbed a halter, walked to the first pasture and, with patience, caught the first mule. The second was easier to catch. He returned with the halters.

"Now, let's see how they react to you, Maggie."

"You want me to catch them?"

"Yep. See how they react to a woman, skirts, and all." He handed her a halter.

She handed him the parasol. He didn't know what to do with it, and finally, put it over his shoulder. Carson and the rancher laughed.

She took a deep breath and walked into the first pasture. The mule faced her, huge ears forward. Mimicking Jim's actions and moving slow, holding out her left hand for the mule to smell. Its nose was wet. She stroked its forehead. It put its head down so she could rub his ears. She slipped the halter over its head and tied the chinstrap and then led it back and tied to the fence rail.

Maggie grinned and asked Jim for the other halter, and then she walked into the pasture to catch the second mule. It watched her approach. She held out her hand. The mule spun, planted its two front feet in the ground, and kicked at her. She jumped back, tripped and fell in the dirt.

The mule looked over its shoulder at her, defying her to get closer. She rolled to her knees and tried to stand. The fabric bound her legs, and she had to pull the skirt above her knees before she could stand up. The mule turned to watch her struggle.

She should walk away, but felt since the men watched, she had to prove she could catch it.

She stood quiet for several minutes, acutely aware the men watched. The mule now faced her, left ear forward, right ear back, not paying full attention. She approached it even more slowly than the first time. This time it let her touch its nose, but then it spun. She fell again, close to the mule's back feet. It looked around at her, waiting. She rolled out of danger, rose and dusted herself off.

"I don't want this one!"

They laughed.

"Yep," Bridger said, "that one is a real son-of-a-bitch."

"Don't swear in front of a lady," Maggie scolded.

Carson turned to the rancher. "Now, we'd like to harness the good one up to a buggy."

She led the mule to a buggy in the barn. Its harness was the same as the one back home.

"I'll harness him," Carson said.

"No, I'll do it," she said.

They stood back and watched her harness the mule without a problem. She then climbed into the driver's seat, tapped the mule's butt with the reins, and drove the buggy out of the barn and around the farm lot, turning, stopping, and backing up.

She set the brake, stepped down, and asked the rancher, "How much?"

"That's my best mule. Two hundred."

"We've looked at others almost as good. One hundred," Maggie said.

"Hundred and fifty."

"Done. If you'll keep the mule until I'm ready. Now I'd like to look at your best mare."

Carson and Bridger glanced at each other and grinned.

They selected a sturdy chestnut-colored mare and paid top dollar.

"I'd like you to put my mule and mare alone in one pasture, so they get to know each other."

She excused herself and found a private place in the barn where she cut out double eagle gold pieces and put them into her purse. She walked back to the farmyard to pay the rancher, feeling much lighter. Her corset still felt like an uncomfortable vest, yet she dared not to shed it.

Where else could she keep her money safe?

Jim Bridger suggested they take dinner at Kelly's Westport Inn to celebrate a successful horse-trading morning. "The place has history. Daniel Boone's grandson ran a grocery there. Many think there's a tunnel from the basement to a stable, which was part of the Underground Railroad, helping slaves escape to Kansas. It's only one mile west. Besides that, the Inn is a place where ladies are welcome, and we men can wet our whistle."

Maggie wanted to ask why a woman couldn't have a drink, but let it pass.

They drove toward Westport in the harsh noon light. Maggie opened her parasol and tried to pat dust off her skirts. "Tell me about the strangest sights you've seen during your adventures, Jim."

"Well, there's an area up in the western mountains that's sure enough interesting. You walk your horse across the ground, and it sounds like you're walking on a drum. Steaming hot water shoots high out of the ground, and there are waterfalls like you never seen before. Then there is an area I call Great-Springs, so hot you can cook meat in, and lower down the hill where the water cools, and you can take a hot bath."

"Sounds wonderful," she said over the sound of the carriage wheels on gravel.

Later, at a table at Kelly's Inn, she ordered hot tea. Carson and Bridger ordered bourbon.

Carson grinned, slow-like. "Tell Maggie about the time you were trapped by redskins."

Bridger drew deeply from his long-stemmed pipe and stood up and rubbed his back. "Sorry. I've still got an arrowhead lodged in my back, and it sometimes gives me trouble."

A waiter approached, and they gave him their food order.

Jim sat down, took a puff on his pipe, and said, "Remember that time like it was yesterday. In the early thirties, I was up in that area we was just talking about. I was trapping with Milton Sublette.

"It was Blackfoot country and them can be mighty ornery, so we ran our trap line early morning and late evening. Well, one evening we heard the sounds of men and horses. We spied sixty or more braves coming at us, all painted for war. We jumped on our ponies and rode like hell-fire through the trees, trying to get rid of them. We rode into new country neither of us knew.

We stopped in some downed timber and fought them till our ammunition was running low, so we jumped back on our ponies and high-tailed it out of there, the Blackfoot hot on our trail. We rode twenty miles or so and found ourselves trapped in a box canyon. There was sheer rock walls on three sides and the injuns blocked our way out. We was in some predicament.

"We fought on till nightfall and then in the morning, backed up against that rock cliff, with no more ammunition and them injuns moved in on us slow like, real sure of themselves. Finally, they were less than thirty feet away, and we could see murder in their eyes, and there was nothing we could do."

Bridger put his pipe on the table, rose, and began to walk away.

"Wait!" Maggie said. "Don't leave till you finish the story. What happened? How did you get away?"

Bridger walked back to the table with a smile. "Bless your heart, Maggie, we didn't getaway. They killed us."

"What?"

Bridger picked up his pipe and walked away, chuckling to himself.

She didn't like Carson's gentle laughter. "What?"

"He tells that story to all greenhorns."

"Well," Maggie laughed, "he sure fooled me."

Chapter 13

After dinner, they drove towards the Alexander Majors house. Sunbeams pierced cracks between clouds. The warmth made Maggie drowsy.

"Now there's some pilgrims, for sure," Bridger said, as they passed several men walking along the road, wearing fringed buckskins.

"What do you mean? Maggie asked.

"Greenhorns. They're from out east and think buckskins are the thing to wear," Bridger said.

"Buckskins are good," Carson said. "West of the Arkansas River."

"I don't understand," Maggie said.

"The pilgrims wear buckskins on the trail between here and the Arkansas," Bridger explained. "And it rains between here and there. Their buckskins get wet and stretch. Pretty soon, they're a-walking on the knees of their pants, and their sleeves get long and floppy-like, and they can't get their hands out easy.

"Well, that gets real bothersome, so they cut those loose ends off and things go pretty well 'til about the time the wagon trains hit the Arkansas River, where the air gets real dry. Then them buckskins shrink, and they're a-walking around through the cactus with tight short pants and sleeveless shirts."

Carson nodded agreement. "Buckskins are good for the dry country, but not between here and there. I sometimes use a dried double buckskin shirt when I'm in Indian country. It deflects arrows. Sometimes." He turned to Bridger. "Tell her what you tell pilgrims about the forest you found up in that Yellow Stone country."

"Yes, sir! I found me a forest up there with petrified trees and petrified grass and petrified flowers, and even birds still a-singing petrified songs. My horses and mules had a mighty hard time feeding on that grass turned to stone." He belly laughed.

They pulled up to an elegant two-story white house – civilized living on the frontier.

"This here is Alexander Majors' house," Carson said. "He ran the finest and largest wagon trains down the trails. Made millions, but then he started the Pony Express and lost it all after the Overland Telegraph Company took the government contract. His son-in-law, Samuel Poteet, runs the wagon train outfit now."

Rebecca, Alexander's daughter, greeted them at the door and led them into the office. Her husband Samuel, a short man with serious gray eyes, rose from his desk and greeted Carson and Bridger as old friends.

Carson said, "Mrs. Hartstone would like to join your trip to supply the army forts along the Santa Fe Trail."

"I see. How many in your party, Mrs. Hartstone?"

"I'll be traveling alone, in my own small wagon."

"Alone? Our wagon train only hauls freight. You would be the only woman." His eyebrows furrowed as he glanced at Carson and Bridger.

"She's capable, and if there's trouble, I'll look after her," Carson said. "I've got a detachment of the army cavalry guarding us all the way to Fort Garland."

Bridger added, "You'll be safe, Maggie. Samuel here has continued Mr. Majors' policy of having every employee sign a contract that forbids swearing, fighting, trouble-making, and the like. Samuel honors the Bible and rests the train on Sundays."

"We've had no trouble, so you can feel safe on that account. I can't account for accident, disease, or Indians," Samuel said.

"That's reassuring," Maggie said.

"How far do you plan to travel, Mrs. Hartstone?"

"At least to Council Grove, and maybe to Santa Fe. I'll book passage to Santa Fe, and you can keep the difference if I leave earlier."

They talked about the details, and she agreed on a fare.

"My men will herd your animals to and from grazing. You will be responsible for hitching and unhitching, as well as collecting your own firewood and cooking. We'll leave within the week.

She told him about the murder of Jenny and George, and how she wanted to locate the killers and turn them over to the law for justice. "I'll offer a reward of fifty dollars gold for information about their whereabouts."

Samuel shook his head. "If they're in Council Grove now, they'll be gone by the time we get there."

"I might discover where they're going," she said.

Samuel stroked his chin. "You'd be time and money ahead if you'd hire someone experienced to chase them down."

"I've considered that. But this is something I have to do personally."

He agreed to put the word out to his employees. "I give the Good Book to all who travel with us." He handed her a leather covered Bible.

"Thank you, but I carry my family Bible," she said.

Rebecca walked into the office. "Sorry to interrupt, but if your business is done, I wanted to let Mrs. Hartstone know that I'm going over to the Binghams' for tea. Perhaps you'd like to join me?"

Maggie knew of the Missouri politician and artist George Caleb Bingham. In fact, she had displayed several of his paintings at

Thespian Hall. She would love to meet him, she said and thanked the men before leaving with Rebecca. The Poteet's man, Jefferson, drove their buggy to the twenty-acre Bingham estate, close to Independence Square.

The white brick house had a wraparound porch with gingerbread trim. A smaller upper porch protruded from the middle of the second story. The roof had three dormers artistically balanced over the upper porch, and a cupola sat on top of the roof. A white chimney rose from each corner of the house.

Mrs. Bingham greeted them and, after a quick, delightful chat over tea and scones, led them to her husband's studio, a log-and-clapboard building northwest of their home. He was pencil-sketching an idea for a new work.

"I'm going to call the painting *Order Number Eleven.*"

Maggie studied the sketches. They were dark and depressing, people fleeing burning homes while Union General Ewing, sitting on a horse, watched guerrillas murder a man and woman.

"General Ewing's forced evacuation of four counties was an act of stupidity. And all to deprive Confederate-allied guerrillas with material support from the countryside. I wrote to the general and said, 'If you execute this order, I shall make you infamous with pen and brush.'

He ignored my advice. He burned houses, destroyed crops, and forced innocent civilians into homeless poverty. My hope is that this panting will forever tarnish his reputation, as I promised."

Maggie looked at the murdered man and woman in the highlighted foreground. She felt as though she'd been kicked in the stomach; the painting brought back the scene of Jenny and George's death with horrifying immediacy. She told her hosts she was late for an appointment and rushed out.

Later, on the buggy ride back to the boarding house, she apologized to Rebecca and told her what had caused her to flee from the Bingham's hospitality.

She arrived back to her lodgings just in time for supper, where Henry pulled out a chair and sat next to her.

"Are you feeling well?" Henry asked.

"I feel fine."

"Ready for our shooting match?"

"Of course."

"Good! I'll teach you how to shoot," he said.

"Don't count on it."

Chapter 14

The next afternoon was sunny, calm, and warm when Henry and Maggie walked to the stable. Jodi rented them a mule and buggy and suggested a place on the edge of town where Henry could practice shooting.

Jodi brought the rig to them, and Maggie started to climb up to sit next to Henry in the driver's seat when she had an idea. "Jodi, do you keep a ledger of the names of owners of horses you stable?" she asked.

He looked at her with his right good eye. His left eye searched the street aimlessly. "Yep. Why?"

"I wonder if the red-headed man who stole my horse wrote down his name."

"Most just sign with their mark."

"Well, why don't we look in any case?" And so they walked back to the stable. Maggie followed Jodi inside, where his father napped on several hay bales.

Jodi pulled down a tattered ledger from a shelf close to the door, running his finger down a column describing customers' horses until he found Traveler's description. He slid his thumb across to the owner's name column and held the ledger up for Maggie to read. Most had indeed signed with their marks – but Red had scrawled his name. *Patrick Doyne.*

Grinning, Maggie walked to the buggy and climbed up next to Henry.

"You look might pleased with yourself."

"I found the red-haired killer's name."

He frowned when she told him it was Patrick Doyne.

"What?" she asked.

"There was a Doyne family in Montgomery County. They mortgaged their plantation to help the Confederacy. The Union replaced pro-south bankers, and they foreclosed. They sold the place out from under them. Mrs. Doyne's heart quit. When her husband found her, he shot himself in the head. They had several kids, all with bright red hair. I heard one joined Bloody Bill Anderson. Must be the one you're looking for."

"Another decent family ruined by fellow citizens."

"Now you know his name, what are you going to do?" Henry asked, slapping the reins on the mule's rump. Its ears flattened, and it refused to move until Henry flicked the reins several more times against its rear.

"I'll think about it," she said.

They drove past Independence Square's courthouse and out into the countryside north of town. He turned down a country road.

"Have you heard from our drunk friend?" Henry asked.

"Mr. Williams? No, he hasn't shown his face."

"He'd rather drink up your money and wallow in self-pity. You were kind to give him money. Kinder still to offer to help him once he got sober."

She checked her bonnet and opened her parasol to block the sun. "I can't force my ideas on someone else."

"So Williams is doomed?"

"His choice."

Henry found an open field lined with hedge apple trees. He reined in the mule and set the brake. They got down, and he walked under the trees, returning with an armful of hedge apples.

"Think you're a better shot than me, Mrs. Hartstone?" he said flippantly. "Now is your chance to prove it." He tossed two hedge apples into the field, about twenty feet away. "Ladies first."

"What are the stakes?"

"I believe we agreed the winner gets his wish."

"*Her* wish, Mr. Herndon."

He smiled. "Your shot."

"I thought you gave ladies a choice. I'd rather you shoot first."

He opened his coat, pulled a Colt Navy.36 from its holster, cocked, aimed, and fired. The hedge apple shattered. He grinned and bowed. "Your shot, Madam."

She waited for the smoke to clear, withdrew the revolver from her sash, pulled back the hammer, aimed at the second hedge apple, and pulled the trigger. It exploded. Gray smoke and the acrid stink of black powder and the sweet smell of hedge apples drifted back to them.

Henry grunted. "Here's a harder shot." He tossed two more targets into the field, twice the distance as the first two. He shot. His bullet hit under the apple, spraying dirt into the air. The intact hedge apple rolled several feet farther. He stared at his pistol as if the miss was its fault. "Goddamnit!"

"You know better than to use that kind of language in front of a lady."

"Sorry."

"You were close, but it looks like you can't hit a bull's rump with a banjo," she said with a glint in her eye.

She shot. The apple split in half, pieces tumbling across the field. "Let's try a harder shot."

He threw a hedge apple high above him, thumbed the hammer, squeezed the trigger, and it exploded.

"Good shot! Let me try." She tossed the target high and shot. Fragments rained down upon them. He grinned and brushed sticky yellow pieces off his shoulders. She laughed. "I should have thrown it further out."

"Final shot. You toss mine, and then I'll toss yours."

She tossed the apple high and far.

His shot shattered the target.

"Good shot."

He picked up another hedge apple. "You're one point ahead. Miss this, and I hit mine, and we'll tie. Hit it, and you win. Don't let the pressure get to you," he laughed.

"Wait! Before you toss it for me, I want to know the stakes," she said.

"Sorry?"

"You missed one target. If I miss this next shot, it's a draw. If I hit it, I win. I'd like to know what you were hoping to win."

"Why should I tell you?"

"Because you're a gentleman. You don't have to confess, but I am curious."

He looked at the sky and the trees and then said, "Had I won, I would have demanded to go with you to look for Patrick Doyne."

She blinked - not at all what she expected.

"We could stop our contest now and call it a tie," he suggested.

"Not on your life!"

He shrugged, picked up a hedge apple, and prepared to throw. "Say when."

She cocked the pistol and pointed it toward the sky. "Now!"

He threw it high and far. Maggie aimed, following the target while it rose. The instant before it stalled, she pulled the trigger. The hedge apple shattered. Tiny pieces fell into the field. Silent, they smelled the sweet scent of the apples and the earth and the bitter scent of gunpowder.

"You're a better shot." He shook her hand. "So, what did I lose?"

"You mean, 'What did I win?'"

"Yes, that too," he said.

"Can't you guess?" she asked.

"I can't imagine."

"You owe me another dinner, Mr. Herndon."

He smiled, and the scar across his cheek throbbed – or maybe that was just her imagination.

That evening after dinner, they danced. Henry was a marvelous dancer, a strong lead and light on his feet. George's dancing had been all technique, as though he had to concentrate, counting each step, flawless but without a soul. Henry's dancing was soulful.

Floating across the floor in his arms, Maggie felt the heat of his body and breathed in his masculine smell. She felt young and happy and wanted again. She could dance with Henry until the end of time, but unfortunately, the band stopped playing for the night. They were the only ones remaining on the dance floor.

"I suppose we must stop," Henry said.

She pulled away. "Well, we certainly can't stand here all night in each other's arms."

"I'd like to hold you in my arms all night."

"Why don't you tip the band, Mr. Herndon?"

They walked arm in arm back toward the boarding house. Two doors past the Red Eye Saloon, they stopped under the post of a gas lamp and read a brass plaque on a door: *Thomas F. Billings, Esq. Attorney at Law.*

"I wonder if he's reputable?" Maggie asked.

"Do you need a lawyer?"

"I might."

"You might ask Mrs. Watson or Mr. Bridger about his reputation."

They were surprised to find Mrs. Watson standing behind the check-in desk at this late hour. She turned toward them.

"There you are, Mr. Herndon and Mrs. Hartstone. Everyone was worried about you missing supper."

"Good evening, Mrs. Watson," Henry said. "Did I forget to tell you why we had to miss supper?"

"You don't like my food?"

Maggie said, "We had an invitation to eat elsewhere."

"I don't give refunds for missed meals."

"Nor do we expect one." Why did Maggie say 'we', like they were a couple? Ridiculous!

"Many people want our rooms, so if you'd prefer to go elsewhere . . ."

Henry ignored Mrs. Watson's complaining and walked Maggie upstairs to her room. When she reached in her purse for her door key, he slipped his arms around her. Maggie stiffened and then allowed her body to relax.

She pressed into him and felt his warmth and the pleasant musky scent of his skin. She reached up and pulled his head down and felt the fullness of his lips on hers, and it was better than good. Henry's lips were warm, alive, and eager. George had hard, somewhat unresponsive lips.

She pulled away and put her head on his shoulder. Why was she comparing Henry with George? Why couldn't she just live in this moment?

He cupped her chin in his hand, lifted her head, and kissed her again. "Give me the key. I'll unlock your door."

"Thank you for being a gentleman, Henry, but I'm capable of unlocking my door."

"You mean?"

"It was a lovely romantic evening, but all good things must end."

"I pictured a different ending."

"You have a healthy imagination." She turned an inserted the key, opened the lock, and opened the door. "Goodnight, Henry." She stepped inside.

He held the door open. "Wait."

"What?" She turned toward him, expecting him to try to push his way into her room.

"I haven't been candid."

"Your wife didn't die?"

"No! It's not like that. When we first met, I never imagined I'd feel . . ." he paused.

"What?"

"It's too complicated to talk about tonight. It's late. I shouldn't have brought it up."

"I want to know."

"It's nothing. I don't want to spoil our evening."

"I had a lovely time, Henry. Thank you." She shut the door and listened to his footsteps fade down the hallway toward his room.

She got ready for bed and wondered about Henry's secret. It would have to wait until tomorrow. She crawled between the bed sheets and, as she reached to turn off the gas lamp, looked at the washbasin. It would be lovely to soak in a bath. She lay in the dark, had an idea, and stifled a giggle.

Chapter 15

Maggie rose early the next morning, poured cold water into her washbasin, and wiped her face and body clean with a washcloth before dressing. Downstairs, Henry had already eaten breakfast and sat on the porch, reading.

She greeted him and sat in the rocking chair next to him.

"Did you sleep well?" he asked.

"I thought about us."

"Oh?"

"You promised to tell me your secret today," she said.

"Perhaps later."

"Afraid of my reaction?"

"You are quite perceptive, Mrs. Hartstone."

"I had another thought about you."

"Oh?" he asked. A hint of suspicion in his voice made Maggie wonder if he resented her refusal to invite him into her bedroom. Did he bear a grudge?

"Since you are a gambling man, I propose another shooting match with known stakes – the loser will rent the Noland Hotel suite for tonight and tomorrow. The winner can use it as *she* sees fit."

Henry blinked. "You mean, 'as *he* sees fit,' don't you?"

She laughed. "The suite, with no additional promises, Mr. Herndon."

"I don't like the odds. If I lose, I could be out my investment without any return."

"You aren't much of a gambler if you won't take a chance on a woman changing her mind."

His eyes looked hard when he reached over and shook her hand. "It's a deal. When do you want to shoot?"

"Right after I visit a lawyer."

She walked to the attorney's office. Thomas Billings, Esq sat across from her at a large oak desk piled with papers. Short and rotund, he was bald with an unruly white beard. The stench of cigar smoke filled the office. He asked how he could be of service.

"I would like to hire you to write a letter on your stationery to a Mr. Patrick Doyne," she said.

"And what would the letter say?" he asked.

"I'll dictate it to you," she said.

An hour later, Maggie walked out of the attorney's office with the letter sealed inside an envelope addressed to Mr. Patrick Doyne with a return address of Thomas F. Billings, Attorney at Law.

She tucked the letter into her purse, opened her parasol, and walked toward Mrs. Watson's to find Henry. She wanted to know about that secret.

A block from the boarding house, a horseman called her name. It was Sheriff Clay. She stopped and shielded her eyes from the sun as he reined to a halt, leaned his hands on the saddle horn, and stared down at the sidewalk.

"I have news, Mrs. Hartstone."

"Good news, I hope?"

"Might call it that. Might not."

"Well, spit it out, Sheriff."

"I sent a wire to the sheriff in Council Grove, asking about the red-haired man and your horse." He sat up and tipped his hat to a woman walking past.

"And?"

"Just got his telegraph. Red left four days ago with a wagon train headed down the Santa Fe Trail."

She felt her heart thump faster. "The sheriff's going after the killer?"

"Nope. Red has too big a head start. Besides, the sheriff has enough troubles in the city."

"That's what all you lawmen say. Too much trouble to catch killers."

"You wanted to know where he was, and now you know where he's headed. That's more than you knew when you walked into my office." He spun his horse and trotted up the street.

She shouted, "Thank you!" to his back.

Henry's rented buggy was in front of the boarding house, and he waited on the porch.

"I sweet-talked Mrs. Watson into making a picnic."

"That's wonderful! I'll bet it cost you extra."

"As I said, Maggie, you are perceptive."

They drove through town toward their shooting area.

"It's time you told me your secret," Maggie said.

A wagon rolled past. A woman and two children sat on the driver's seat. The father walked alongside the ox, the lead rope in his right hand, and a stout staff in his left. The wife's face looked hollowed by exhaustion.

"It's not important," he said.

"Are you in the habit of breaking promises, Mr. Herndon?" she asked in a light, teasing tone.

He snapped the reins against the mule's haunches and said, "I believe honesty is a basis for a long-term relationship."

"We don't have a relationship," Maggie laughed. "Much less a long-term relationship."

"What I was trying to say is that I'm beginning to develop feelings for you, Maggie."

"I'll bet you say that to every gal you try to bed."

"Dammit! Will you just listen?" Henry snapped. "I don't want something to arise in the future that might alter your feelings because you think I've been dishonest."

"What are you trying to tell me, Henry?"

"I'm Ephraim's nephew."

She gripped the wagon's sideboard so hard she thought her fingernails would break. "Ephraim told me he had a nephew."

"He knew I'd been thinking about starting a new life out west. With my wife and children gone, there was nothing to hold me to the place."

"And so here you are. What a coincidence."

"When you decided to chase the killers, and Ephraim could not talk you out of it, he wrote and asked me to look out for you."

"He *what*?"

"Asked me to protect you."

"He *hired* you?"

"I was headed west eventually. It made sense."

"No one asked me!"

"Ephraim said he broached the subject with you, but you were too stubborn to listen."

"Not stubborn, Henry, *determined*!"

"Ephraim told me not to tell you because you'd be insulted if you knew he'd sent me to protect you."

"I never wanted to drag anyone else into my problems. I can protect myself. I can certainly shoot better than you!"

"Ephraim loves you like a father, Maggie."

"My father would never have tried to control me." She rocked back and forth.

"Well, that's the issue I didn't want to spoil our relationship if one were to develop. Ephraim loves you and didn't want to see you come to harm. Don't be hard on him."

They rode in silence. Maggie wondered how Ephraim was getting along managing both plantations. Had many of the slaves run away? All of them? Was *White Haven* producing enough revenue to pay the taxes? Was the other half of her gold still hidden? It was a comfort to think she had a buried reserve, if and when she needed it.

Henry parked the buggy under the shade of an oak tree and placed the picnic hamper on a blanket. It contained freshly baked dark bread and cheese, a bottle of wine, and a bottle of water.

They sat, and he placed plates and cups on the blanket. He offered Maggie a glass of wine.

"Let's celebrate after I outshoot you," she said with what she hoped was a wicked smile.

They ate.

"You're quiet today, Maggie. I hope it's not all my news."

"The sheriff told me he's just learned the killers were starting down the Santa Fe Trail. Now I know where they're going."

"That's excellent news! Now you can wire the sheriff in Santa Fe to be on the lookout for them. It might be wise to offer a large reward."

"I've already done it."

"Good. Now you can return to Boonville."

"And what? Sit in my parlor and knit, hoping in vain to hear about their capture?" She thought about returning to her former life on the plantation, waiting for *guerrillas* to knock on the door, directing the slaves, running the place, listening to her tea group gossip, trying to return a bit of culture to the community. It felt wrong.

Henry stood and offered her a hand up. "Shall we have our match, then?"

He collected an armful of hedge apples and offered her the first shot. She imagined each apple thrown to be one of the killers.

She handily outshot him and laughed gaily. "Since you owe me the suite, I'll be happy to pay for dinner."

"And after dinner?"

"Two dances."

"And after that?"

"That's what will make this evening exciting. We won't know until the time comes." She kissed him lightly on the cheek. "Now, let's pick up our things and drive back to town. I need to pack my valise while you arrange for the suite. I can hardly wait to take a real bath."

Maggie met him in the Noland Hotel's lobby. He smiled and held out the key. When she reached for it, he dangled the key above his head and laughed. "I'll escort you to your suite, Madame."

She moved her hand toward her pistol. "I'll shoot you if you try to misbehave – before I'm ready."

They walked up the wide staircase and down the hall toward the suite. He opened the door for her and allowed her to walk first into the room. The suite was as lovely as he'd promised, with a living room, a separate bedroom with a massive four-poster bed, closet, a bathroom with a toilet, and, best of all, a huge bathtub.

She turned on a faucet. "I can't imagine they would have running water, cold and hot, too."

"Maggie, even the Romans had running water," he said.

"Still, this is the frontier. *Amazing!*" She felt the thick towels and ran her fingers across two robes folded on a table.

She turned and pulled him close, kissed him, and then pushed him away.

"I'm going to take a bath so that I'm clean for you, so I need privacy. Go downstairs and make supper reservations. I'll be freshly bathed when I meet you there at six."

"Take a bath later. Or better yet, I'll scrub your back."

"Think of me in the tub." She led him out and locked the door behind him.

She undressed, took down her hair, brushed out the long braids, and filled the tub, immersing herself in the deliciously hot water.

After soaking, she washed her hair and body until she could no longer stand to be in the scummy water. She stepped out, wrapped her body in a towel, drained the tub, rinsed it out, and then refilled it. The tub felt so good. She soaked until the water turned cool. She emptied it a second time and filled it again with even hotter water.

When her skin seemed like it would be eternally wrinkled, she towel-dried and brushed her hair but decided not to braid it just yet. Would Henry like it down? The robe felt delicious, and she found a chaise lounge in the living room where the afternoon sun shone warm and bright.

Her emotions were a surprise. She'd never expected to be attracted to anyone but George. Wasn't her rage enough to snuff out any desire or feelings? How could her heart have room for both blinding hatred and seductive temptation? Perhaps it didn't.

Maybe she was starting on the road toward forgiveness and peace. Or it could be that Henry was merely a way for her to escape sorrow and anger. The answer was beyond her. The warm sun beat down on her, and she nodded off.

Sometime later, she shivered awake, squinting through closed eyelids. The sun was low. It was time to get dressed for dinner.

She put on her best dress and started to walk out of the suite. George appeared, leaning against the wall next to the door.

"Are you going to make love with him?"

Her hand covered her locket. "Of course not. How could you even think such a dirty thought?"

"Henry seems nice enough. You need to move on with your life, Maggie. Give up your hunt and settle down with him."

"That's ridiculous. You're the only one."

"Think about it, Maggie," he said, fading into the wall.

Henry met her in the lobby. "I've not seen your hair down. It's beautiful."

They had a lovely dinner and afterward danced more than twice. The band finally stopped for a break.

"It's getting close to bedtime," Maggie said.

"I hope the lady has changed her mind."

Maggie took his hand and hurried him up the broad staircase, thinking everyone in the lobby must be watching, knowing what they were hurrying for a tryst. She hoped Henry didn't notice her blushing face.

She led him down the wide carpeted hallway, lined with landscape paintings. They stopped at the walnut door with Suite #4 spelled out in brass letters. She turned and kissed him, tasted his lips, and lingered in his arms.

He nibbled her earlobe and whispered, "Shouldn't we go in?"

She dropped the key when she tried to insert it into the lock.

Henry bent down, picked up the key, and grinned as handed it to her.

She opened the door.

George sat in the lounge chair, facing the door.

She gasped, hand on her chest.

George smiled at her and then looked over her shoulder at Henry. "Looks like you two are getting friendly."

Maggie moaned.

She spun toward Henry, kissed him hard, and pushed him back into the hall, and shut the door behind her.

"What's wrong?" Henry asked.

"I . . . I just can't."

He cupped her chin and looked into her eyes. "Can't or don't want to?"

"I want to, but I can't. I don't know. I can't explain."

"You don't have you talk about it. I expect it's too soon. There's no rush."

"There are too many memories. My husband, and that strumpet hanging on you. You're right, it's too soon. I'm sorry. So sorry."

Henry kissed her on the cheek, turned, and walked away.

She watched him stride down the hall toward the staircase. She leaned against the door, covered her face with her hands, and shook her head. Would George always appear at intimate moments? Was he jealous?

Still, Henry didn't protest. If he wanted her badly, he could have shown it. Now that's ridiculous. George is dead. He is not real. He's a figment of her imagination, of her needs, of her guilt. What would have happened had she invited Henry inside? Would have George disappeared? Or sat and watched? Or, god forbid, would have he interrupted them with a running flow of judgments?

She turned, opened the door, and looked into the room. The lounge chair was empty.

"George? Where are you? We need to talk." She searched the suite. George was gone.

She stood in the middle of the living room, hands tight fists, eyes closed, and thought her buggy driver, Sam, was right. She was going crazy.

And what about Henry? He was the only man other than George that attracted her. What was he thinking? That she was a tease? She believed women who teased men were cruel. Did Herny think she couldn't make up her mind? On the other hand, if he genuinely cared about her, why didn't he make a stronger protest? Or did he think she felt, given George's murder, an intimate relationship was premature?

She hoped so, but couldn't escape the feeling she'd pushed Henry away forever.

Chapter 16

Maggie rose early to walk to Mrs. Wilson's to meet Kit Carson. Without his help, getting her mule and horse to her buggy at Hiram Young & Company would be a logistical nightmare.

She dreaded the thought of meeting Henry. What could she say? Fortunately, she did not see him. She changed out of her fashionable dress into a travel dress.

When she returned to the porch, she found Carson, dressed in civilian clothes, waiting for her in a buggy on the street in front of the boarding house.

"I dropped Bridger off at the ranch where you bought your stock. He'll ride the mare and lead the mule to Hiram Young's, where we'll pick up your new wagon."

She climbed into the driver's bench next to Carson and popped open her parasol. Carson flicked the reins and prodded the mules into a plodding gait. They wove through traffic jamming the street: carriages, buggies, carts, wagons, and cowboys on horseback driving a herd of longhorns.

Maggie covered her nose with her handkerchief to ward off the stench of dung and sweat and waved away tiny flies that swarmed around her eyes, hoping that they would flock back to the animals to suck their blood instead of hers.

Carson cut her a swift glance. "Still of a mind to find the killers?"

"Yes."

"One of them might kill you," Carson said with a voice so soft he might have been thinking aloud.

Maggie stayed silent.

They nodded a greeting to a man and woman riding in a slave-driven buggy, and Carson sighed after they passed. "Sorry. Shouldn't have said that."

"You're right. But as I told you on the boat, I have nothing to live for."

"It's the way you die you should worry about. You should pray, as I do, that death will be fast."

"I don't know what else to do."

"It's none of my business, but you could take up with some nice gentleman and lead a happy life." He paused. "Like that Mr. Herndon, for example."

Maggie clenched her fists.

"My experience is that you can love more than one person," Carson continued. "I've had two loves and been married three times. Don't like to talk about the first two. Squaw men aren't favored in a civilized society."

"Tell me about your wives," she said, happy to keep him talking about himself.

"I met Singing Grass at a Green River trapper rendezvous in '36. I had to fight a duel for her hand. Darned near kicked the bucket when that trapper's bullet singed my hair. I loved her mightily. We had one daughter, but Singing Grass died giving birth to our second daughter. And that girl died when she was two. Fell into a kettle of boiling soap in Taos."

"Oh, my God! What a tragedy. Did you raise your first daughter?"

"Couldn't. I was a trapper and explorer. I took her to live with my sister in St. Louis. She grew up, got married, got divorced, and died in the California goldfields."

"I'm so sorry. What about your second marriage?" Maggie asked.

"Jumped too fast to a Cheyenne woman named Making-Out-Road. She wanted to continue the traveling ways of her tribe. I wanted to settle down. She divorced me in the way of her people by putting my personal property outside our tepee."

"I'm sorry."

"Needn't be. Two years later, I met Josefa. She was the daughter of a wealthy Mexican couple living in Taos. I had to join the Catholic Church before I could marry her. And now we have seven children, and I love her more than anything."

"So, you're happy now?"

"Happier than ever before. I'd thought my life was over when Singing Grass died, but given time I found Josefa. Something you might want to think about, Maggie, before you rush in where angels fear to tread."

"I'll think about your words. Thank you."

They approached the Hiram Young & Company building. Jim Bridger leaned against the trunk of a shade tree in front, waiting for them. Her mule and mare stood at the hitching rack.

"Found you a saddle that'll fit you, Maggie," Bridger said.

"That's so nice of you, Jim, but I don't ride," she said.

He laughed. "You'll learn fast if Injuns chase you."

She smiled in return. "I'll bet you're right."

They found Mr. McCoy in his office, who led them to her new buggy. It looked perfect: small, durable, and sturdy, but what did she know? He showed her the spring front seat with the concealed compartment below. A toolbox hung from the front, above the tongue. A fifty-gallon water barrel was attached to the left side, and a feedbox and second water barrel hung on the right. The front wheels were smaller than the rear for easier turning. All were made from seasoned hardwoods – the spokes and rim –while an iron tire bound each wheel.

McCoy said, "The air gets mighty dry once you get west of the Arkansas River, the spokes and rims dry out and shrink. They'll break down unless you soak the wheels in water to swell them to fit. But in case they break, I included extra spokes, and two felloes and iron plates."

Maggie noticed that Mr. McCoy had included a grease bucket that hung from the rear axle assembly.

Bridger knocked his fist against the wagon bed. "See you've made it watertight, so it'll float in deep water."

Maggie looked at him. Was he kidding?

"We sewed three sheets of canvas together for a rainproof cover," McCoy continued. "You can draw the ends together in bad weather or for privacy."

She glanced at Bridger and Carson. Each man nodded his approval, so she accompanied Mr. McCoy to his office to pay the balance.

Bridger and Carson brought the mule and mare to the wagon and hitched up the mule without a problem. They tied the mare's halter rope to the rear of the carriage.

She climbed into the driver's seat and took the reins. Carson joined her, while Bridger followed, driving Carson's buggy. The large bay mule's large floppy ears moved back and forth as it walked. It responded well to her commands and seemed to pull her wagon without effort.

"He'll need a name," she said.

"It," Carson suggested.

"You don't have to explain. I know a mule is an 'it,' but I prefer giving it a male name."

"Better hurry, or you'll end up calling him 'Stupid' or 'Stubborn.'"

He directed her to a store that sold merchandise for wagon trains. She reined to a stop outside the store and set the brake. Bridger parked alongside.

Inside, the clerk handed Carson a list of items necessary for a wagon trip. He glanced at it and passed it over to Maggie. "Might be easier if you'd read it out loud instead of each of us looking at it separately."

The look in his eyes confirmed his secret: he was illiterate.

She read: "Ax, hatchet, set of augers, shovel, pickax, saw, mallet, hammer, plane, nails, rope, tallow for the grease bucket, a twelve-foot chain, horseshoes, hammer and nails, and a light wagon jack."

Bridger said, "Other than the tallow, ax, and hatchet, you won't need any tools, because you'll be traveling with Samuel's wagon train. They'll have everything and will fix anything for you."

"I agree," Carson said. "No sense in adding weight. Make it harder for the mule to pull."

Maggie studied the list. "I'd feel better if I had everything I might need."

Bridger chuckled. "So they leave you in the dust. You're all alone. Break a felloe on your rear wheel. Know how to use those tools to fix it?"

"I'll feel more comfortable with those tools than without them."

Carson and Bridger cut a glance at each other as if to say, "Just like a woman."

She ignored them and told the clerk that she'd buy the recommended tools.

While the man gathered up the items, she read aloud the recommended cooking utensils: "Dutch oven, kettle, skillet, ladle, tin tableware, butcher knife, skinning knife, paring knife, lantern, matches, and extra-large safety pins."

She thought the recommendation of large safety pins was strange. "Do I need to add or subtract anything from this list?"

Carson shook his head. "Seems good to me."

Bridger nodded his agreement.

"Good. Now how about the food?"

She read the recommended amount of food per person: 150 lbs. Flour, 100 lbs. Bacon, 25 lbs. Sugar, 50 lbs. Lard, 15 lbs. Coffee, 4 lbs. Tea, sacks of beans, rice, and dried peaches and apples. Eggs, cornmeal, salt, pepper, vinegar, and molasses.

"Well, I don't drink coffee, so I certainly don't need that."

Bridger rubbed his chin. "Well, even animals like coffee mixed with water to kill the chalky taste."

"You must be teasing me," Maggie said.

"Nope. Unless you hit a clear spring, the water can taste terrible. Gotta avoid bad water, or you'll get cholera and die of the flux," Bridger said.

"How do I keep eggs from breaking?" she asked.

"Pack them in the cornmeal," Carson said, "and then use the meal to make cornbread."

"Better buy two sheepskins and blankets for sleeping," Bridger suggested.

She paid her bill while Carson and Bridger hauled the merchandise and packed it in her wagon.

They stopped at the feed store and, after calculating the amount needed for the trip, she bought shelled corn and feedbags for the animals.

Fully loaded, they drove the wagon out to Samuel Poteet's place and parked it at the barn near his other wagons.

"Samuel's men guard the place, so you don't have to worry about having anything stolen, Maggie," Carson said. Samuel told me we're pulling out at dawn day after tomorrow, so you'll want to sleep in your wagon tomorrow night."

She thanked them for their help and asked if they would join her for dinner tonight at the Noland Hotel. They were delighted at the prospect of having a good meal.

Chapter 17

Maggie looked for Henry to invite him to dinner with Carson and Bridger.

He sat in a rocking chair on Mrs. Watson's porch, reading a book. He looked up at the sound of her footsteps on the stairs and flashed a smile, standing to greet her and stepping closer for a kiss. Maggie sidestepped his advance and sat in a rocking chair next to his.

"You're reading a book," she said, avoiding the subject of last night.

He picked it up from the coffee table between them and handed it to her. "I bought it for you. I hope you like poetry. It's *Leaves of Grass*, by Walt Whitman. It might make a good companion for your travels."

"That's very thoughtful, Henry." She leafed through the pages. It hadn't been available in Boonville because of its explicit sexual imagery.

They watched a group of cowboys trot past, horses lathered in white sweat, hoofs kicking up puffs of dust. The creak of saddle leather broke the silence.

"Looks like they're going to stop at the first saloon," he said.

"I invited Mr. Carson and Bridger to join me for dinner. You're welcome to join us."

Henry's eyes clouded before he flashed his smile. "Wild horses couldn't keep me away."

Several hours later, Maggie was the first to arrive in the dining room. The maître d' led her to an empty table for four. When Carson and Bridger came, the maître d' looked as though he was on the verge of an epileptic fit, simultaneously thrilled to have the famous mountain men in his dining room and frightened about what might happen.

They ordered drinks when Henry joined them: straight-up whiskey for Carson and Bridger and a bottle of red wine for Maggie and Henry.

Bridger held up his drink: "Here's a toast to Maggie's adventure!" He slugged down his whiskey and set the glass down with a loud thump. He waved his arm for the maître d', who hurried over, head bowed as if to duck trouble.

"We'll have another round!"

The maître d's head bobbed as if on a spring. "Another bottle of wine, as well?"

"Hell no! Can't you see they haven't even started on that first bottle?" Bridger said.

Henry turned to Carson. "Maggie tells me you met President Polk in Washington."

"I carried the news of our conquest of California from General Fremont to the President. It was an interesting experience to cross the country and be in Washington."

The maître d' produced the menus with a flourish. Bridger looked at Carson and raised his eyebrows. Both men were looking at the list uneasily – neither could read.

"Henry and I ate here the other night. I had the wildfowl, and he had the buffalo tongue. Both were delicious. But I've heard the scalloped oysters and the pigs head are excellent," she suggested.

Bridger put down his menu. "Never had oysters. Think I'll try the wildfowl instead."

"I've had plenty of buffalo and birds. I'm going to have the pigs head, even though it seems to be the wrong end to eat," said Carson.

After they ordered, Bridger said, "Hear about how Kit won the Battle of Adobe Walls?"

Carson said, "It was more like a draw. And lucky for us."

"Kit had three thousand Kiowa and Comanche warriors gunning for him, but he beat 'em with just a couple hundred men."

"Tell us about it," Henry said.

"The Indians had been raiding, and General Carleton wanted to put an end to it. So he sent me down to their winter camps with about four hundred men to punish them. Thank God I took along two mountain howitzers, or we wouldn't be here today.

"There were too many Indians, and I called a retreat. The Indians started a grass fire to block our way, but I had the boys start back-fires. We got out with our skin intact."

"It was a great victory! Taught 'em a good lesson," Bridger crowed. "Now, you ever hear of a glass mountain?"

Maggie and Henry shook their heads. Carson smiled and relaxed in his chair, shaking his head.

"Well, this here is a true story, or I ain't the greatest mountain man who ever lived. I was up in that Yellow Stone country, where a man can catch a fish in the deep cold water and pull it up through the hot water, and it'll cook perfect-like. I was hungry and set up my lean-to at dark.

In the morning, around dawn, I look out from under my buffalo robe and there, not twenty-five feet away, stands a big elk with its head down eating grass.

"I picked up my rifle and took careful aim and squeezed off a shot, expecting that elk to fall dead. But it never even looked up. I looked around to see if anyone might be about to see the worst shot I ever made.

"I reloaded and shot again. That elk never moved. I figured it must be stone deaf, and I shot once more. It just stood there pretty as a picture. Well, I figured my rifle was plum wore out, so I pulled out my knife and gave that elk a charge with a mind to slit its throat.

"Not six steps from my lean-to I hit a wall of glass. It was a solid mountain of glass. I jumped on my horse and spent the day riding around that mountain and discovered that elk was on the other side, miles away.

"That mountain was a huge magnifying glass. And I tell you that is as true as if I was sitting here, which I am."

Henry asked, "Is that the mountain that Indians used to make arrowheads and spear points?"

"Same one. Where'd you hear about it?"

"Read about it in a newspaper," Henry said.

"Huh."

The waiter brought their food.

Carson said, "Maggie, you'd better buy yourself a rain slicker because there's likely to be afternoon thunderstorms. Get one of them yellow slickers. It'll turn your skin yellow, but keep you drier than the other makes."

Bridger picked up a duck leg and pointed it at her. "And you'd best buy a couple of dark-colored gingham dresses. The dresses you wear have too much material, wide skirts and all. Won't do on the trail."

Carson nodded his agreement.

Henry said, "What do you gentlemen think about Maggie going off alone after the murderers of her husband and daughter?"

Bridger shook his head. "Ain't smart at all." He looked at Maggie. "If I weren't contracted by the army next week, I'd go with you."

Carson said, "I've already told her I'd join her in her hunt if I hadn't been assigned to the command of Fort Garland."

Both men turned toward Henry.

He held up his hands as if to fend them off. "She refused my help."

"Why are all of you men talking as if I wasn't sitting here? I've told you that it's my problem alone. I don't want to get innocents involved."

Bridger laughed. "No innocents here."

Henry said, "You tried to get help from the law."

"And that wasn't much help, other than 'Yes, we saw them. They're headed down the Santa Fe Trail. No, we're too busy to catch them,'" she said.

Bridger turned to Henry. "If she don't want help, it's her business. And if she wants to kill herself, it's her business. On the other hand, it's a free country, and she can't stop anyone from traveling close by if you catch my meaning."

Maggie threw her napkin on the table, excused herself, and walked away.

After she'd calmed down, Maggie walked back to the table. They stood. Henry pulled out her chair.

"They have wonderful ice cream. Shall we have some for dessert?" Maggie asked, changing the subject.

After they ordered, Carson turned to Maggie. "I think it would be best for you to sleep in your wagon tomorrow night, so you'll be there at dawn for hitching up and rolling out."

"I'd be happy to take you out tomorrow afternoon, Maggie," Bridger said.

Carson and Bridger said their farewells. Maggie and Henry watched them leave; Bridger slapped the maître d' on the butt as he left, sending the menus flying. They all laughed heartily.

Henry and Maggie ordered a glass of sherry.

"They're quite fond of you, Maggie."

"They have good hearts."

"I'll miss Bridger's stories," Henry said.

"I haven't laughed that much in a long time."

He raised his glass. "Laughter eases the pain in life."

"We laugh a lot."

"I feel better now that I know the cavalry will protect the wagon train," he said.

"I'll be fine. Now you can return home and assure Ephraim you've done your job of protecting me."

His face reddened, making the scar across his cheek look deathly white. He picked up his glass and sipped sherry. Strains of a waltz drifted through the dining room.

Chapter 18

In her Noland Hotel suite the next morning, Maggie took her last luxurious bath before the trip. She soaked in hot water and wondered if George would have disappeared if she had invited Henry to spend the night. Or would have he interrupted? Still, George might have left them alone if she'd invited Henry inside the suite.

However, she would have been a nervous wreck, worrying that he'd pop up, maybe even sit on the bed with them, and make devastating comments. Good Lord, she had to be sick to even think about George watching her make love to Henry.

Disgusting.

She sank in the water and put the washcloth over her face, feeling its warmth on her puckered eyelid.

She still needed George, but she also needed Henry. She ran her fingertips across her body in a futile effort to relieve her physical desire.

She dressed.

There was a knock on the door. It was Henry.

"I bought a going-away present."

She invited him in, and he handed her a flat package. They sat on living room chairs, and she tore the wrapping paper off a rectangle box, finding a palm-sized two-barrel derringer.

"Oh! That's a surprise." She had expected something more romantic.

"I'm told that Ladies of the House carry this model."

"I suppose the ladies showed you where they kept it, then."

He smiled and handed her a paper bag, from which Maggie pulled a garter belt with a wide elastic band. She grinned, thinking of him inside a woman's' store, looking at intimates. "You bought these for me?"

"The band holds the derringer, and the garter belt keeps it from falling."

"Oh, it's very romantic," she said, lifting her skirts to put on the garter belt. He turned toward the window. "Don't tell me a man of your experience is embarrassed to see a lady's legs?"

"Just looking at the weather."

"Uh-huh." She slipped the elastic band over her foot, raised it to her thigh, clipped on the garter belt, and slid the flat derringer inside. "Is this the way your ladies wear them?"

He turned around and looked. "No. They wear the gun on the front of the leg, or the outside of their thigh."

She slipped the derringer around her leg. "You've certainly done a lot of research on my behalf. You can tell Ephraim I'm fully protected."

"Don't be mad at me for wanting to help you. You need a backup just in case. Each barrel shoots a .41 caliber bullet. Not any good for distance, but up close it has knockdown power. It shoots the upper barrel first, and then the second barrel."

"Well, you'd better show me how it works, and I can get used to carrying it during my last minute shopping."

"Later," he said. "Your stitches need to come out. I'll help you."

She gave him her fingernail scissors and tweezers. He had her lie on the chaise lounge and then disappeared into the bathroom. She heard the water running and imagined he was washing his hands.

He returned and covered her neck and blouse with a towel and then placed a hot washcloth over her face. The damp heat felt good, and she felt her muscles relax.

After the washcloth cooled, he removed it and bent close to examine the stitches. His eyes were beautiful. Maggie had noticed his eyes before but had never been this close. The whites were bright, and his iris seemed to sparkle as if covered with tiny diamonds. They were honest, kind eyes. His black pupils were so large she felt as though she could see into his soul. She thought he must have a good soul.

His fingers touched her cheek and traced the scar and stitches. His hands were warm and gentle, and she imagined his hands caressing her body.

His voice brought her back.

"I'll cut the knot off the top stitch and then use the tweezers to pull it out. Then I'll work down and pull out each stitch. The skin has grown around the string, so it will hurt when I pull them out."

"Wait." She touched his hand. "Let's try it another way."

His brow furrowed. "What?"

"Cut off all the knots first and then pull out the stitches.

"Why?"

"I want to put off the pain and get the hard part over at once, rather than anticipating pain with each stitch."

He smiled. "That makes sense. I'll do it your way, but it's still going to hurt."

He was right, pulling them out hurt like heck. Maggie fought from crying, even though he handed her his handkerchief for tears that streamed down her cheek.

"All done."

"Thank goodness."

"You were a brave patient." He cupped his hand behind her neck, bent over, and kissed her forehead.

She felt the heat of his lips long after he went to the bathroom. He returned with a hot washcloth and placed it over her face.

She covered his hand and pressed it against the cloth. He didn't try to move.

After the fabric cooled, he raised her hand and kissed her fingers. He removed the washcloth and examined her face with those gorgeous eyes. He smiled. His smile was another thing that made him handsome.

"I'll be right back." He returned with her hand mirror. "Take a look."

She raised the mirror and gasped. The eyelid had returned to normal; her eye no longer bulged. She smiled. She could live with a scar.

There was a knock on the door. Maggie stood up while Henry opened the door. It was the maid, wanting to know if they wanted the room made up.

Henry told the woman to come back later, turned, and laughed. "Well, that broke the spell."

"I'm sorry, but I do have some last-minute things to buy." She agreed to meet him later.

Shopping, she bought several dark-colored gingham dresses and a bright yellow rain slicker for the trip. She returned to the boarding house, where Mrs. Wilson looked at her with suspicion.

After supper, Maggie changed into one of her new dresses and packed her trunk. She walked downstairs, placed her Bible on the check-in counter, and paid Mrs. Watson for the lodging bill.

The woman took the money and said, "You are the most exasperating client I've ever had. You and Mr. Herndon should get married and be done with sneaking around in sin."

Maggie smiled. "Thank you for your kind thoughts, Mrs. Watson. Now I understand why you're a grass widow."

"My husband has not divorced me!"

"I'll bet he's not eager to return to you."

The woman's face flushed, and, for once, tongue-tied.

"I'll wait for my ride on the porch." Maggie picked up her Bible, turned, and walked out.

Henry rose from his rocking chair when she arrived. "If you're packed, I'll be happy to get your trunk."

She thanked him, sat down, and watched a Mexican bullwhacker drive an ox-pulled wagon down the street. Was the man taking the cart out to Samuel Poteet's farm to join the wagon train?

She thumbed through her Bible to passages about forgiveness. If she could forgive the killers, she could return to Boonville now and continue leading her life as before, almost as if she had never left. She could buy newspaper ads in Santa Fe, offering a reward for the murderers' capture, dead or alive. That should bring justice. Maybe.

And then there was Henry. He was fond of her and kept hinting about his "feelings." She couldn't imagine living in Boonville with Henry. Not at *White Haven*, not surrounded by memories of Jenny and George. They would haunt her.

She closed her eyes and shuddered at the scene – Jenny lying in her mortally wounded father's arms, her dead eyes staring at the heavens above. Dress around her waist and blood on her thighs. Maggie felt flames of anger rise within her. Would she ever find peace?

Maggie heard heavy footsteps approaching. Henry carried her trunk through the doorway and lowered it on the porch next to the stairs. He straightened up, pulled out a handkerchief, and wiped his face, glistening with sweat. The scar on his cheek seemed to throb in rhythm with his heart. She touched her scar and wondered if it throbbed when she became emotional.

He took off his hat and wiped the inside band with his handkerchief. "I signed on with Samuel Poteet's outfit as a night-rider to watch over the stock."

Speechless, Maggie stared at him. She found a smile and asked, "You aren't returning to Missouri?"

"Nothing to go back for."

Jim Bridger drove up in a buggy. He set the brake and hopped out. "Ready to go, Maggie?"

Bridger mounted the steps, picked up her trunk, and tossed it in the back seat. "Come sit with me. Maybe we can start some rumors." He laughed.

She sat next to Bridger on the driver's seat. Thank God, he did not try to dissuade her from going. He was uncharacteristically quiet during their trip to the Poteet farm.

The two hundred acres were full of oxen and crates and barrels and men loading wagons. It looked like controlled chaos.

Bridger parked next to her wagon, loaded her trunk, and helped check to make sure she had everything. He reorganized the barrels and crates and supplies so that she had space to sleep. He kept fussing until she wished he'd go.

"Well, I think you got almost everything you need, Maggie, except I made you something that might help on your trip." He walked back to his buggy and returned with a wooden plank and two pieces of iron rod welded in the form of an S on one end and an L on the other.

"What in the world is that?" she asked.

"Let me show you." He hooked the iron rods over the back wagon wheel and placed the board on the bracket. "Now you got yourself a work table. Won't have to grub around in the mud while fixin' dinner 'n' stuff."

"That's a wonderful idea. Thank you!"

"One more thing," Bridger said, walking back to his buggy. He returned and handed her an elk-skin bag with a shoulder strap. The flap had beautiful beadwork. "It's my 'possibles' bag. Useful to carry a flint 'n' striker, and balls'n'powder, and jerky'n'pemmican, and other things."

"It's beautiful."

"Yep. Useful too. My first wife made it for me. It was too fancy looking for me to use, but I held on to it, and now I'm glad I did. Looks right pretty on you."

She kissed him on the cheek, raising an embarrassed blush on his rugged face. "You'd better get on and let me get settled in before night-fall."

He mounted his buggy and drove off. Maggie waved at his back, and he doffed his hat and waved it above his head. She wondered if the stories were true: could he see behind his back?

Carson and Bridger had been an enormous help. Even though they didn't agree with her decision to go after the murderers, they respected her. They had a better attitude than Henry. On the other hand, maybe Henry cared more because he felt he had more to lose.

Perhaps Carson and Bridger were respectful because, as mountain men and Indian fighters, they knew revenge quenched the flames of rage. In any event, their respect gave her self-confidence to carry on with her quest.

She turned her attention to the wagon, inspecting the contents of each barrel and crate and sack, imagining when and how she'd use each item. The sheepskins and blankets made for surprisingly comfortable bedding. She pulled together the drawstrings in the ends of the wagon's cover and discovered she had privacy.

She wondered what she could fix to eat without gathering firewood and burning a fire in the middle of the pasture. Someone called her name. She looked up to see Rebecca Poteet.

"Samuel told me you were here. We'd like you to join us for supper."

"You're a Godsend. I was just trying to figure out what to fix."

They walked across the pasture toward the house. There was low rumbling in the west as thunderheads billowed white on the horizon.

At the house, Rebecca served beef stew and biscuits. Samuel joined them.

"I understand this is your first wagon train, Mrs. Hartstone, so let me lay out what I expect from you: we work from can-see to can't-see. At dawn, one of my men will bring your animals. You will immediately hitch up your mule and tie your horse's lead rope to the back of your wagon. Your wagon is now parked directly behind the lead wagon. You are to follow close behind.

"Once we hit an open country, we travel four abreast. You will continue to follow that lead wagon. There will be five groups of twenty wagons following you, each group a mile apart. We start at dawn, travel until midday, stop, and allow our stock to graze and rest.

"At that time, you will gather firewood or buffalo chips, cook, and eat your dinner, and then do repairs or rest until midafternoon, when we hitch up and travel until dark. Once we have stopped for the night, we circle the wagons and graze the stock, cook supper, and sleep.

"I will be on horseback, managing the wagon train. There will be scouts sent ahead to look for the best places to stop and graze and to look out for Indian trouble. Since General Carson has a contingent of cavalry, I don't expect any problem.

"Be wary of rattlesnakes when you get off your wagon, and don't drink or use any water that's not flowing from a clear spring. Drinking dirty water is a sure way to get cholera.

"The Good Book commands rest on Sundays, so that will be a day of rest and prayer. Besides that, just follow orders and you'll be fine."

Maggie nodded and listened to thunder in the distance. "I'd better get back to my wagon before it rains." The air had the acrid scent of hot iron. Thunderheads boiled close. She climbed into her wagon and drew the end canvas as tight as possible. She hoped she wouldn't get soaked.

The first raindrops hit her wagon's canvas like rifle shots. She remembered that Mr. McCoy had said that they'd sewn three layers together. She hoped that would be enough to keep her dry. Maggie sat on a crate, wondering how she could sleep dry if the rain flooded the wagon box. She shook out her yellow slicker and put it under the sheepskins, raising the raincoat's edges against the crates and barrels.

The rain came in driving sheets, as though the ancient God Zeus had decided to take retribution on the world. She chose to sleep in her dress in case something happened to force her outside. Tired of sitting, Maggie cozied onto the sheepskins and pulled the blanket over her. She'd forgotten a pillow. She opened the trunk, took out a towel, and rolled it before sticking it under her head.

The rain tapered off, and she stared at the canvas cover. Finally, she lit the lantern and read several poems from *Leaves of Grass*, and thought about Henry.

Chapter 19

Maggie's sheepskins and blankets were warm, yet she couldn't sleep, thinking about tomorrow's start, fearing she'd oversleep. The wind snapped a loose canvas back and forth. A man coughed. Oxen bellowed. Sporadic drops of rain drummed against her wagon top. A man yelled. Laughter.

Footsteps approached her wagon. They paused. She cocked her gun. The footsteps retreated. All that, plus the croaking of frogs and the screeching of an owl, brought black and foreboding thoughts to mind.

Had she made a terrible mistake?

Finally, dead silence. Or was Maggie asleep?

Hours later, she woke to the smell of coffee and frying bacon. Voices. A curse.

Happy to already be dressed, she threw off the blanket, tied a bonnet over her disheveled hair, loosened the drawstring to the canvas at the back of her wagon, and peeked out.

It was still dark. Lantern-lit man-shadows slithered over the grass, casting ghosts upon white wagon canvas. She should have brought a chamber pot. She stepped out, hid in a shadow, relieved herself, and then laid out the mule's harness.

Waiting for her animals, she found the coffee pot, but she'd forgotten to gather firewood the night before it had started raining. She put the pan back in the wagon and drank a dipper of water from the barrel.

"Here are your animals, Mrs. Hartstone." A short curly bearded man as thin as a willow branch handed her the lead ropes to her mare and mule.

"We're harnessing up now?" she asked.

"Yep. Can't hold up the train," the man said over his shoulder as he walked away.

The mare tossed her head when Maggie tied its lead rope to the back of the wagon. Then, as she led the mule toward the front, the horse tugged against the line and whinnied. The mule dug in its two front hooves and jerked back, nearly toppling her over. She tugged and pulled, but the mule he-hawed and refused to move. The mare stomped the ground.

She looked at the darned mule in the leaden gray of dawn. The animals had bonded. Inseparable. She was in a stalemate. She wasn't strong enough to drag the mule into the traces, and it wasn't about to take another step forward.

If she couldn't get the mule in its harness, she'd make the train late. She'd have to ask for help. Lose respect. She wasn't sure she had anything to lose. She wiped her forehead on her sleeve and thought.

Finally, she led the mule back to the mare, untied the horse's lead rope from the wagon, and led both animals to the front. The mule was happy. So was the mare. All was well.

After that, it was only a matter of tying the mare's rope to the brake handle, backing the mule into the shafts, settling the collar, and hooking up the trace chains without trouble. Maggie decided to leave the mare near the mule until they left.

Maggie was too nervous to eat now, but pulled out several pieces of jerky and put them in Bridger's "possibles" bag for later.

Samuel Poteet rode up on a short gray horse. "You all set?"

"I think so."

"Better tie that horse to the back of your wagon. My first order will be 'Head 'em up!' That means to get ready. Each of my drivers will yell his name and 'Ready!' When everyone is ready, I'll shout, 'Head 'em out!' That wagon in front of you will start moving. You follow it."

She nodded and led the mare to the back, tied the lead rope tight, ignored its neighing, and climbed into the driver's seat. In spite of the chill, she wiped the sweat off her forehead. She picked up the reins and waited for the signal. It came sooner than she expected, and they moved out.

Three hours later, the sun burst from the horizon and cast long shadows in front of her. The mule settled into a plodding gait. She managed to keep a proper distance from the lead wagon, and the mare settled down. When they rolled into the open country, the wagons spread out as planned: four abreast, five lines deep.

Other groups of wagons followed, separated by a mile or more. Where was Henry? She stood up on the seat and looked around, but couldn't see him.

The rain had softened the ground, yet her wagon moved well. The mule pulled without effort. Grass grew tall, and soon there were yellow and blue and red wildflowers dotting the landscape as far as she could see. Meadowlarks flew out from the path of the wagons. High overhead, two red-tailed hawks circled, waiting to catch a rabbit startled by wagon wheels.

Two of General Carson's cavalry saluted as they trotted past to check on the following groups. She guessed Kit, and the guards were scouting in front of the wagons.

Maggie thought the sky was blue as she imagined the ocean, even though she'd never seen it. The air was crisp and clean from last night's rain. Her wagon wheels rolled over rich black soil. The sun shone upon her. Its warmth soon lulled her into a peaceful state. All was right with the world except for the two killers she sought.

She'd made the right decision. What would it feel like to have Henry sitting next to her? She discarded the thought. She liked being in charge of her own life, with nobody telling her what to do. Still, it would be nice to have someone with whom to talk.

After the sun climbed to its highpoint, Samuel Poteet trotted in front of the wagons, his left arm making a circling motion. The cart in front came to a halt, while the other three wagons pulled up and stopped alongside it. The caravan behind pulled up, too, making a giant square.

Maggie set her brake and, following the actions of the other drivers, unharnessed her mule and tied him next to the mare.

Soon the same man from that morning took her animals to pasture. Maggie spotted some bushes at the nearby creek and collected dead twigs and branches to make a fire. A half-hour later, the water boiled, while bacon and eggs sizzled in her frying pan.

She put Bridger's metal hooks over the rear wheel and placed the board over the top to make a table. Thankful not to be sitting, she stood at the table and ate out of the frying pan.

Her leg brushed the wheel and felt the derringer on her thigh. She was surprised how quickly she'd become accustomed to wearing it.

Pouring her second cup of tea, she noticed that the other drivers sat in groups, eating and chatting. Even though there were people around her, she felt alone.

Carson, wearing his uniform, rode up. "How are you getting along, Maggie?"

"I'm doing just fine."

"Good. Have you checked your wheels for loose spokes and felloes?"

"Thanks for reminding me. Have you seen Henry?"

"Not yet, but if I do, I'll give him your regards. I'd like to stay and chat, but I need to check on my men with the other wagon groups." He tipped his hat, wheeled his horse, and rode off.

She watched him trot away before washing the frying pan and cup and collecting more firewood, putting it in the wagon for supper. Returning, she tested each wheel's felloes and spokes. They were tight.

She crawled into the wagon bed and looked at her Bible and Whitman's *Leaves of Grass*. She picked up the poetry book, climbed down, and leaned the table board against the wheel as a backrest, and began reading. The poetry transported her to another place.

Later that evening, as they drove into a setting sun, mosquitos rose and swarmed her face and hands. She tied a scarf over her bonnet and pulled it around her face to provide protection. She pulled her hands into her sleeves. Still, she had to slap the mosquitos that landed on the exposed part of her face. She listened to their whine and felt miserable.

At dusk, Samuel Poteet called a halt. The wagons circled, and the men took their animals to graze. Exhausted, Maggie made a cold camp. She sat on the ground and ate several pieces of jerky, tearing them with her teeth and chewed because she was hungry like an animal – not like a lady there, either.

It seemed like yesterday when she'd sat at the head of the dining room table with Jenny and George, and rang the little silver bell to have Sally bring the meal.

She laughed out loud. "Well, George, what do you think of your civilized wife now?" There was nothing but the breeze swishing the grass. The old loneliness that she'd felt so often in Boonville rolled over her like a black fog.

Soon she crawled into the wagon to lie on the sheepskins. She heard nothing but buzzing mosquitos. She pulled the blanket over her head to escape the biting insects, tossing and turning, muscles sore from the day of unusual activity.

And then she heard a guitar. She listened to the music and remembered what fun she'd had dancing with George at Boonville's Masked Ball. George held her in his arms, and he squeezed her and nodded toward Jenny, disguised as an Arabian princess.

A young man asked her to dance. He was the first man to dance with her, other than her father, of course. After flubbing the first several steps, Jenny was flawless. She looked at Maggie and grinned.

It had been one of many marvelous nights before the war changed everything.

The next afternoon, the monotony disappeared when the front wagon spooked a rabbit. It bounded off, clearing the grass in long jumps. A red-tailed hawk high above folded its wings and dove toward the fleeing animal. At the last moment, the bird spread its wings, timing the rabbit's next jump. Its talons pierced the rabbit's skin. The hare squealed a pitiful sound as the hawk lifted its prey high into the blue sky.

Maggie marveled at the beauty of the horror.

Carson reappeared and told her Henry was riding with the group behind her and that he sent his regards.

Sending his regards didn't satisfy her. Why hadn't he visited her? He worked nights, guarding the stock, so he was free when they were on the trail. Had her refusal to make love that night at the Noland pushed him away?

Another day, sure she was developing blisters from sitting too long, she slowed the mule and jumped off, and walked alongside the animal as she held the reins. It was a blessing not to be sitting on the wooden bench all the time.

During the noon break, she cut long grass, piled it thick and level on top of the driver's seat, covered it with spare canvas, and tied it down with a rope. Now sitting was more comfortable. She was more than pleased.

Samuel Poteet called a halt another evening, near a clear-running creek. Sunday was for rest, prayer, and repairs, and to allow the animals to rest and graze.

Surely Henry would come calling.

The next morning, wanting to look good for Henry, Maggie gathered soap and clean clothes and walked along the creek bank, hoping to find a private spot to bathe and wash her filthy dress and unmentionables. The men had walked downstream to bathe, so she walked upstream.

She'd gone about half a mile when she spotted a five-foot bull snake stretched out on the mud bank. It saw her and curled into a defensive coil, opening its mouth to hiss a warning. A frog jumped out of its mouth. It blinked at Maggie and then hopped to the edge of the bank and plopped into the water.

Farther along the creek, she found a bend where the water riffled into a waist-deep pool. Satisfied she was alone, she placed her revolver and derringer on the ground. She slipped her dress over her head and gagged on the stench of her body odor. She knew she smelled, but was surprised that it was that bad.

Naked, she waded into the pool, the cold water raising goose-bumps. She washed her hair and body and then, finally, her clothes, hanging them on bushes to dry. She waded back into the pool and washed all over again. She climbed out and sat on the grass and brushed her hair, and then raised her arms and stretched to let the sun warm her body.

"You still have a beautiful figure," the man's voice said.

Startled by the sound, she covered her breasts and spun toward him. George sat on the creek bank.

"Oh. It's you. You surprised me."

"You seem to have adjusted to the trail well," he said.

"I miss you."

"Thought about taking Henry's advice and call off this silly hunt?"

"Why don't you join me, so I'd have someone to talk to? I get so lonely, and you just can't imagine how boring it is to sit in the wagon, or walk alongside, all day long, day after day, alone with nothing but my thoughts."

"You can change that, Maggie. Why don't you ask Henry to join your wagon group?

"Why are you pushing him on me?"

"Because I don't want you to be killed."

A flock of crows exploded from a nearby tree with a raucous cawing. Something moved through the bushes toward Maggie. No time to dress – she reached for the pistol, cocked it, and pointed it toward the sound. A doe stepped out and stared at her. Maggie exhaled lowered the gun.

George had vanished.

The deer spun and disappeared. The same thing had happened once before when Maggie visited George and Jenny's graves at *White Haven*. Was the repetition a coincidence? Some sort of cosmic signal?

The sun warmed her body, and she reclined on the grass, eventually falling into an exhausted sleep. Several hours later, in the creeping shadows of an oak tree, she woke. Her skin hurt. She pushed her finger against her chest. When she relieved the pressure, she knew she was sunburned.

"You should have dressed before taking a nap." George appeared again.

"Stop nagging. Come back to the wagon with me."

"You know I can't. People would hear you talk and think you're going crazy."

"They might be right. Think about joining me on the trail."

He nodded and faded from her sight.

She dressed in clean clothes, as the washed clothes were just about dry. She felt almost human again.

When she returned, there was a piece of paper nailed to her the side of her wagon. She hoped Henry had been looking for her and left a note, but when she read it, it was an invitation to join Samuel Poteet and Kit Carson for supper. Well, at least she'd be able to talk with someone.

She brushed her hair and left it long instead of weaving her usual braids. She tied it back with a piece of yellow ribbon; her long hair might protect the back of her neck from insect bites.

She found Poteet's camp several hundred yards in front of the lead wagon. He had a tent, and an iron tripod spread over a small fire and camp chairs. *Chairs!* The men stood to greet her and handed her a cup of tea – Samuel had remembered she was a tea drinker.

Carson asked how she was doing, and then they talked about the next leg of their trip toward Council Grove. After a supper of ham and beans and cornbread, Samuel stirred the fire and began telling her stories of past adventures.

"How many more days will it take to get to Council Grove?" she asked.

"We're making good time," Samuel said. "If everything goes smoothly, we should be there in six or seven days."

She looked into the fire. Everything seemed to be taking an eternity. Perhaps it seemed so long because she had no one to talk to, to break up a monotonous routine and plodding rhythm.

Carson walked her back to her wagon. Before she said goodnight, she asked, "Will you do me a personal favor?"

"Of course."

"When you see Henry, tell him I need to see him."

Chapter 20

Maggie snuggled into her sheepskins, pulled the blanket over her head and thought about Henry. She could not sleep, imagining footsteps, the tapping of an eager fist on her wagon, a whispered greeting.

The next morning, she watched a bullwhacker walking on the side of the front wagon use his whip to behead a rattlesnake. He offered to share it with her at dinner. She was proud she didn't gag. Its white meat tasted like chicken.

She thought of her life with George and Jenny. And each memory ended with the image of them lying in front of the house – closing Jenny's eyelids, pulling her skirt down and then holding the love of her life in her arms, watching him slowly die. She heard the echo of her scream when she threw herself over their bodies in an insane effort to keep their souls from departing.

And she remembered the image of Jenny's ghost waltzing around the fallen piano, singing "Gone forever! Gone forever!" before disappearing through the parlor wall.

She imagined confronting the killers, what terrible things she would do to them. She felt that her journey was turning her into someone else, hardening her like pottery fired in a kiln. She wasn't sure she liked that feeling.

From her driver's seat, she watched the back of the front wagon or stared at the never-ending sky, watched hawks float in lazy circles overhead, the swish of her mule's tail, the endless prairie of swaying grass. She was insignificant, nothing more than a speck of dust in the wind.

Where was Henry?

And each day, when the sun evaporated the sparkling dew on the grass, swarms of green flies rose to attack her mule and mare while she waved the horde away from her face. Later, when the sun lowered beyond the horizon, waves of mosquitos emerged to destroy all thoughts, throwing her into an irritable mood that might have been bearable had she been sharing the evening with someone.

There were times she thought about Henry's kiss. But how could she think about anyone but George? She slapped the reins hard against Sonny's haunch. His ears flattened as if to ask why she should take out her guilty feelings on him. What had he done wrong?

Kit had delivered her message to Henry, and he still hadn't appeared. She had pushed him away. She slipped back into gray loneliness.

Six days after her bath in the creek, she felt grimier and smellier than she had before. She hoped the noon break would be next to a stream where she could clean up, but when they stopped, they were far from water. She dipped some water from her barrel to wet a cloth and wiped her hands and face.

She had just finished eating when Kit Carson rode up and dismounted. "We should get to Council Grove tomorrow, right after crossing the Neosho River," he said. "We'll be spending several days to repair wagons, replenish supplies, and rest the animals. The great-grandson of Daniel Boone, Seth Hays, is my cousin. He built a trading post where he rents rooms to travelers."

"Do any of those rooms have tubs?" Maggie asked, desperately. "A bath would be wonderful!"

"Don't get your hopes up. The inn might be full. Council Grove is where smaller wagon trains and other travelers gather to join bigger caravans. The trail west is much more difficult because it goes directly through Indian lands, Kiowa and Comanche. They've been stirred up by news of the Sand Creek Massacre."

"Will it be dangerous?"

"Probably not, since we're a large train and have a contingent of cavalry. But you never can tell."

"George, my husband, mentioned something about the Post Office Oak...?"

"Yep. Travelers used that old tree as a post office from the twenties up through the forties. They used it to leave messages, like water source locations, Indian troubles, and other information. People also left letters there. Those traveling east took eastbound letters to post in Independence. Those going west took those to Santa Fe. Now Seth's store is the post office."

She would write to Ephraim to tell him about the trip and Henry. But what should she say about Henry? That he'd done his duty, and she appreciated Ephraim's help, or should she tell him that she resented him disregarding her wishes? Why upset him? It wouldn't hurt to be kind.

"I'm surprised we haven't passed a Mexican wagon train carrying goods from Santa Fe to Missouri. Could meet one in the Grove," Kit said.

"Why do they call it Council Grove?" she asked, not that interested in the answer, just desperate to talk with someone, though, to hear a human voice rather than be alone in her thoughts.

"A council between the Kaw and Osage Indians and our government was held in 1825 under an old oak tree. The Indians signed a treaty to allow passage through their territory in exchange for $800 cash, plus tobacco, calico, ribbons, and other goods. Now that tree is known as the Council Oak. That covers the first part of the town's name.

"The last part, 'Grove,' was for the mile-wide stand of walnut, hickory, and oak forest. That's the last hardwood you'll find headed west. Wagon trains use it for repair and timbers for the rest of the journey. And unused timbers are lashed under the wagons for maintenance. So that's how Council Grove got its name."

They looked up to see Samuel Poteet's approach. He dismounted, tied his horse to her wagon, and accepted a cup of tea, nodding at Kit. "If you're going back to check our other groups, I'll ride along with you."

"If you see our friend Henry Herndon, say hello for me," Maggie said.

Samuel said, "I'm sure he'd like to hear that. He asks about you every time I see him."

"Why hasn't he ridden up to say hello?" she asked.

Samuel said, "I suppose he's respecting his contract."

"Contract?" she asked.

"He joined the train at a discount. The deal was that he'd provide a horse and rifle for protection, and I'd provide meals and shelter under one of the wagons. He wanted to guard this first group, but I assigned him to guard our second group of wagons."

Maggie exhaled. Still, Henry could ride in her wagon during the day, when he's not working at night. Maybe he'd found another woman to ride with, but she remembered Samuel said she'd be the only woman on the train.

Carson tossed the remains of his tea on the grass. "Suspect we'd better git. Thanks for the tea, Maggie."

She watched them ride down the trail toward the second wagon group, and then washed the tin cups and whistled a happy tune. She hadn't whistled in a long time.

Samuel hadn't yet called the noon halt the following day when Maggie spotted a lone horseman riding toward them. He rode on a black quarter horse, directly toward the wagon in front of her. Henry Herndon slowed to a trot and reined in to walk alongside her.

"Mr. Herndon!" Maggie exclaimed. "What a surprise!"

He tipped his wide-brimmed hat and smiled. "I brought you a gift from Council Grove."

"How did you pass me without my seeing you?"

"I rode out before dawn, right after my night guard shift. You were asleep in your wagon." He leaned toward her and handed her something.

She looked at a key that said, "Hays House – Room 2", and then up at his beautiful smile.

"The room has a tub. It was the last room. I thought you'd like to soak in a bath."

"That's not hard to figure," she said.

"I have to get back to my duty. See you in town." He spun his horse and loped back toward his station.

She watched him until he was out of sight, holding up the key and allowing herself a smile.

Several hours later, they stopped at the bank of the Neosho River. Samuel spurred his horse across the river at the shallow ripples. The water was no more than two feet deep, but a strong current flowed over a stony riverbed. He gave a signal, and the first wagon slid down the short mud bank into the river and began to cross.

Maggie gave that wagon space and then flicked the reins on the mule's rump, but it didn't move, so she slapped harder. It refused. She heard shouts of encouragement from wagons behind her. The damned mule wouldn't budge.

She jumped off the wagon, ran to the mule, took the reins, and pulled it toward the river. The mule's long ears flattened against its head. Its front legs dug into the earth. She ignored more shouting for her to move on. She tried to move the mule twice.

She shouted, "You son-of-a-bitch!" and then ducked her head and looked to see if anyone had heard her swear.

She dropped the reins, ran to the back of the wagon, untied the mare, and led it next to the mule. Its ears snapped forward, it nudged the mare's side. Maggie picked up the mule's reins and, leading both animals, pulled them down the bank. The wagon's shafts pushed the mule, and they plunged into the river.

About three quarters across, the mare tripped and bumped Maggie. She fell forward, desperately holding on to the lead rope and reins as she sank under freezing water. The current swept her skirt over her head. She swung a slow arc underwater and downstream of the animals and wagon.

She held onto the rope with her right hand and tried to use her left to push off the bottom. The weight of the gold coins in her corset pressed her down. Water gushed into her mouth. She couldn't breathe. She was going to drown.

The rope and reins slipped from her hand, and the rushing current rolled her sideways. She clawed the shirt from her head and rolled onto her back. The force of the water pushed her to a sitting position. She skidded on her butt against the gravel and jammed her heels into the streambed. The current against her back pushed her forward and up. She pushed off the bottom with all her might. Stumbling, she rose to her feet, coughing and gasping for air. She fell again, but stood up and steadied herself against the current.

Clearing water from her eyes, she saw the mule had pulled her wagon across the river. It grazed with the mare on the far bank.

That goddamned mule!

Dripping wet and determined to ignore the cheers of the train's bullwhackers, she climbed up on the driver's seat and hupped the mule into location behind the first wagon. She still had her two guns, but they would have to be cleaned and reloaded. The room key lay on the wagon floor.

After the train crossed the river, Samuel led them to an area on the edge of town where there was grass for feed and room to circle their wagons. She got off, unharnessed the mule, tied it next to the mare, and tried to wring her dress dry.

The usual man came to collect her animals for pasture. For the first time, he smiled at her. "Proud of you, Mrs. Hartstone. You done good."

"Thank you. Would you call me Maggie?"

He nodded, "I'm Jake." And he walked away with her animals.

She watched him go and thought her river crossing fiasco had been a gift. The crossing had earned her the respect of the men, and she'd finally found a name for the mule – "Sonny," short for "Son of a Bitch."

She packed clean clothes and her hairbrush in a handbag and walked toward town. The hotel key gave a pleasant weight to her pocket. A bath, and later, a conversation with Henry over dinner would be wonderful.

Chapter 21

Water dripped from Maggie's skirts as she walked through Council Grove's confusion of wagons, soldiers, Mexican freighters, Indians, homesteaders, and gold-seekers littering the dirt streets. There were many more Indians here than in Independence. She avoided direct eye contact with them, still noticing the differences in tribes' clothes and bearing, but could not tell the difference between Kiowa and Comanche and other tribes.

The Hays' Store was a two-story frame building with an outside stairway that led to the rooms. There was as a dining and meeting room downstairs, as well as a trading post, courthouse, post office, and printing office.

Charles Gilkey, the Hays' hotel clerk, ignored her wet clothes and greeted her with a pleasant smile and led her to her room.

The bedroom was plain; walls of rough-cut wood, an adequate bed with a chamber pot underneath, a dresser, and an unfinished armoire. The highlight, of course, was the tin bathtub. An employee carried buckets of hot water upstairs for her bath. She soaked until she thought her skin would wrinkle.

Later, after she had dressed in clean clothes, Mr. Gilkey told her where she could find a lady to wash her filthy dress and underthings by noon the following day. And after that, it was time to meet Henry at the Hays House dining room. It appeared he had also cleaned up. She suspected he'd bathed in the river.

Henry looked at her over the dinner menu. "The selection isn't like Noland's."

"That's not what I remember about Noland's."

He flashed the white smile she loved. "You must be thinking about that maître d'," he said.

"No," Maggie said, "although he was memorable, too."

"Then, it had to have been the décor."

"That was lovely, but it was something else."

"Wait! Let me guess." He picked up his wine glass, studied it, sipped, and then said, "It was the music from the band in the lobby."

"Wrong again." She hadn't had this much fun in ages.

"Ah! I know. It was when we danced the waltz."

"You're a wonderful dancer, Henry, but that's not what I remember."

The waiter interrupted and took their orders. They watched him leave.

Maggie looked at him over the lip of her wine glass. "You were saying?"

"I remember holding you in my arms, dancing with you."

"Yes, that was wonderful. You're quite light on your feet."

"What are you planning for tomorrow?" he asked.

"I'm going to talk with the sheriff and ask around for information about the killers."

"Still bent on finding them, then?"

"I've had a lot of time to think about it between Independence and here."

"Forget them. Let's go to Denver City instead."

"It's lonely traveling by oneself," she said.

"And boring."

"Yes," she agreed.

"It would be nice to travel together."

"Why didn't you ride in my wagon during the day?"

He looked away. "I thought you didn't want me."

She leaned toward him, instantly regretting the edge to her voice, "We aren't innocent youngsters, Henry. Kit Carson told you I wanted to see you, yet you ignored me. So I'll ask again. Why?"

He wiped his mouth with his napkin. "You act as you want me, and then you push me away. You don't know what you want, Maggie. I feel like you are playing with my emotions, so I gave you time to think things through."

"I don't need time to, as you put it, think things through. I know what I want. I'm first going to carry out justice for Jenny and George. After that, I want to get on with the rest of my life."

"But . . ."

"Let me finish."

He nodded and sat back in his chair.

"You hint at a relationship, whatever that means, and at the same time, you have saloon whores hanging all over you."

"Sweet Jesus Christ!" He grinned.

"What?"

"You're jealous."

"I'm what?"

"Shows you care about me."

"Does not!"

"Then what does it mean?"

"It means I didn't expect this. I still love George."

"And I still love my wife. Always will, but they are dead, Maggie. It's time to move on."

Other diners stopped eating to listen. She stared at them until they looked away. "We seem to be the entertainment."

He simply sat there and gave her his gorgeous white smile. "What do you propose, Maggie?"

"All right, Henry. What would you think about me explaining our situation to Samuel; my uncle hired you to protect me, so you need to move to my group?"

"We're entering Indian country. I'd think Samuel would be happy not to worry as much about your safety."

"You'd protect me?" she asked.

"You're a better shot, and you can protect me. I'd even be happy to pay Samuel a little extra for your protection."

After dinner, they walked outside for fresh air. The sound of a string instrument drifted to them.

"Is that a mandolin?" asked Maggie.

"Kit Carson told me about an Italian monk who lived as a hermit in a cave up on the hill. He spoke nine languages and ate only cornmeal mixed with water or milk. He played the mandolin. The priest left and walked the entire 550 miles to Las Vegas, New Mexico, where he performed miracle cures."

"Too bad he's not here. We could have sought his blessing," Maggie said.

"I didn't know you were religious."

"I get confused by the contradictions in the Bible. I feel the Old Testament is about retribution – an eye for an eye – while the New Testament is more about love and forgiveness. Still, I believe there is a greater power, and we can use all the help we can get."

They returned to the Hays' House, and he walked her to her door. She thanked him for dinner, kissed him on the cheek, and said goodnight. Inside, she waited, hoping to hear him knock.

When he didn't, she sat at the table and cleaned her pistols. She was washing the fouled black gunpowder from her hands when she heard his soft knock on the door. She smiled, dried her hands, and opened it a crack. He stood in the hall.

"Oh, it's you. What do you want?" Maggie asked.

"To hold you."

She opened the door and pulled him close, kissed him, and felt his passion, before pushing him away. "I want to get ready for you. Go downstairs and have a drink and then come back and knock on the door. I'll let you know if I'm ready."

"But . . ."

She ran her tongue across the scar on his cheek. "I want to be perfect for you."

"Hurry," he said in a strained voice.

She shut the door, undressed, and hung her clothes in the armoire. She scrubbed her hands to wash off the foul-smelling black gunpowder.

She opened the window and threw out the washbasin's dirty water, refilled it with clean water from the pitcher, and cleaned herself a second time that day.

Naked, except for her locket with the clipping of George's hair, she slipped between the sheets and waited. She'd sworn never to remove the pendant - but she couldn't wear it while she made love to another man. She slipped it over her head and hid it behind the base of the oil lamp on the bedside table.

She remembered her disappointment that George had not had a picture taken to put in the locket so she could remember him. She'd clipped a bit of his hair before the burial and placed it in the pendant.

She waited for Henry and prayed George would not spoil their tryst. Soon she wondered if a saloon hussy had caught his attention.

Just when she decided he wasn't coming, she heard a soft tap on the door. "It's unlocked," Maggie said. "Come in."

He opened the door and sat on the bed, staring at her. "I thought you might change your mind."

"Why?"

"You said you needed privacy before getting into bed. I thought you might not be ready for me."

"I'm not a woman who changes her mind."

He laughed, stood up, walked to the window, put his hands high on the drapes and pulled the curtains tighter before he slipped off his coat, hung it over the back of a chair, and paused.

"What's wrong?" she asked.

"I feel modest, for the first time in my life."

"That's ridiculous. Take off your clothes and get in here with me."

He grinned. "You smell lovely."

"It is a lavender-scented soap."

He covered her eyes with a hand towel. "If I can't see you, you can't see me."

She giggled, listening for the sound of his clothes rustling to the floor. She heard him put his gun on the bedside table, listened to the sheet rustle as he raised it, and then felt his body weight on the mattress. Her nipples felt deliciously hard against the sheet.

A wave of his body heat washed over her. He didn't touch her, so she arched her back and then she felt him move. The hand towel that blindfolded her slid off. He lay on his side next to her, and she looked into his gorgeous eyes.

He reached for her.

They merged into one sinuous being, moving to an unheard rhapsody, moving faster and faster toward its climax. It was as if a dam ruptured inside Maggie.

"It's so good! Oh god, George!"

Maggie's God threw ice water over them, shattering their enchantment.

Henry moaned and rolled onto his back.

She stared at the ceiling. "I'm sorry. I'm so sorry, Henry."

He remained silent.

She reached for his hand. "It was my first time since George died."

He kissed her fingertips. "It was the first time for me as well."

"Really?" She turned her head and looked into his eyes.

"Feel guilty?"

"Yes," she said, "but not as much as I thought. You?"

He rolled toward her. "Let's do it again without guilt. But this time, try to remember my name."

Chapter 22

They woke in each other's arms before dawn. He caressed her cheek with his forefinger and said, "I don't want to leave you."

"Don't."

"I'd ruin your reputation if anyone sees me leave your room."

"You can't hurt the reputation of a needy widow." She kissed him. "I want to travel together."

"I'd like that, but since I ride all night, I sleep most of the day."

"I'll ask Samuel to switch you to ride with my group," she said.

"He'll never permit lovers to travel together."

"My uncle hired you to protect me."

"Ephraim is not your uncle."

"That makes us related. You'd be my cousin."

He laughed. "Kissing cousins."

A few minutes later, he slipped out of her room.

Maggie stretched her arms overhead and then touched his side of the bed; the sheet was still warm. Her fingers brushed across her nipples and belly, tracing the scar from Jenny's birth, and then glided down between her legs. Her fingers lingered a moment longer than necessary, and she shuddered in the aftermath of joyful love-making.

That's what love-making was: pure, innocent joy, a cresting wave of happiness, an undulating surge that swept the reality of life – war, death, pain, uncertainty, fear – into a whirlpool of peaceful oblivion, leaving only an otherworldly rhapsody of contentment.

The sad thing was that the peaceful oblivion couldn't hide reality for long. Maggie would always carry the pain of Jenny and George's murders. Now, after making love to Henry, she felt she had violated her loyalty to George. That guilt became another new reality.

But why should she feel guilty? George died over a year and a half ago and besides, even grieving widows had needs. Everyone needs love.

Best of all, George hadn't appeared while she was in bed with Henry. His judgment would have pushed her into the abyss. Or had she thought she was making love to George?

Maggie bathed, dressed, and had breakfast before going shopping for a chamber pot. On her way back, she stopped by the stables to ask after Patrick Doyne and Traveler, both of whom the stable hand remembered.

"He had a mean-looking friend," he said.

"What do you mean?"

"Musta been shot in the face. The guy had a twisted mouth off to the side of his face."

So they were still together! She found the *Kansas Press* newspaper office, opened the door, and stepped into the pungent scent of ink. She introduced herself to its owner and editor, the Reverend J.E. Bryant.

"When was the last wagon train to Santa Fe?" she asked.

"If I remember, it passed through a week ago. It was the first headed west. I wrote about it. Let me check."

He walked to the counter, pulled musty issues of the weekly from a shelf, and placed them on the countertop. He scanned the front pages.

"I was wrong. The red-headed man and his partner passed two weeks ago. Read for yourself."

She did. Reverend Bryant described an unusually beautiful horse – a spotted Tennessee Walker with a black head and neck and a flowing white tail and mane. Her skin tingled.

"Did you talk with the rider?" she asked.

"Don't think so, or I would have written about it."

"He has red hair and beard," she said.

"Sure, I remember him. But I didn't talk with him."

She returned to the hotel. Charles Gilkey, the clerk, stood behind the desk, sorting keys. He looked up and asked if he could help her.

"I understand that the first wagon train heading west passed through several weeks ago. I'm curious if a gentleman by the name of Patrick Doyne stayed here."

The clerk opened the register, ran his finger down the column of names, stopped, and tapped his finger. "Yep. He sure did."

"Do you remember talking with him?"

"Don't know. I talk with so many travelers. What does he look like?"

"Red hair and beard," she said.

"Oh, *him*."

"What?"

"Said him and his partner were going to homestead, but they didn't look like homesteaders. His partner was scary looking."

"Anything else?" she asked.

"They were trouble. Got drunk, beat up some men, and tore up the place."

"Anything else?"

"Nope. Why are you looking for them?"

"He owes me money."

"Be careful."

She thanked him and walked to the launderer's to pick up her clean clothes. After dinner, she checked out of the hotel, and, after buying Jake a small gift, walked back to her wagon.

Maggie found Jake sitting with his back against a tree. He scrambled up and tipped his hat.

"Something I can do for you, Maggie?"

"I appreciate you taking care of my animals." She handed him a paper sack.

He opened it. "Tobacco!" he exclaimed. "Thanks."

She checked her wagon. Nothing had been disturbed.

Henry stopped by later to help her. He untied the tallow bucket and greased the wagon axles. They started a fire, cooked, and ate supper together.

"I talked with Samuel," she said.

"And?"

"He agreed."

"Do you always get what you want?"

"Yep, but it'll probably be the day after tomorrow before he can find a replacement for you."

"We have a long way to go, so I suppose I can live without your company another day or two."

The fire died to embers, and the sun fell into the horizon. A figure loomed out of the dusk.

"Everything all right, Maggie?" Jake asked, staring at Henry.

She introduced the men.

"Henry is the nephew of an old friend. He and I have traveled together from Boonville." She left the rest to Jake's imagination.

"Uh-huh. I'm close by if you need anything, Maggie." Jake walked away.

"Competition?" Henry asked.

"Maybe, if you don't join me soon," she said.

"The sooner, the better. I'd better ride back to my wagons and do my job."

She watched him ride away and disappear into the dusk.

The wagon train came to life before dawn. Samuel Poteet rode up and said good morning, "Henry will join your wagon group tomorrow."

They heard approaching hoof beats. Maggie shaded her eyes from the rising sun and recognized Kit Carson.

Carson reined to a stop, nodded to Maggie, and said to Samuel, "One of my scouts reported a pilgrim family named Hasberg is stranded up ahead with a broken axle. A family of three: father, mother, and a young boy. They are alone."

Samuel shook his head. "Danged fools. We should leave them be to teach them a lesson, but I'll send several of my men with the makings for a new axle."

So, Maggie thought, that's why the wagons carried rough-cut timber tied under their beds since Council Grove.

Maggie slipped back into the familiar, dull routine. At the midday break, Jake told her there would be little firewood, but suggested she collect dried buffalo dung.

"It burns pretty good, but it takes more than you think to cook dinner," he said.

"I haven't seen any buffalo."

"They've been shot out of here. When I first started, there were thousands and thousands. We'll see some farther west. Point is, don't have to see buffalo to find their shit," Jake said.

"Are you going to gather chips now?"

"Not my job, but if you'd like, I'll go with you. Show you how."

He cradled a rife in his arms as they walked north of the wagon trail on hard packed sandy soil – so different than the rich black loam they traveled through from Independence. He showed Maggie the first pile of dung, less than a mile from the wagons. She bent to pick it up.

"Nope! You want real dry ones," he said.

Several minutes later, they found perfect flat gray round droppings. Maggie held her breath and picked one up. It was gray, lighter than she'd imagined. Thankful it didn't smell, she bent and lifted the second chip. A huge brown spider clung to the bottom. Maggie screamed, dropped the dung, and retreated.

Jake laughed. "Shoulda told you. Spiders and all sorts of things hide under 'em. Closer to the desert, there'll be scorpions. Be careful of them tails. Make you mighty sick." He flipped over the pie. The spider clung on. "Look here," he pointed. "This here is a tarantula. They grow to the size of a man's hand, with its legs spread out. Real hairy and ugly as sin, but harmless." He picked it up, put it in the palm of his hand, and showed it to her. "Want to hold it?"

"NO!" Backing up, she tripped but managed to keep her balance. "Keep it away."

Later, after picking up a skirt full of dried buffalo droppings, they walked back toward the wagons. Jake studied the ground on their way back, falling silent and looking over his shoulder. Once, he told her to stop while he listened.

"What's wrong?" she asked.

"Nothing. Just looking."

"You weren't watching like that when we walked out."

"Spotted fresh horse prints."

"I saw them. So?"

"They ain't been shod."

"There were a lot of Indians in Council Grove. Seemed harmless."

"No such thing as a harmless Indian. Got your pistol on you?"

"Yes." She touched the handle.

"If'n they come, save the last shot for yourself. Injuns do terrible things to womenfolk. Let's get back to the wagons."

She made a fire with the buffalo chips. They burned fast, so she needed all she'd gathered. She'd make a sack to hold them in the future.

That afternoon Samuel led the distressed family's wagon, pulled by two mules, into the train close behind Maggie. The driver, Hasberg, a large, sunburned, raw-boned man, glanced at her and spat brown juice from a tobacco wad in his cheek.

His wife, a thin and worn-down woman, wore a calico bonnet and worn black dress, and sat next to him. A little fair-haired, freckle-faced boy looked over their shoulders. Maggie thought he must be eight or nine years old.

"Pull in behind Maggie and follow her."

"I got two mules. She's got one. I'll go in front," the man said.

The woman put her hand on her husband's arm, "Now, Haz . . ."

He jerked his arm away, fist high, raised as if to hit her.

"Control your animals and fall in behind her," Samuel said in a voice that made Maggie think of steel.

Hasberg yanked hard on the reins, jerking the mule's heads roughly to the side, and fell in behind Maggie's wagon.

Maggie heard the Hasbergs arguing. Soon her mare, tied to the back of her wagon, began to snort and whinny. She looked back just in time to see her mare kick at Hasberg's mules who were nosing the mare's butt.

"Back your mules off," Maggie shouted.

"Make yours go faster, lady."

"Don't you know how to drive? Slow them to the pace of the train, or you'll cause a wreck."

"I know how to drive my goddammed mules!"

"Don't swear in front of a lady."

"Sally ain't no lady, and you ain't no lady neither."

"Now, Haz."

Maggie shot them a look. The boy disappeared.

That evening they gathered up to form a circle with the wagons. Samuel told her to park inside next to the lead wagon. He ordered Hasberg to park behind her. He complained, but pulled in and set the brake.

The wagons were closer together than usual. The men chained the front of each one to the rear of the one directly ahead.

Maggie felt a sense of foreboding. She wished Henry were with her. He'd join her tomorrow.

She checked her guns before retiring. The wool blanket scratched her face, and she listened to insects whine and the sound of a horse nicker. It took forever to fall asleep.

Sometime in the middle of the night, Maggie's neck stiffened, and her head came up off her blanket quickly. Something was out there. She picked up her pistol, leaned on her elbows, and listened. The camp seemed to be asleep. And then she heard them: coyotes.

But no, she'd heard the yipping of coyotes almost every night in Missouri. She knew the sound of coyotes. This howling was different: wolves.

Or Indians?

She rubbed her queasy stomach.

Howls from her far right. Several minutes later, there were howls from the left. A pack of wolves signaling each other? Indians signaling before an attack?

She leaned back against the flour sack to better watch each opening in the wagon's canvas top. She half-cocked the Colt pistol and waited. The howls grew faint as if the Indians or the wolf pack had lost interest in the wagon train and had moved away. She listened for sounds from other wagons. Silence, as though no one stirred.

She pulled the blanket around her shoulders, gripped the gun and waited. She overheard Sally ask Hasberg if they were safe.

"Ain't nothing out there except coyotes and wolves. Ain't no Indians in this god-forsaken country."

Chapter 23

The next morning, Maggie reined Sonny behind the lead wagon, waited for the start, and listened to Hasberg bitch about how the wagon train would slow them down.

Soon, Henry rode up, tied his horse next to her mare at the back of the wagon, and climbed into the front seat. She looked around to see if anyone watched, then kissed him on the cheek.

They fell into a long silence where they simply soaked up each other's presence.

"When we stop for the night, you can toss your bedroll under my wagon. It won't exactly be as intimate as the Hays House, but having you under me will be a great source of comfort."

"Under you?" he laughed. "You know I like being on top."

"We have to be careful. Samuel thinks you are my cousin."

"We won't have a problem. I ride the night shift, so I'll only see you while we're traveling in daylight."

"Oh, darned."

"Besides, I'll be in back, sleeping most of the day, while you're driving."

"At least we'll share meals and be able to talk with each other, and that will make the trip much more pleasant." Besides, she thought, his presence might keep her mind off of George and Jenny.

He reached for the reins, but she pulled them away. They laughed.

"Funny isn't it?" he said. "We wouldn't have met if it weren't for this war."

"It's changed, everyone. George and Ephraim talked about the coming war, but I argued no one was stupid enough to start one, and if there were war, it would never reach Missouri, much less Boonville. How could I have been so naïve?"

"It wasn't only you, Maggie. Many of us didn't think there'd be a war. What's the old saying, 'No one believes the sky is falling until they get hit by a part of it.'"

"I could have never imagined that, after the naval battle of Fort Sumter, that Boonville would be the first ground battle."

"Well, from what I hear, it was more of a skirmish than a real battle."

"You wouldn't think that if you'd been with me caring for the dying and wounded."

"In a sense, everyone's been wounded."

Soon Henry's head nodded, and she suggested he climb in the back of her wagon and get some sleep. Soon his soft snoring made her smile.

Late that afternoon, Henry rode out to look for a grazing area for the stock.

Once they settled into the pace, Maggie stepped off and walked beside her mule and overheard Sally suggest they should also walk.

"I bought two damned mules, and I ain't walking nowhere."

Maggie shook her head and felt gratitude for her time with George. And Henry wasn't abusive. Had she been lucky or used common sense in picking her relationships?

She wondered if Hasberg was always nasty, or he was out of sorts because he broke down and had to be rescued? Maybe his stinking attitude was a result of an injury to his male pride.

"Hi!" The boy walked next to her.

Maggie's hand flew to her locket. "Oh, you startled me."

"I'm Josh, and I'm nine years old." His freckles and crooked tooth smile made him look darling.

"I'm Maggie. Where are you from, Josh?"

"Saint Louis. My dad worked in a shop. He thinks we are going to get rich."

"How so?"

"I don't know. Maybe find gold or something." He picked up a pebble, looked at it, and tossed it aside. "Mom and I didn't want to go. I miss playing with my friends."

"What was your favorite game?"

"Hoop and stick. I'm pretty good."

"That was my favorite game when I was your age. I used to beat the boys."

"A girl can't beat boys."

"My father didn't like me to play with boys. Said it wasn't befitting of a lady, but I snuck out and played. And beat all the boys in our neighborhood."

"Huh. I bet you couldn't beat my friends and me."

Maggie laughed. "Probably not."

A giant grasshopper flew from beneath their feet, wings making a whirring sound. It landed in the grass several yards in front. Josh spurted ahead, fell to his knees, and captured the hopper. He brought it back to Maggie and opened his hands to show her. The grasshopper struggled to get on its feet and spurted dark juice on Josh's palm.

"Yuck! It looks like Dad's tobacco juice." The boy tossed the hopper aside and wiped his palms on his pants.

"Josh, stop bothering that woman and git back here," Hasberg yelled.

"He's no bother," Maggie shouted over her shoulder.

"Git back here. Now."

"I guess I've got to go," Josh said.

"It was fun talking with you, Josh. Come back anytime."

That evening, after Samuel called a halt, Maggie walked to the back of her wagon to tie the mare. Hasberg ripped the bridle off the lead mule's head, the steel bit clanked against its teeth. The mule jerked up its head and reared. The bit fell out.

"You son-of-a-bitch!" Hasberg slammed his fist into the mule's nose. The animal staggered, dazed, head down. "That'll teach you to stay while I unharness you."

Maggie shook her head and turned away, noticing several of the other teamsters watched.

After supper, she noticed Josh chasing fireflies. She found an empty jar and called the boy over. "Let's catch some and put them in this jar."

They scampered after the fireflies, running, jumping, laughing, and catching about twenty. Maggie screwed the lid on the jar. "Look, Josh, you've made a lantern. Show it to your Mom and Dad."

Josh held the jar over his head as he ran to his wagon.

She heard loud voices, and several minutes later, the boy came back and handed her the jar.

"He said I should get rid of it."

Maggie was silent for a moment. "He's right. We don't want them to die. Let's let them go."

He huddled close to her as she unscrewed the lid, and they watched the fireflies crawl out and fly away, their yellow lights switching on and off.

"You should go back to your folks now, Josh."

"Can't I stay?"

"We'll walk together tomorrow, so you need your sleep."

The boy hugged her and, head down, shuffled back to his wagon. Later that night, Maggie woke to angry voices from Josh's wagon.

"Oh! Please don't."

Maggie heard the sound of a hand slapping flesh.

"Oh . . ."

Maggie shouted, "Stop it."

"None of your dammed business!" Hasberg screamed.

It was quiet after that, but Maggie had trouble sleeping, thinking Hasberg was such a fool for not being grateful for the safety of the wagon train.

The next morning, when Jake brought Maggie's animals, he said, "Pretty disgusting goings-on with the man of that family."

Maggie nodded. "Too bad someone didn't beat some sense into him."

"Yep." Jake walked away to leave Maggie to harness the mule and tie the mare to the back of the wagon.

She watched Hasberg bridle the lead mule. The mule looked humbled and passive.

That afternoon Josh walked with her while Henry slept. They watched small birds fly close to her wagon's wheels, landing and hopping along, spurting into the air to catch fleeing insects.

"Birds are smart," Josh said.

"Yes, I've wondered whether intelligence or experience taught them that wagon wheels moving through grass provide a feast?"

"What do you mean?"

"Is the knowledge passed on from one generation of birds to the next? How long do the birds live? There was so much I don't know about nature."

"I don't know," Josh said.

"Maybe you will learn that in school."

"Uh-huh."

"Tell me a story," Maggie said.

"I don't know no stories."

"Use your imagination. I'll start a story, and you finish it. There once was a nine-year-old boy who was on a wagon train, and . . .?"

"Oh, I see. A boy was on a wagon train heading out west. One day Indians attacked and shot the little boy's father with an arrow. He died. His mother was sad, but the boy helped his mom escape. He saved an orphaned wolf pup, and they became best friends, and one day, the wolf took the boy to a creek full of gold, and they were rich, and they lived happily ever after."

Maggie wiped her eyes on her sleeve.

"Something in your eye, Maggie?" Josh asked.

"I liked your story, Josh."

They walked in silence, and Maggie wondered if Josh realized he'd revealed his attitude and emotions about his father. She hoped not. Imagination and wishful thinking would not help him out of his situation.

She pulled him close, and they walked together.

Chapter 24

The grass whispered behind them. Maggie turned and watched Josh's mother, Sally, hurry to join them. The woman had a purple bruise under her left eye. Embarrassed for the woman, Maggie looked away, trying not to stare. Was that how others felt when they noticed the scar on Maggie's cheek?

They walked in silence until Sally said, "I'm sorry you have to hear our arguments."

Josh spurted ahead, pretending to chase grasshoppers.

"What's the problem?"

"Haz says the wagon train is too slow. He says we can go faster alone, and he wants to go ahead, but I don't. I'm afraid of Indians and want to stay safe for Josh's sake."

"You're right, but don't tell your husband I said so. He dislikes me enough as it is."

"He was not always like this. I think he was embarrassed about the broken axle and not knowing how to fix it. He was a clerk at a mercantile store. There are a lot of things he doesn't know but thinks he knows, if you know what I mean."

"Did you bring a musical instrument?"

"Wasn't enough room, but I brought my mother's full-length mirror."

Maggie's fingers sought the ridge of the scar on her face. "I cut my cheek during the first week of the trip. I wonder what it looks like now."

"Me, I think you look beautiful. That scar gives you a look of mystery."

"Not much mystery here."

"Well, come over after dinner break and see for yourself."

Henry climbed out of the wagon and walked with them. Sally excused herself and returned to sit with Hasberg.

Henry and Maggie walked, hands sometimes brushing, on purpose. They listened to Hasberg and Sally squabble.

"Listening to that makes me happy to be a widower," Henry said with a grin.

"Treat me that way, and I'd put you out of your misery," she said.

They walked in silence, lost in their thoughts.

"Ever kill a man, Maggie?"

"I shot Mr. Beckly on the ship."

"I meant killed someone?"

"Why?"

"It's not all that simple. You kill a man, but in your mind, he never dies. He's with you forever. You're changed. Not for the best."

"What brought this up, Henry?"

"You might want to change your mind about going after those killers."

She gave him a hard look and fought to keep silent.

The mirror wasn't full length, but a full three-quarter glass bordered by a scrolled cherry frame. Maggie stared at a thin sun-tanned stranger whose face she barely recognized. After recovering from her initial shock, she had to agree with Sally's judgment: the woman in the mirror was beautiful with a mysterious aura.

"What's she doing in my wagon?" Hasberg stood at the rear, fists on hips.

"She just wanted to look at the scar on her cheek."

"Where'd you get cut, in a whorehouse?"

Maggie spun, climbed down, and slapped Hasberg.

He cocked his fist. "Why you bitch, I'll . . ." Words failed when he felt the barrel of her Colt revolver pressed against his groin. His fingers uncurled to form a useless shield. His voice cracked. "You'd better git on back where you belong."

"Don't beat them again." Maggie turned away, surprised by her calm, icy words. Maybe she was getting used to this new world. As she climbed into her wagon to wake up Henry, she noticed Jake leaning against a tree, watching.

That night, as Maggie slipped toward sleep, Hasberg began to shout at Sally.

Sally screamed, "I don't care what you do, I'm not giving it to you."

Maggie wished Henry wasn't out riding the stock. She peeked out from the bottom of the canvas top and saw little Josh standing outside, a three-quarter moon casting a long shadow of the boy toward her.

"Josh, come to me. Hurry."

The boy ran to her wagon, climbed up, and scampered over the front seat into her arms. She covered him with her blanket and held the shivering boy tight.

A few minutes later, Hasberg shouted, "Josh? Where the hell are you? Git back here right now."

Maggie yelled, "Josh is spending the night with me. Now quiet down and let everyone sleep."

"You bitch!"

"Told you not to swear in front of a lady."

"And I told you, you ain't no lady." He continued to berate Sally.

"I'm sorry," Josh whispered.

She held him tight until they drifted off.

Sometime during the night, Maggie thought she heard footsteps. She pulled out her pistol, thumb on the hammer, waiting for Hasberg to climb into the wagon. There was a muffled grunt, and thrashing in the grass. Muted voices. A moan. And then quiet. She listened for something else but finally drifted back to sleep. Her left arm held Josh, the revolver gripped in her right hand.

The next morning, Hasberg walked to Maggie's wagon. His face was bruised and scratched. Black and blue swelling closed his left eye. "Josh can ride with you."

"What happened to you?" Maggie asked.

"Fell and hit my head last night."

"Sorry," she said, not feeling the least bit sorry.

Henry rode up and watched Hasberg walk back to his wagon.

"What was that all about?"

"He gave Josh permission to ride with us today."

"Huh." He glanced around to see if anyone watched and gave her a fleeting kiss.

That evening, when Jake came to gather her animals, she asked, "What happened to Hasberg's face?"

"You told us to beat some sense into him. Let's see if it takes."

"I didn't literally mean to beat him up."

"Sure fooled me." Jake tipped his hat and walked away.

Chapter 25

After she'd harnessed Sonny the next morning, she spotted Samuel and waved him over.

"Find those missing oxen?" she asked.

"How'd you know about that?"

"Henry told me. What happened?"

"Indians tried to steal them. Four braves. I rounded up the animals and pushed them through the brush toward our wagons. Thought the Indians would mount up and ambush me, but they didn't. I never saw them again. Can't ever tell what an Indian will do."

Maggie once again pulled in behind the lead wagon, watching dust rise from its wheels, listening to the clink and clank of her cart. Henry arrived and, after a stolen kiss and few words, climbed into the back to sleep.

Maggie watched vultures float in lazy circles on rising air currents, red heads scanning the ground, waiting to use their sharp beaks to tear up carrion, waiting for a death feast.

She thought about Jenny and George, music and laughter, and friendship and love. She again thought about how badly Jenny had wanted to take dance lessons. Why had she refused to grant permission? She'd been stupid to tell Jenny she was too young. The real reason was

Maggie's fear that her daughter might get involved with the wrong sort of boy who would lead her into sin. Now Jenny would never dance again. What kind of mother had Maggie been?

She climbed off the wagon to walk beside Sonny.

Why had she argued with George the morning before his death? Why did she pick on him about being late to the luncheon? She'd placed her role of being hostess ahead of her husband and daughter. On the other hand, if they'd not been late, if only they'd gone to the luncheon with her, they wouldn't have been home when the killers arrived.

Rage flickered out of its hiding place, and burned in her belly. Her hands shook hard, and the reins flicked Sonny's back. She stepped down to walk alongside the mule. The soles of her feet had hardened; the rest of her had hardened as well.

"Why, Momma?" Jenny's voice.

Maggie stumbled and righted herself. Jenny sat on the wagon bench. She wore the bloodstained dress she'd worn when Maggie found her in George's arms.

"Why did they do it?" The girl's anguished face ripped at Maggie's heart.

A hallucination.

Yet . . .

"I miss you so much, Jenny."

"I want to know why they did it."

"They were evil animals born by war."

"Evil," Jenny repeated.

"I'm looking for them. I'm trying."

"That's good."

A man shouted from the lead wagon. "You alright, back there?"

Hasberg joined in, "Who's ya talking to?"

Maggie realized she'd stopped. "Yes. Coming." She turned back to Jenny.

The seat was empty.

Henry called from inside the wagon, "You all right, Maggie?"

"I'm fine. Just had to stop for a moment."

She climbed into the wagon and put her hand on the seat, hoping to feel Jenny's warmth. The canvas was cool.

An overwhelming sense of despair settled over her. Everyone she'd cared about, except Henry, was dead.

Was she a black widow? Why did everyone she cared about die?

Living at *White Haven* after the death of her family had been like sleepwalking through a dense gray fog: lonely and depressed. Her dream of Jenny's wedding, helping with the births and raising grand-children, growing old with George, surrounded by loving generations on the plantation, had been destroyed by the war. There would be no family, no children, no grandchildren.

She had grown so depressed. One day, after Ephraim gave her the pistol and had taught her how to shoot, she'd visited the graves high on the bluff overlooking the river. She sat on a bench next to the three tombstones – she'd commissioned one with her name and birthdate for herself - and told George and Jenny that she could no longer live without them. Maggie cocked the revolver hammer and put the cold steel muzzle to her right temple. She waited, thinking either George or Jenny or both would say, "Don't shoot yourself. Don't join us."

But they were silent.

Her finger tightened on the trigger.

A screaming apparition exploded, rising from below the bluff. It rushed toward Maggie. Inches from her face, the black specter rose, cawing its displeasure. Maggie froze, unable to squeeze the trigger.

She lowered the gun. A black crow came into focus. The bird flew to a nearby oak, settled on a branch, stared at her with beady eyes, and, with an angry voice, demanded she not desecrate this holy ground.

Was the bird a signal, or was she losing her mind?

It was on that bluff overlooking the Missouri River, sitting next to the graves of her beloveds, angered by the lack of justice when she decided to change the purpose of her life. She would gain new skills necessary to track down the killers and seek justice.

So began her journey.

After the noon dinner break, Maggie untied the mare from the wagon and watched Hasberg reach down to bridle his lead mule.

"Your lead mule seems tame now," Maggie said.

"Yep. A good beating makes women and mules easier to work with." He stroked the mule's forehead and slid his hand down to its muzzle. The animal slowly raised its head and then seized Hasberg's thumb between its teeth. The mule's teeth ground down through skin and bone and, ignoring the man's screaming, calmly spit the bloody thumb onto the ground.

Hasberg shrieked and held his ruined hand close to his chest and ran in little circles until he fell onto the ground, kicking and moaning and crying.

Maggie grabbed a roll of cotton cloth and a pitcher of water. She poured the water over the stump of Hasberg's thumb and then, ignoring the gathering crowd and Hasberg's sobbing and cursing, used the cloth to staunch the blood flow.

Josh stood in front of his mother, who held his shoulders. Maggie thought the boy looked embarrassed rather than sorry for his whining father.

Henry, Samuel Poteet, and Kit Carson rode up and dismounted. Maggie told them what had happened.

Poteet nodded, "Never piss off a mule. He'll remember."

Carson said, "Better cauterize it to stop the bleeding and infection."

"No! I don't need that. I'll be all right," Hasberg pleaded. "Oh god, it hurts so bad." He rolled to a fetal position and squeezed his hands between his legs.

Maggie said, "You've got to think about your wife and son. We're going to make certain you don't die."

They built a fire and heated a small cast iron skillet red-hot. Henry and three other men held Hasberg down while Maggie took the bandage off the stump. She helped Jake pin his arm steady against the ground, thumb stump up. Carson wrapped a heavy cloth around the skillet's handle, picked it up, and pressed it down on the bloody stump. Hasberg screamed and passed out while his skin sizzled. Maggie and Jake coughed from the stink of burning flesh.

Maggie had never before seen flesh on fire. She poured water over the stump, to quench the burning fat, and then she dried it with a clean cloth and wrapped his hand. The men picked up Hasberg and carried him to his wagon.

Josh helped Maggie pick up the soiled rags, and they threw them in the fire.

"Thank you, Maggie."

She hugged him and told him to help his mom.

Henry volunteered to drive their wagon until Hasberg recovered enough to drive.

Three days later, during a Sunday rest day, Hasberg, with a bandage over his hand, hitched up his mules.

Josh ran to Maggie and Henry. "Dad says the wagon train is too slow. We are leaving."

"You can't. It's too dangerous to travel alone," Henry said.

"Can I stay with you, Maggie? Please?"

Impossible. Josh couldn't be with her when she caught up with the killers. Yet the boy didn't need to be rejected by another adult.

"You can stay with me if your father agrees."

Josh stuck his hands in his pockets and kicked at pebbles while he made his way back to talk to his father.

Henry watched him walk back to his wagon. "Looks like we might have our first child. We'll be a family."

She poked him in the ribs.

"Hell no, he can't go with you!" Hasberg shouted. "He's my son. Who do you think you are? Keep out of our way." He slapped Josh on the butt and ordered him to climb into the wagon with his mother.

In spite of Carson and Poteet protesting that he would put his family in danger, Hasberg drove out of camp, shouting the wagon train was too slow.

Josh stood in the back of their wagon and waved to Maggie. They watched the Hasberg family disappear.

"I should have fought harder to keep Josh. I'm afraid I've condemned the dear boy to a terrible fate."

Maggie thought there are moments when one choice affects the rest of a person's life. Perhaps it's you who makes that choice, but the young are at the mercy of decisions made by others: parents, relatives, friends, and other authority figures. The young are innocent victims.

Henry put his hand on her shoulder. "It was his father's choice, not yours."

She was silent, praying, pleading with God to keep little Josh safe.

"You all right, Maggie?"

"I was thinking about Josh. How I wish I would have been stronger against Hasberg."

"What's done is done, still . . ."

"Still what?"

"I miss my family something fierce. Miss the kids. Feel bad I couldn't help them grow up," he said.

"I know. I feel the same. I looked forward to growing old, surrounded by grandkids, but . . ."

"Too bad we didn't keep Josh. We could have gone to Denver City together and had a family."

She flinched. Henry had mentioned it before, but having another family had never crossed her mind.

He looked at her, obviously waiting for her reaction.

The idea was a shock, yet not farfetched; no, she couldn't have children, but that didn't mean she couldn't have another family.

He took off his hat and wiped the sweat off the inside band. "So, what do you think?"

"I . . . what makes you interested in Denver City?"

"Gold. About three years before the war, a man named Simpson discovered gold at the meeting of waters of the South Platte and Cherry Creek. There've been other strikes up in the hills west of Denver City. People from all over are heading there. Where there are new people, there's a business opportunity."

His answer, for some reason, disappointed her. Perhaps it was because her mind was wrestling with the concept of creating a new family.

He settled his hat. "So, what do you think?"

"I think your gift of the Leaves of Grass was a savior to relieve the boredom of the trip."

Her night with Henry in Council Grove had been lovely. Their lovemaking was fantastic – all but at its climax when she screamed George's name. At the same time, she was becoming attached to Henry, emotionally as well as physically. She never thought she'd be able to love anyone but George.

Later, after supper, the herders drove most of the stock to safety inside the circled wagons. The spare horses and oxen pastured on grasslands outside the wagon corral watched over by Henry and other nightriders. Kit Carson posted his soldiers as sentries near the wagons.

She waved goodbye to Henry and settled in for the night. She wished he would be with her, even if he were sleeping under the wagon. Still, she was happy he was nearby. She pulled up her blanket and drifted off to sleep, imaging family.

Sometime after midnight, Maggie awoke to gunshots.

Chapter 26

Maggie thought she'd had a nightmare. Then she heard more gunshots. The night was pitch black, and she heard shouts from nearby wagons: "Injuns! Injuns!"

There were more gunshots from the area that Henry guarded.

Footsteps ran toward the perimeter wagons. Maggie fumbled for her revolver, slipped the derringer into her garter, and crawled toward the driver's seat, peeking out from underneath the canvas.

A full moon cast yellow light on the wagons. Shadowed men leaned against wagon wheels, rifles pointing into the dark, waiting for an attack. Her labored breathing sounded loud, her heartbeat thudding in her ears.

Men were calling to one another: "Seen 'em, Bill?"

"Nope!"

"You, Jake?"

"Think I seen sumpten out on that rise."

"Hold your fire 'til you know what you're shootin' at!"

Thank God her wagon was on the inside of the defensive circle. But what to do? Was Henry safe?

A shadow moved near her. She cocked her pistol and aimed.

"Whoa there, Maggie! It's Jake. I come to look after you."

She hoped he didn't hear her exhaled breath of relief as she let down the pistol's hammer.

"There's plenty of us to fend them off, so don't you worry none."

She backed into the wagon and slipped on her dress. Jake crouched on the floor in front of the driver's seat, rifle pointing over the wooden side. "Join me here now, but if there's gunfire, I want you on the wagon floor. Lie flat in between them boxes for cover."

A few minutes later, someone shouted, "Riders coming!"

"Don't shoot! Them's ours!"

"Drop that chain 'tween them wagons. Let 'em inside!"

She heard the metallic clanking of iron chains. Three horsemen rode out of the dark into the fire lit wagon circle, with two riders supporting the rider in the middle who slumped over his saddle horn. Once inside the ring, the two uninjured men lowered the wounded man to the ground.

Maggie cut a piece from her roll of cotton cloth, grabbed a pot of water she'd boiled for tea, and ignoring Jake's command to stay in the wagon, climbed down and ran to the wounded man. She recognized his face and gasped.

Someone shouted, "Don't leave your posts! Injuns could be following!"

Henry lay on his side, an arrow penetrating his back. Maggie knew how to treat injuries, plantation accidents, and bullet wounds, but had no experience with arrow wounds, especially a buried arrowhead.

Samuel Poteet and Kit Carson ran up and knelt next to Henry.

"What happened out there?" Carson asked the wounded man.

Someone held a lantern, its light wavering and faint.

Henry said through clenched teeth, "Ambushed. Musta been hiding in a bush. Shot me from behind as I rode past."

"Were there other Indians?"

"A group of five or six tried to stampede the horses, but our nightriders shot at them. Think they chased them off."

A shout came from a perimeter wagon: "Driving in the stock!"

Samuel said, "Looks like we didn't lose anything."

Maggie cradled Henry's head in her lap to keep it off the ground. "Let's attend to his wound. Please."

"What are ya thinking?" Samuel asked Carson.

"Could be a small band trying to steal our stock," Carson said. "Or maybe they're setting up an ambush, waiting for us to chase them. I'm of a mind to wait and see. Scout it out in daylight."

"What about this wounded man?" Maggie shouted.

They knelt and examined the arrow. Henry moaned when Carson cut off his bloody shirt.

"Above the lung and below the shoulder bone. Have to push the arrowhead out. Hold Henry tight." Carson wrapped both hands around the shaft. "Son, this here's gonna hurt!"

He jammed the shaft forward, quick and hard. Henry screamed as the arrowhead ripped through the skin of his chest. Samuel cut off the iron arrowhead, and Carson pulled the shaft back out.

"I need to pour whiskey on the wound, so he don't get an infection," Maggie said. "Who's got whiskey?"

No one spoke; Samuel Poteet forbade liquor on the wagon train. Finally, Samuel said, "I have whiskey in the medical kit in my tent."

Maggie's fingers probed the wound. The arrow and shaft had formed a channel from his back through to his chest. Blood was seeping out, but not pumping, so the arrow had not cut a vein or artery. That was good. But Henry had lost a lot of blood. The entire wound channel might become infected by the dirty arrowhead and shaft.

Samuel returned with a half bottle of whiskey. He pulled the cork.

"Give it to me," Maggie said. "Hold Henry down." She took a deep breath, put the bottle to her lips, and filled her mouth until her cheeks bulged, and the brown liquid dribbled from her lips. She handed the bottle to Samuel, dropped to her hands and knees, pressed her lips tight over the wound on Henry's back and, with all the force she could muster, blew the alcohol into the wound channel.

Henry screamed.

"Turn him over so I can do his chest." Maggie took another swill from the bottle, opened Henry's chest wound with her thumb and forefinger, closed her lips over the hole, and forced a mouthful of whiskey on the bloody mess.

Henry moaned and passed out.

Maggie sat back on her heels and asked for the whiskey again. This time she put the bottle to her lips, took a slug, sloshed it around her mouth, and, instead of spitting it, out swallowed it, savoring the burning sensation as the drink wove its way to her stomach.

"Good medicine." She handed the whiskey bottle back to Samuel. His look made her think she was not acting like a lady. To hell with what he thinks.

She asked Jake and another man to sit Henry up so she could dress the injury. She wrapped a bandage around his shoulder and upper body. Blood soon soaked through the white cloth. She hoped the blood would quickly clot.

"He can't ride," she overheard Samuel tell Carson. "Lost too much blood to walk, and laying in a freight wagon without springs might rupture his wound."

"My wagon has springs. It would be the most comfortable ride for Henry," Maggie said.

Carson and Samuel looked at each other.

She said, "I'll sleep on the ground under the wagon, like the rest of you."

Samuel said, "If you're sure about that, I'll have your meals brought to you. Jake can look to repairs on your wagon and harness up your mule."

"That would be kind of you. I'll arrange the inside of the wagon to make a bed for Henry."

During the following days, Maggie found that caring for Henry eased her mind. She read him the Bible and Walt Whitman poems during the noon and evening breaks. He continued to be in a stupor. On the third day, Henry became feverish. By evening, he began uncontrolled shivering. He didn't respond to her questions.

She had to do something to break the fever. She pulled the canvas ends as tight as possible and then stripped Henry naked. She took off her clothes, crawled next to him, spooned her body into his, and pulled the blanket over them.

The other men might notice she was not sleeping under her wagon, but she wasn't about to keep up appearances for the sake of their perception. They could think what they wished. She wrapped her arms around Henry and prayed, wondering if her plea to God would help or hurt.

Henry's fever spiked and broke sometime in the middle of the night. Maggie lay next to him, felt his regular breathing, and knew he'd made it through the crisis. She should put on her clothes and climb under the wagon; to hell with everyone knowing. She remained until dawn with Henry in her arms.

After they started, he continued to bleed because of the rough jostling of the wagon. Maggie wrapped his wounds every day until they ran out of clean cotton cloth. He grew weaker. Perhaps there would be a competent doctor at Fort Larned. She prayed he'd make it to the fort.

That night, Maggie checked on Henry and then crawled under her wagon onto the sheepskins. A full moon painted the land with a pale light, brushing nearby wagons into black silhouettes. She listened to the snuffling of oxen. It amazed her that she could feel comfortable sleeping on the ground when, several months ago, a small lump in the mattress of her four-poster drove her to call Sally to remake the bed.

Later, she didn't know if it was minutes or hours, her eyes snapped open. Something moved on her hair. She froze.

A spider. Huge.

It crawled over her head and moved down. Hairy legs stopped on her ear. One leg probed inside. She stifled a scream and held her hands tight together so she wouldn't try to brush it away and get bitten.

It paused on her ear for an eternity. Would it try to burrow into her ear canal? Oh, God! The spider moved onto her cheek and began to follow the scar. She could no longer endure the tension and slowly raised her hand to protect her mouth. The tarantula – she guessed it was a tarantula – crawled upon the back of her hand. She gently lowered the spider to the ground in front of her face and watched the giant spider walk away in the moonlight.

Body trembling, her heart was beating so loud she thought Henry sleeping above her would wake. Still, she hadn't panicked. Maggie handled her fear of spiders pretty well – considering. She smiled, wishing Henry had witnessed her small victory.

The next afternoon, the wagon train crossed a bridge across the Pawnee Fork. The road led to Fort Larned. Maggie expected the outpost to look like a fort, square with tall stone walls and a massive iron-reinforced gate. Instead, the fort was a collection of wooden buildings built around a central parade ground, with a barracks, officer's quarters, the quartermaster storehouse, stables, and other buildings she couldn't identify. The civilian sutler's store on the periphery sold commercial goods to soldiers, travelers, and Indians.

Despite an impressive number of soldiers marching in the parade ground and a squad of cavalry troops trotting past, the fort didn't look exceptionally safe.

She drove Henry to the fort's infirmary, where an army doctor took charge.

"You rest, and I'll visit you soon."

Henry nodded and tried to touch her hand, but was too weak.

Samuel directed four freight wagons to unload their supplies at the storehouse; the rest parked in the wagon yard. The pasture surrounding the fort had been eaten down, so he directed that the animals graze on better grass under guard several miles away. He seemed uneasy about this arrangement.

Later, he told Maggie that Kiowa braves had stolen over two hundred horses and mules from the fort's corrals. That affirmed Maggie's first impression – the fort was vulnerable.

She watched another wagon train cross the bridge toward the fort; its bullwhackers wore sombreros. Mexicans were heading east, toward Council Grove.

The fort commander, Captain Thomas Moses, Jr., found Maggie a room with a bath and invited her to dinner.

That evening, Maggie dined with Captain Moses, Kit Carson, Samuel Poteet, and the Mexican wagon master, Epifanio Aguirre, a charming, portly man with a long drooping mustache who was surprisingly fluent in English. He told them that his wagon train had left Santa Fe and traveled the Cimarron Route in spite of the current Indian troubles.

Señor Aguirre turned to the captain. "Your killing Cheyenne Peace Chief Lean Bear stirred up even more hostility. We are fortunate the

Indians know the difference between you Americans and us Mexicans. They do not bother us."

Carson turned to Maggie and whispered, "President Lincoln presented Chief Lean Bear a peace medal in Washington. Later, when the cavalry appeared at his village, Lean Bear wore the peace medal on his chest. The Chief approached the soldiers holding up an American flag and an official document signed by the President, stating that he was peaceful and friendly with whites. The soldiers shot him dead."

"Indian attacks have increased since then," Captain Moses said.

"Particularly after the Sand Creek Massacre," added Samuel.

Maggie turned to Señor Aguirre. "I'm looking for two men. One has bright red hair and rides a spotted Tennessee Walker with a black neck and head, and a pure white mane and tail."

"Oh, that horse. *Magnífico*! I tried to buy it, but the red-headed man acted insulted and rode away."

Maggie flinched and accidentally knocked over her wine glass.

Chapter 27

After the waiter cleaned up the spilled wine, the Captain began to tell a story. While he was distracted, Maggie whispered to Señor Aguirre. "Tell me about meeting the red-haired man with the magnificent horse."

"He and his companion were camped at the Middle Spring on the Cimarron Cutoff. He told me they had heard about some fertile bottom ground in the canyons north of Rabbit Ears Mountain. If so, they would stake out a homestead. But I think they are looking for gold.

"I told them of a family traveling alone on the Trail about a day ahead of them. Riding over that Trail alone is a dangerous thing to do, by the way. They said they'd catch up and protect them. The red-haired man's companion had a war wound, making his face look evil. They didn't look like the protecting kind if you know what I mean."

Maggie listened with dismay. Hasberg couldn't have been stupid enough to risk his family by taking the Cutoff. "Was it a family of three, a father, mother, and little boy?"

"Yes. The father seemed, how do you say . . ."

"Arrogant?"

"Precisely. May I ask why you are interested in that family?"

Carson interrupted, "Middle Spring is close to the Point of Rocks. Back in '49, the army asked me to guide a rescue mission to save Mrs. White. She was traveling with her husband, James, a veteran of the Trail, her baby daughter, and a Negro servant, plus some other travelers.

"They traveled west with a wagon train led by a well-known wagon master by the name of Aubry. After they passed what was considered the dangerous part of the trip, the Whites and several others decided it would be safe to leave the slow-moving train and advance to Santa Fe alone.

"The group paused near the Point of Rocks when a band of Apaches and Utes approached and asked them for presents. Jim White sent them away, but they returned, attacked the settlers, and killed everyone but Mrs. White, who they took away along with her baby and her servant.

"I guided the soldiers to the scene. It took another ten days tracking the Indians over some of the most challenging trails I ever followed.

"When we found their village, the Indians took flight. We chased. I found Mrs. White's body, still warm, an arrow through her heart. Never seen a woman so abused. They threw the baby in the river."

"That's a terrible story," Maggie said.

"Indians do terrible things when they capture white women," Samuel agreed. "Normally, I would not mention that at this table."

The Captain nodded.

"I suspect we've been equally unfair to their people," Maggie said.

"Mrs. Hartstone, you need to understand that Indians are not humans. They are savages," the Captain said.

Carson said, "Point of the story is, don't leave the safety of the wagon train if you want to stay alive."

There was an uncomfortable silence.

Maggie finally spoke. "Several of you know two men murdered my daughter and husband. Just as you know that I will do whatever it takes to bring the law of our civilized society down upon their heads."

The silverware shook when Kit Carson slapped the table. "Maggie, I'm telling you not to go after them. You'll never find the first spring. You and your animals will die of thirst if the Injuns don't kill you first."

"If I remember correctly, Kit, you told me that your policy after an attack was to take swift revenge."

"This is different. You need a guide, someone to protect you. Don't go, Maggie. You'd be better off living with bitter thoughts than dead."

The waiter brought the main course: buffalo hump, potatoes, and beans. They ate in silence until Maggie put her napkin on the table. "Thank you, Captain, for a fine dinner. Gentlemen." She pushed back her chair.

Señor Aguirre touched her elbow, holding her back. "You are certain of your decision?"

"Yes."

"And you know the dangers?"

"We've discussed this several times before."

The rest of the men looked on.

Señor Aguirre nodded. "In that case, I have an idea."

Chapter 28

Señor Aguirre introduced Maggie to Juan Pedro, his mixed-blood guide for the Cimarron Cutoff. Juan nodded a greeting, eyes watchful.

He was short, thin, and wiry, with long black hair and hard eyes. He could be taken for an Indian if it weren't for his brightly colored serape and the giant broad-brimmed, high-crowned sombrero that cast a shadow over his hawk-like face.

"Juan knows the Kiowa and Cheyenne," Señor Aguirre said. "He can communicate through sign talk."

He knows the trail and the water holes. He's in love with a new wife and wants to get back to Santa Fe before she gives him his first son."

Juan nodded, the sombrero hiding his eyes.

Señor Aguirre continued. "The Indians are fighting Americas, not us Mexicans. You would be safer if you were to hire Juan to guide you."

"That sounds agreeable," Maggie said.

"Juan is a good family man. You will be safe with him. You should follow his advice, even if you don't agree, because he knows in the ways of the trail."

Juan nodded again.

They settled on a price. Maggie paid in gold coins, which Juan gave to Señor Aguirre for safekeeping. She also bought two extra horses, and gifts for Indians and two additional water barrels at the sutler's store. Maggie would supply the food. Juan would provide his horse and guns.

Señor Aguirre handed her a colorful serape. "You would be safer to wear this if you encounter Indians."

Later, she walked to the fort's hospital and found the doctor.

"How is Mr. Herndon?"

"He'll make it unless his wound gets infected. There's not a lot I can do. He's lost a lot of blood and won't be able to travel for some time."

"How long?"

"At least several months."

Henry stirred when she walked to his bed. His voice was weak. "I wasn't very good at protecting you."

She smiled. "You're going to be fine. But you're going to have to rest and get well."

He faded out for a long moment and then opened his eyes. "Are you going to stay with me?"

She'd been dreading the question. "I discovered the men I'm looking for are just ahead of us. And I hear that fool, Hasberg, has taken his family on the Cimarron Cutoff, and they are just ahead of the killers. They're a danger to the Hasberg family. I'm going to try to catch up and turn them in."

"Oh." He showed no emotion but closed his eyes. He was quiet for a long time.

His eyes flickered open again, and he seemed to have trouble focusing on her. "Where are you going to turn them in?"

"That depends where I find them."

He faded out again. Maggie waited next to his bed until she was sure he was asleep and then turned to leave.

"I thought you might give that up and go with me to Denver City."

"You know I made a vow to avenge the killing of my daughter and husband. I'd like to stay here with you and, after you've healed up, go with you. I'm very fond of you, Henry, but I have no choice. We can have no chance for a future together until I fulfill my pledge."

"They'll kill you." He raised his hand to reach for her. His arm fell limp on the bed. His eyes shuttered and closed.

"We'll meet again, I promise. Know that you are the only man who I've loved, other than my husband. You are charming, smart, and brave, kind and a wonderful lover."

He opened his eyes and the corner of his lips raised. "I love you, Maggie." His eyes flickered as he fell back to sleep.

She kissed him on the forehead and whispered, "Until we meet again."

She joined Samuel Poteet's wagon train, which headed toward the Arkansas River. Silent Juan rode next to Maggie's wagon during the day and slept under it during the night.

And then, one day, Juan pointed to a shallow part of the river. "We leave here."

Maggie turned Sonny westward.

A short time later, Samuel and Kit Carson rode up to say goodbye.

"Why cross at Mulberry Creek instead of the regular crossing?" Carson asked.

Juan said. "Fewer eyes watch this crossing."

Carson nodded.

Samuel rode close to Maggie in the driver's seat. "Still time to change your mind, Maggie. This is your last chance. There's no turning back."

"Thank you for your kindness and help, Samuel, but this is my decision. Please don't let my action weigh heavy on your mind."

"You're a fine woman. Just remember: if the Indians are about to capture you, use your pistol on yourself. May the Lord protect you," Samuel tipped his hat and trotted back toward his wagon train.

Carson approached her and handed her a hand-drawn map. "Here's the best map I remember of the Cutoff." He cleared his throat. "Well then, Maggie, I won't say goodbye, but 'until next time.'"

"Until we meet again," she said.

He spun his horse and loped away.

Juan directed her to the river, where they filled their four water barrels before crossing.

"From now on, we change wagon animals often to save their strength," he said. That was the last thing he said for quite some time.

Having Juan ride with her was almost as bad as being alone. He never uttered an unnecessary word, and never showed facial expressions.

The earth soon turned hard under a relentless sun. Her wagon wheels rolled over short grass so dry it broke like shards of glass. She baked in the middle of the day and froze during the night. Several days later, she harnessed a fresh horse and observed, "I've noticed more wagon tracks recently."

"We joined the trail," Juan said.

She opened a barrel for a dipper of water. Their supply was shrinking fast. "How far is it to the Wagon Wheel Spring?"

"Two, three days. Maybe."

The land looked the same in every direction: flat, barren, the horizon distorted by rising heat waves, the sky hot white. Vultures soared in languid circles high above.

They rolled along. Maggie noticed something strange on the ground ahead, something large and square in contrast to the smooth windblown landscape. It looked out of place. A half-hour closer, the image became clear. An upright piano had been tossed from a wagon and abandoned. The lower half had broken off, giving the impression the piano was being swallowed up by the earth.

She stopped her wagon next to the piano. Juan came back to her and reined in his horse to a halt.

"I can't believe anyone would leave a piano here."

Juan shrugged his shoulders, turned his head, and spat tobacco juice in a high arc toward the back wagon wheel. "They needed to lighten the load. Probably ran out of water."

A rattlesnake slithered out from the shade of piano. If it crawled close, it could strike one of the animals. Maggie pulled her revolver and thumbed the hammer.

"No!" Juan said.

She released the hammer. "Why?"

"Sound carries."

She slid the pistol into her sash. They left the piano behind and trudged on toward the sun on the western horizon weaving through more family heirlooms thrown away by travelers desperate to reach water.

Chapter 29

The harsh landscape turned depressing and frightening when they passed the remains of a wagon. Sun-bleached human bones scattered along the way.

"Why, for God's sake, weren't they buried?"

"Who wants to die of thirst to bury them?"

She started to object but realized survival trumps civilized behavior.

The next evening, thunderheads billowed on the horizon, breaking the monotony of clear skies. Clouds boiled upward, the swirling masses creating brilliant whites and foreboding dark shadows.

"The sky is angry. We stop now."

They picketed the animals to graze on the sparse grass. The building storm blocked the last sunlight, and the distant booming of thunder reached them.

Night fell, a blackness Maggie had never before experienced. Lightning began, jagged streaks crisscrossing the sky, flashing the black into crackling and pulsating sheets of sterile light. She counted the seconds between the jagged bolts and thunderclaps. She saw the image of herself as a frightened little girl and her mother holding her, telling her the thunder was the sound of potato wagons rolling across the sky.

"Cover-up now. Maybe rain. Maybe not." Juan slid under the wagon and put his head on his saddle for a pillow.

Maggie drew the canvas top tight and covered anything that might get wet. She crawled on the sheepskins and watched the light show on the canvas.

The thunder became unbearably loud and frightening. It was louder than a thousand potato wagons.

"Come!" Juan shouted.

"What?"

"Now!" He opened the canvas and dragged her out and put his arm around her waist and ran until they were about a hundred yards from the wagon. He pushed her to the ground, fell over her, and covered both of them with his serape.

She breathed in his fetid breath and tried to push him away, but he held tight, arms tensing with each lightning flash.

"God's spears!"

She felt her hair rise and heard a sizzle. A lightning bolt exploded to the ground halfway to the wagon. A sharp metallic scent assaulted her nostrils. Hell must smell like this, she thought.

The mules brayed, and a horse screamed as lightning bolts struck nearby. Lightning zipped across the sky, looking like a crazed giant spider spinning a brilliant white web against a black otherworld.

The dry storm rolled on.

Juan rose and looked at the wagon. "Lightning hit next to the wagon."

Still on her back, she looked at his silhouette and realized he'd just saved her life.

They walked back to check on the animals. Two horses had pulled their picket stakes and now wandered, heads down to search for something to eat.

"Damn!" Juan walked over to one of her two new horses. It laid on its side, still, eyes open and glassy, tongue hanging out, with a burn scar on its side. She covered her nose from the stink of charred horsehair.

"Is it dead?" It was a stupid question.

"Meat," Juan said, reaching for his knife. He sliced through the hide along the spine and cut out the two back straps. Maggie marveled at the speed with which he worked.

He handed her the two long, round, heavy pieces of meat. "Might die of thirst, but with a full belly."

She wrapped each back strap in cloth and put them inside her wagon.

The next afternoon, they changed and watered the animals. Maggie looked in each of the water barrels – almost empty.

"No more water after they drink tonight," Juan said.

"Where's Wagon Bed Spring?"

Juan raised his chin, pointing somewhere ahead.

"How far?" she asked.

"One, two, three days."

"How long can we go without water?"

"Horses not long. Maybe one day. Mules a little longer."

"What about us?"

"Longer."

She mounted the driver's seat and hupped Sonny forward.

That evening, as the blood-red sun sank toward the earth, she saw dots of white on the far horizon. She pointed.

Juan nodded. "Tents at the spring."

The next afternoon, they met a group of cavalry, who escorted them to the spring – nothing more than a dimple in a barren and featureless landscape surrounded by tents and soldiers and horses. Her animals smelled the water, and Maggie struggled to hold them back as they rushed to drink.

The camp commander introduced himself. "Indians have been active lately, so you'd best camp here and wait for a large wagon train headed to Santa Fe."

"Did a family of three pass through here? They were traveling alone."

"I warned the father and suggested they wait with us and then join a wagon train, but he was stubborn. Their little boy was interested in our camp and the soldiers."

"Did you see a red-haired man on a spotted horse? His partner had a face wound."

"They came through a day after the family left. Why?"

"Just wondered. Met them before."

"How long will you camp with us?"

"We will leave in the morning." She looked at Juan. He nodded.

"I have a cavalry patrol leaving in the morning for the Middle Spring and on to the Point of Rocks. You can travel with them. After that, you'll be on your own."

That night Maggie begged God to keep little Josh safe.

Middle Spring, only eight miles west of Wagon Wheel Spring, was an easy day trip. They camped under the shade of cottonwood trees and refilled the water barrels.

The cavalry guard turned back at Point of Rocks, a high promontory overlooking a creek meandering through a long valley filled with cottonwoods.

Maggie watched the soldiers trot away until they were mere dots on the barren horizon.

Juan pointed to the high cliff. "Indian lookout place."

"No Indians?" she asked, hoping she was right.

"Not yet." Juan turned away.

Maggie followed.

Chapter 30

Juan began to vomit just before they camped for the night. Later, after she picketed the horses and Maggie forced him to drink some hot water, he staggered to his feet and stumbled as far as possible before dropping his pants. His diarrhea was pure brown-green liquid.

She prayed he didn't have cholera. It could be fatal.

Throughout the night, she heard him vomiting, accompanying loud gas explosions. Could she live without him?

The next morning, clear and windless, Juan could barely move. He refused to drink or eat.

"What can I do to help you?" Maggie asked.

"Go," he said with a weak voice, before turning on his hands and knees to dry heave.

"I'm staying with you. You need liquids."

"Leave me water and go.

"I don't know the way."

"Follow wagon tracks. Follow the sun west."

"I'm staying."

"You stay, you get sick. You stay, and we both die. Not enough water for animals to stay a day or two and then get to the next water."

"I can't leave you here to die alone."

"I catch up after I'm better." He struggled to his feet and lurched to the other side of the wagon to drop his pants. The stench was a poisonous fog smothering their camp.

He was right. But Maggie still had no idea where they were in this desolate desert.

She remembered the hand-drawn map that Carson had given her and showed it to Juan, who pointed weakly to their location. The drawing had an arrow pointing north, so she could use Ephraim's compass and find out where to go for their next water source.

She left food and water for Juan and his horse, waved goodbye, and headed west.

She looked out at the terrifyingly empty prairie with an endless sky and the sun that bore down without compassion, and she shrunk into the realization that her life was insignificant.

Alone.

She had once been Mrs. Margaret Hartstone, the wife of a loving husband and mother of an adoring daughter, and a respected leader bringing civilization to a frontier town.

The Civil War and the killers ripped away her entire life. She was now nothing more than an empty vessel of revenge, her quest meaningless.

That night, Maggie lay under her blanket and looked up at the infinite wash of stars in an unpolluted black sky, and she realized that humans as a whole vastly overestimated their importance to the universe.

Everyone is alone.

The next afternoon, moving like a solitary ant crawling over a barren desert under circling vultures, Maggie saw a mirage. Several feet above the heat waves on the horizon, shadowy forms appeared, bouncing up and down. Horses, feet never hitting the earth, coming directly toward her. Maggie reined to halt.

She studied the movement. Indians?

Had they seen her? Of course, they had.

She watched what she'd hoped to be a mirage form into solid images. Closer now. Warriors? She set the brake and checked her Colt revolver and the derringer on her thigh. She took off her sunbonnet, tucked in loose hairs with shaking fingers, and settled the hat before tying it securely.

She could do nothing except wait for them. Or she could do something they didn't expect.

She scrambled into the bed of the wagon and found the bright red blanket. She threw it over her left shoulder, jumped out, and walked twenty paces in front of Sonny. She waved the blanket over her head.

The mirages stopped, then moved closer. Now Maggie could make out horses and humans. She waved the blanket one last time and held it wide before her, settling it on the ground. Forcing herself to move with slow, confident motions, she searched for the rocks to anchor the blanket's four corners.

Back in the wagon, her hands shook as she opened the trunk and selected several of each kind of trinket she had bought at the Fort Larned store: various sized beads, buttons, bright ribbons, a piece of Mexican tin, three iron arrowheads, needles, and thread. She wrapped them in a cotton cloth and tied a piece of string around the top, knotting it in a bow, so she could quickly open the satchel.

She put on the serape that Señor Aquirre had given her and then picked up one of the cloth-wrapped horse back straps. The meat had aged and formed a thin hard crust that kept it from spoiling.

The Indian ponies now kicked up puffs of dust as they loped toward her. They were still several hundred yards away. The four braves wore no shirts; two carried bows, and one carried a lance and a war club.

Maggie strolled back to the blanket and sat cross-legged on its edge. She pulled the Colt revolver from her waist sash, checked the primer caps, half-cocked the hammer, and lowered the pistol to her lap before hiding it under the serape.

She folded her arms across her chest and waited and prayed to God to help her survive.

Chapter 31

The warriors galloped toward her, their horse's hooves hammering the desert floor like a drum, its vibrations assaulting her body, bearing down upon her like the Four Horsemen of the Apocalypse. They would run over her and stomp her to death like she squished a spider underfoot. Maggie fought from flinching. They swerved just before the blanket, spraying her with stones and dust. Screaming, they circled the wagon. Maggie tried to calm her shaking hands.

The braves reined in their horses and circled the wagon. They smelled of sweat and grease, their faces painted in hideous colors. One warrior had painted his face red with white dots, and an eagle feather hanging from the long braid hanging on the left. The hair on his right side was short.

She remembered Kit Carson telling her that Kiowa warriors cut the hair on the right short so it would not catch in a bowstring when releasing an arrow. A jagged white scar ran from the top of his left shoulder and across his chest. His right nipple was missing.

They reined to a halt in front of the blanket, horses blowing and prancing. Maggie spread her arms in welcome. The braves slid off their horses, held their reins, looked at each other, said something she couldn't understand, and then they sat cross-legged on the edges of the blanket.

They used sign language and a few words. Their tone of voice reminded her of angry conversations between George and the bankers, who wanted him to mortgage the plantation and donate the money to the Confederate cause. Some warrior's words were harsh and guttural. Was that a normal conversational tone, or was it anger?

She pointed to the cotton sack on the blanket. With great patience and ceremony to raise their curiosity, she opened the bag and dribbled out the contents.

Eager hands reached for the trinkets. Two braves argued over the arrowheads.

The heated discussion erupted and then died when she held the cloth-wrapped tenderloin high over her head and bent forward, placing it in the center of the blanket. She made a show of unwrapping it.

The braves nodded, took the trinkets and meat, and stood up. The brave with a black band painted across his eyes began to walk toward Maggie's wagon. The scar chest man grabbed his arm and stopped him. They argued, shouting, and pointed at her. The man with the black band repeatedly looked at her and made other motions.

Maggie understood: Black Band wanted to take her with them. Under the serape, she gripped the handle of her revolver; her thumb pulled back the hammer, and index finger on the trigger.

Black Band took a step toward her. Under the serape, she pointed the muzzle at him. She'd shoot through the cloth.

Scar Chest's fist hit under Black Band's ribs, doubling him over, gasping for air. The other braves stood silent, watching. Scar Chest pointed at Maggie and then held his nose. The others laughed.

Maggie's trigger finger relaxed.

Several minutes later, Black Band straightened, held his nose, laughed, and then mounted to his horse.

Scar Chest nodded to Maggie, jumped on his horse, kicked it in the ribs, and galloped off with the others close behind.

Maggie's hands shook, breathing fast and shallow. Fearing she might accidentally pull the trigger and shoot herself, she dropped the revolver in her lap. She'd lower the hammer after she regained her composure.

Several minutes later, she put away her gun, picked up the blanket, and tossed it in the back of the wagon. She watched the Indians ride away until their heat-distorted images disappeared over the horizon. Her hands still trembled as she held onto the wagon wheel spokes for balance to relieve her bladder.

Back on the driver's seat, Maggie touched her Bible and thought there was a God after all. She thanked Him for His help in acting on her prayer. He'd helped her survive.

The next day, a dark silhouette shimmering in the heat waves appeared on the distant horizon. She stopped and watched until she felt sure the object wasn't moving before she steered towards it. An hour later, vultures flapped into the air as she approached a broken wagon.

"Oh, no," she said over and over as she approached the wreck.

The wagon's rear wheel had broken off. The canvas top was in tatters, flapping in the wind.

Sonny shied. Her horses nickered and pranced.

Maggie's fingers tightened against the reins as she drove closer.

The smell of rotting flesh hit her. She gagged. The three decomposing bodies sprawled on the ground were the remains of Hasberg and Sally and young Josh. Caked blood covered their scalped heads.

They didn't have to scalp Josh.

Sally's skirt was high around her waist, her drawers tangled on her right ankle.

The image of Jenny flashed into Maggie's mind. She leaned over the side of her wagon and vomited.

"Damn you!" she screamed.

The contents of the Hasberg wagon not stolen were strewn across the ground. A crippled table lay slanted nearby, surrounded by pieces of dinner plates and scattered clothes. A gust of wind tumbled Sally's bonnet across the desert, over and over as if, once freed, it wanted to flee the grisly scene.

"You bastard!"

Pieces of Sally's prized mirror lay scattered across the ground. Each shard reflected different scenes: a white cloud floating in a blue sky, a vulture tearing open Hasberg's stomach, a severed arm, and Sally's naked lower body. A large piece of the mirror reflected Maggie's image, sitting in her wagon, alive. She shuddered, and realized there was no God.

"Move on," said a voice.

Maggie jerked the Colt from her waist sash and spun around.

Juan, looking like death itself, had followed her and approached unnoticed. She had been so focused on the tragedy she hadn't paid attention to her surroundings. If Juan had been an Indian, she'd be dead. Another lesson learned.

"Glad you made it. Who were you swearing at?"

"God."

Juan shrugged his shoulders. "Tracks back there looked like you had a powwow with Indians."

"You need to teach me to sign."

He nodded.

"Indians must have killed them," she said.

He walked his horse around the scene. "Not Indians. Shod horses. Two white men. Pretending to be Indians."

"We should give them a decent Christian burial," she said.

"The ground too hard. Wolves need to eat, too." He turned and spurred his horse forward.

"You bastard!" She watched him turn his back and ride off.

She set her wagon brake, found a shovel with her tools, and leaped off the wagon. She jammed the shovel into the ground, but the wind-packed dirt wouldn't yield. She pushed her foot against the top of the shovel's blade. The earth refused to surrender.

She stood on top of the shovel's blade and jumped, and her feet came down with all her weight, and she fell off without denting the ground. Sweat ran down her face and poured out of her body and darkened her dress.

She threw the shovel against the earth, looked to the sky, and reached her hands overhead and screamed. The sound disappeared into the desert.

"We will cover the boy with rocks."

She spun toward the voice. Juan sat on his horse and spit brown tobacco juice to the side and dismounted. She wiped tears from her eyes with the sleeve of her dress.

They gathered rocks and covered Josh's body. She was too exhausted to make a cross.

"We leave the other two for wolves."

She looked at Hasberg. "That bastard deserves to be eaten and shit out by wolves."

Later, as they crossed the prairie, Juan began teaching her the basics of sign language.

That night, after they'd eaten and were ready for sleep, she said, "I'm sorry I didn't act like a lady this afternoon."

"What?"

"Lady's don't swear," she said.

"Why not? The Great Spirit would not have given women a tongue unless He expected them to use it."

Chapter 32

Two days later, at McNee's Crossing on the North Canadian River, they came across a wall tent set under the shade of cottonwood trees. Smoke curled from a campfire. Four horses, tethered to a picket line, watched them.

Juan called out a greeting. Two men stepped from behind the tree trunks, pointing rifles at them.

"Whatchu want?" asked the tall, bearded man wearing a plaid wool shirt.

"Going to Santa Fe," Juan said.

"Alone? Just the two of you?" the shorter man, wearing a buckskin shirt, asked.

"Looks like there are just two of you," Juan replied.

"We's four."

"Where the other two?" Juan said.

"Gone prospecting."

Maggie stood up from the seat, stretched her back, and asked, "One of them has red hair, riding a paint horse?"

"Why you want to know?" the short man asked.

"I'm his sister. Have important family news."

"Sister? Hell, you can't be Red's sister, you got black hair."

Maggie laughed. "That's what everybody says. Different father."

The tall man grinned. "Someone slipped in between the sheets while the old man was away?"

"My daddy was shot dead in a card game. Mama married again and had Red. That's why we look different," Maggie lied.

"Ain't what he told us."

Maggie's hand cradled the handle of her pistol. Juan turned in his saddle to face the tall man. The serape hid his gun hand.

"Either you or Red is a liar," Maggie said.

"You calling me out to be a liar?" the tall man shifted his feet for a shot.

"If my no-good brother told you different, he's lying to you. Cut to the chase. I need to talk to him about family business. Where'd he go?" she asked.

The short man grinned. "I do believe he knocked you up!"

Maggie stood straighter. "Look like I'm pregnant?"

The tall man lowered his rifle. "Oh, hell. All right. Tell you where they went if you give us something."

"Sure, I'll give you something," Maggie said.

The men looked at each other and grinned.

She disappeared inside the wagon and returned to the driver's seat with a bundle wrapped in cotton.

"What is it?" asked the short man.

"Come and see for yourself," she said, unwrapping the parcel.

The short man approached the wagon. She used both hands to show them the tenderloin. "Meat."

"Hot damn. Ain't had meat in forever." He reached for it.

She pulled it out of his reach. "Tell me where my brother is, and it's yours."

"Red and his partner and the squaw went to look at the canyon country north of Rabbit Ears Mountain."

"Truth?" Maggie asked.

"Swear on the Bible," he said.

"Doubt you've ever held the Good Book." She handed him the meat and nodded to Juan, who stood guard as she drove the wagon away.

A few minutes later, Juan rode up next to her and nodded. She thought she detected a smile.

That afternoon, through the heat waves, she spotted Rabbit Ears Mountain shimmering on the far horizon. She finally had something to look at besides the flat desert that made her feel as though she was an insect pinned to one unforgiving spot for eternity.

The distant mountain gave her a sense of perspective and purpose: a direction, a goal even though her movement was imperceptible. Still, the black mountain thrusting out of the desolate flat gave her hope.

Three days later, they rode past the north shoulder of the mountain. Juan led them across the flat desert and stopped on the edge of a slope that dropped hundreds of feet into a vast canyon area.

"There." Juan pointed to valleys rimmed with cliffs and steep hills that rose once again to the prairie. Creeks meandered through the bottoms, giving life to lush grass and trees. It was as if God had used a serrated knife to cut a zigzag rip through the barren desert, to hide a Garden of Eden.

How would she find the killers in that expanse of nooks and crannies, stretching as far as the eye could see? A marshal would scoff at the idea of searching such a large area. She'd have to locate their precise location.

"Where is the nearest law office?" Maggie asked.

"Santa Fe," Juan said. "Law won't come here."

"Why not?"

He shrugged. "Too far. Besides, it's haunted."

"What if the marshal isn't superstitious?"

"Too many hiding places, escape routes. Never catch them. Might not be down there. Marshal would not go on a goose-chase."

Maggie set the brake and climbed off of the wagon. She used her hand to shield against the sun as she looked for a sign of life. There could be thousands of Indians hiding down there, and she wouldn't see them.

"Will you go down there with me?" she asked.

He shook his head. "I go to Santa Fe. You come with."

She didn't want to go down in those canyons alone. She closed her eyes and heard Jenny's voice: "Why? Why did they do it?"

She'd made a vow to her daughter. Maggie would die someday, anyway. Better to die now trying to make a difference than to live as a bitter, grieving old woman.

She would use the attorney's letter to trick them, maybe capture them and haul them to Santa Fe. Turn them over to the marshal and make sure they got their just punishment.

She had to go for Jenny. For George. For Josh and others in the future.

"Will you show me the way down?"

He nodded. "You make a big mistake."

She followed Juan down the slope. The drive was more accessible than it looked, and they stopped at the bottom in a grassy meadow next to a meandering stream.

Juan reined in his horse to look at tracks in a patch of bare earth. He circled the hoof prints several times and then nodded.

"What are you looking at, Juan?"

"Two sets of shod horse tracks heading up the canyon. One set of unshod tracks following them."

"An Indian?"

"Sí. His tracks are on top of the others, so he's following. You come back with me."

Maggie flipped the reins against Sonny's haunch and moved to where she could better examine the tracks. She had a bad feeling about going on alone. "What do the shod tracks tell you?"

"A white rider led a packhorse."

She set the wagon brake, climbed down, and stared at the tracks. It would be easy to return with Juan. Safer. He walked around a bush to relieve himself. She heard a voice from the wagon behind her.

She reached for her pistol and spun toward the sound.

Jenny sat on the driver's seat. "Don't stop now, Mother. Please find them."

Maggie blinked and shoved her revolver back into her waist sash. Sand seemed to fill Maggie's throat, slurring her words. She could only utter her daughter's name.

"Bring them to justice if you love me."

"I will," Maggie croaked.

Juan stepped from behind the bush, gun drawn. He glanced around. "I heard a voice."

The wagon seat was bare. "I was thinking out loud. I'm going to stay down here."

Juan nodded and mounted his horse. "I have a baby coming soon, maybe a son. Adiós, Maggie. Good luck." He spurred his horseback up the hill.

Maggie called out her thanks. She watched him ride away and felt as though she was shrinking into a pinpoint in a hostile world. Juan disappeared over the top without waving.

She was alone.

All alone.

She exhaled and took several deep breaths. How to find them? Follow the horse tracks, of course. She hupped Sonny and rode on. Soon a high-pitched noise and clacking sound caught her attention.

She stopped, set the brake, climbed down, and discovered the spokes on the left rear wheel were loose, and the iron tire had slid an eighth of an inch off the outer edge of the rim. There was nothing she could do now, but to soak the wheel and continue.

Two lonely and fearful days later, the tracks led toward a lush valley that ended in a cul-de-sac. Maggie reined in Sonny and studied the scene. At the north end, the land undulated upward to a rocky bluff. Juniper trees spotted the side hill. Near the center of the meadow, a spring bubbled out of the ground, the grass was tall, and cottonwoods provided shade.

She spotted something white, almost hidden by tree trunks – a tent.

Birds chirped. A raven cawed somewhere to her left, another answered behind her.

Someone was camping there. Where was he? Or them?

A sudden breeze puffed like a giant's breath, and she felt its pressure against the back of her neck. She shuddered. An instant later, the breeze changed and swayed the grass and danced through tree branches and leaves, floating a shower of puffy white cottonwood seeds across the meadow.

As she watched, the wind shifted, carrying the bitter scent of charred wood from a dead campfire.

A horse nickered. A black and white spotted horse, ears forward, looked at Maggie.

Traveler!

Chapter 33

A rope from Traveler's halter led to a picket stake. Everyone told her Red rode Traveler. He must be close.

Another sorrel horse grazed fifty feet to the left. Nothing else moved. Maggie adjusted her revolver and then flicked the reins against Sonny's haunch. The mule pulled her wagon closer. She heard a metallic screech and a snapping sound. The back of her wagon crashed to the ground; the wheel snapped off the axle.

Maggie's mare whinnied. Traveler and the other horse whinnied back. Sonny hee-hawed. That would alert anyone around. She waited, favoring the height of the wagon seat and the protection of it's wooden sides. Nothing moved.

"Hello!" She retrieved the lawyer's letter from the secret drawer under her seat and slipped it into her waist sash. The back of her hand touched the gold coins sewn into her corset.

No answer. Where was Red? Where was his partner?

Convinced the killers were not close, Maggie stepped down from the wagon and walked toward Traveler. The horse moved to the end of his picket rope to greet her, nodding and nickering. He recognized her, even after all this time.

She scratched his ears and recognized George's saddle leaning against a nearby tree. The bridle hung from the saddle horn. Traveler nuzzled her with his velvet-soft nose.

A man stepped from behind the trunk of a tree. His rifle pointed at her chest. "That horse don't cotton to strangers!"

"Don't shoot!" She raised her hands.

"How come he lets you get close to him?" Black greasy hair fell over the thin man's shoulders from under a wide-brimmed felt hat. His distorted mouth twisted to the left side of his face, upper lip extruding from his beard like a piece of raw sausage.

"Would you please aim that gun someplace else?"

"You know that horse?" he asked.

He wore a long, striped cotton bushwhacker's shirt with large pouch pockets on either side of the chest to carry spare revolver cylinders for quick reloading.

"Like I say, he don't like strangers. Why you?"

"He must like women."

"I like women." The wide leather belt circling his shirt held a holster for a revolver and a Bowie knife. "Who are you?"

"My name is Maggie. I represent Thomas F. Billings, Esq., Attorney at Law."

The twisted-mouth man cocked his head and lowered the rifle muzzle toward her feet. "Huh?"

"I'm looking for Mr. Patrick Doyne from Missouri."

He cradled the rife in his arm and scratched his neck. "Why are you looking for him?"

"Where is Mr. Doyne?"

"Why do you want to talk with him?"

"I have a letter from Thomas F. Billings, Esq., Attorney at Law, to Mr. Patrick Doyne." She pulled the envelope from her waist sash and waved it at him. "Do you know where I can find him?"

He ran his fingers through his beard, thinking. Something flashed between the junipers high on the hillside behind him, but when she focused on the spot, nothing was there.

"I'm Patrick Doyne. Show me the letter."

He leaned the rifle against the tree trunk, walked toward her.

"Patrick Doyne has red hair."

He stopped, hand on his holster. "How'd you know that?"

"Says so in the court records. Besides, everyone saw him riding that horse," she pointed to Traveler. "Why did he give the horse to you?"

"Traded for an Indian squaw I caught. Show me the letter." He walked toward her, hand out.

She held up her hand. "Stop!"

"What, for Christ's sake?"

"Don't use the Lord's name in vain."

"What?"

She turned and walked several steps back, edging closer to her wagon before she turned toward him. "Aren't you Patrick Doyne's partner?"

"Why'd you think that?"

"People said he had a partner who looks like you."

"Who told you that?"

The mule brayed and the mare, still tied to the back of her wagon, whinnied in response.

"The men camped at McNee's Crossing told me. So, where is Patrick Doyne now?"

"Why?"

"If I can find him and get him to the nearest town before the deadline, an attorney can certify he is Patrick Doyne. He'll get his family's plantation back. He'll be richer than finding gold out here.

You and he can go back to Missouri to claim the plantation and live like kings."

He scratched his neck. "I'd be rich?"

There was another movement on the hillside behind him. It must have been an animal or her imagination. She turned back to him. "You'll have more money than you can imagine."

A mourning dove cooed.

He looked up, and beyond her, eyebrows furrowed. She heard her breathing and water rushing over rocks in the stream. His greed would do the work for her. He would help her find Red and, if she played it just right, she could lure them to Santa Fe, where she would have the sheriff arrest them.

"Red took his squaw and headed out to explore some side canyons. Said he'd be back soon."

"Let's go find him."

"Your fee can't be that much money."

"Two hundred greenbacks to look for him. Another four hundred if I find him."

"That's a lot of money."

"Not enough. If you help me find Red, you'll be rich, and if you're nice to me, I might go back to Missouri with you."

"Huh." A crooked smile creased his lips. "Ladies liked me a lot before I got shot in the jaw."

"What's your name?"

"Bobby."

She felt giddy with excitement. "Well, Bobby, saddle up Traveler, and let's go."

He nodded and walked toward the saddle, picked it up, paused, and then dropped it on the ground. He turned toward Maggie. "You called that horse by name."

She paused, "Popular name. Robert E. Lee's horse is named Traveler."

"You're lying." His hand slid toward his holster.

She'd have to do it the hard way. She pointed at the ridge behind him. "Is that your partner?"

The killer looked over his shoulder. "Ain't nobody up there."

She pulled her pistol at her waist sash, but its hammer caught in the fabric. She clawed the cloth away.

It was as if time slowed, and she was trapped in molasses while he moved in real-time. The killer spun toward her. Her fingers caught the fabric, and, instead of clearing the revolver, she tangled it with more cloth.

He opened his holster flap; his fingers closed around the handle of his pistol.

She finally pulled her revolver free of the tangled mess. She cocked it and raised her pistol to aim.

He had his pistol pointed at her. He pulled the trigger.

Maggie's body rose as if a mule had kicked her in the chest. Her revolver flew from her hand, spinning away in slow motion. She landed on her back, pain jolted through her left shoulder and arm, and the world turned black.

Chapter 34

Maggie floated, drifting through a black void. Unbearable pain scorched her mind, propelled her through a haze of consciousness. She slowly became aware of her surroundings – lying on the ground, looking at the sky, a fuzzy image of the twisted-mouth man searching her wagon, her pistol on the ground, too far to reach. He would kill her if he discovered she was still alive.

She wanted to scream in agony from the searing pain in her chest. She bit her lip, stifling a moan as she watched the twisted-mouth man through partially closed eyes. She pulled out the derringer hidden in the holster on her leg and cocked it. Its short double barrel was barely visible in her hand. She hid the gun in a fold of her skirt and waited, knowing he'd come for her. She smelled the acrid scent of black powder from his shot, heard his boots scuff on the ground, coming closer. She shut her eyes and waited.

The sounds of his footsteps came near. Stopped. Maggie felt him yank her skirt up to her waist.

She watched him through a slit in her eyelids. He fell to his knees between her legs, undoing his belt. She jammed the derringer barrel deep into his belly.

His eyes bulged. "What that hell?"

She pulled the trigger, the explosion muffled by his clothes and skin. She cocked the derringer again, keeping the barrel close to his chest as he rose and fell backward onto the ground, legs jerking. She pulled the trigger and heard a metallic snap. The gun didn't fire.

She pulled her skirt above her knees, rolled over and, using her right arm, crawled to her revolver. She picked up the gun, stood up, and stumbled toward him. She cocked it and pointed it at him. He moaned and held his belly.

"Why'd you shoot me?"

"You killed my daughter and husband."

"Did no such thing!" Blood and yellow liquid ran between his fingers.

"Remember Boonville?"

He rolled to his side and then to his back. "Where's that?"

"Don't lie to me. You know Boonville is in Missouri."

"That weren't me."

"Yes, it was. That's my husband's horse."

"Red did it! Not me!"

"Why'd you let him do it?"

"A-feared of him." He moaned and held out a bloody hand to her. "Help me. I hurt awful bad."

"That's what my husband said. It took a long time for him to die. I hope you'll take longer."

Moaning, he scooted on his butt back to lean against a log. "I didn't do nothing."

"Which one of you violated my daughter?"

"Weren't me! I respect the ladies. It was Red. He done it. Red shot your husband, too! He's a killer." His right hand dropped toward his holster.

"You steal my daughter's silver cross?"

"Red done it. Said he was gonna find a woman and give it to her. He took the cross and got him a squaw. Gave that cross to her." His fingertips raised the leather holster flap.

Pain shot through her. She felt dizzy. Her eyesight blurred, her left arm paralyzed with pain. She felt the spot on her upper chest, wondering why she wasn't dead or bleeding. Her fingers traced a cupped gold coin – the twisted-mouth man's bullet had hit the center of the coin. Gold had saved her life.

The twisted-mouth killer moaned and looked at the blood and guts leaking through his fingers. "I don't deserve none of this."

"Really?"

"I was handsome before a Yankee bullet hit my face. People liked me. But after they sewed me up and discharged me, I had nothing. I looked like a monster. People were afraid of me; laughed at me. Kids ran from me. Couldn't get a job. Couldn't even beg for food."

"So how did you survive?" she asked, hoping to hear more details about George and Jenny.

"I was mad, and I wanted to get even. I could shoot. I joined up with Bloody Bill Anderson's bunch. They didn't care what I looked like, so long as I could kill. And I killed good. Red joined up, too. He was green so I showed him the ropes. We thought we could do better on our own, so we . . . oh, God, it hurts!"

"That's what my husband told me after you shot him. Remember that as you suffer," Maggie said.

"You ain't gonna leave me like this?" His fingers touched his revolver.

"I hope it takes a long time," Maggie said. "What's your name?"

"Bobby. Mama done named me Bobby."

The twisted mouth man raised his revolver toward her. Its muzzle wavered.

Maggie raised her gun, aimed, and shot him in the chest.

His revolver fell into the dirt, and he slumped onto his back.

She heard galloping horses and looked toward the sound. She thought she was hallucinating, but when her vision cleared, she realized the warriors were all too real. Five braves bore down on them. They wore war paint, their faces bearing designs in red and yellow and black, making them look hideous.

The leader reined in his horse, slid off, and landed in a crouch behind Bobby's body. The warrior grabbed the man's hair and pulled it high. Maggie watched as he scalped the dead killer, cutting off the hair on top of his head.

Raising the bloody scalp over his head, he looked at the sky and screamed an animal shriek that carried hatred, sadness, and revenge. His scream echoed from nearby hills.

Maggie, frozen with fear, yet mesmerized by how easy the knife sliced through the killer's scalp and shaved off the skin containing his hair, making Bobby into a bloody bald corpse, just like the Hasbergs.

She watched, fighting fear and nausea. She held her pistol at her side. *Shoot yourself in the head before you let an Indian take you*, Kit Carson had said.

The brave stood tall and looked at her across the dead killer's body. Black eyes locked on her. His short hair fell to the bottom of his right ear lobe, while a long braid wrapped in fur fell over his left shoulder. The left side of his face was black and the right half yellow, with red dots. He had high cheekbones and a long straight nose, full lips, and white teeth. He wore a necklace of bear claws, while a deerskin breechclout folded over a belt, its flap covering his genitals. Leggings wrapped his legs. They were attached by leather loops to the belt that held his breechclout. Beaded deerskin moccasins covered his feet. A bronze chest and muscular stomach bore a white scar.

He was missing a nipple.

It was Scar Chest; the man who'd saved her after she had given them gifts and meat at the blanket powwow on the prairie.

She stared into his eyes and recognized a shadow of recognition and sadness. Beyond that, his eyes seemed honest and curious, not hostile.

The other braves slid off their horses. They pointed at Maggie and argued with him. He shook his head and said something with an empathic voice. She slowly raised her Colt .31 across her chest, put her thumb on the hammer, and let it down. She tucked the revolver into her waist sash, and waited.

The other braves ran to ransack her wagon. One man opened her trunk and threw clothes out until he found a chemise. He slipped it over his head, jumped off the wagon, and, whooping, spun in circles.

Scar Chest offered the bloody scalp to her over Bobby's body. Frozen for a moment by the gift offering, she held up her palm and shook her head.

He again pushed the scalp toward her.

She wouldn't touch the scalp. She held up a finger, walked to the wagon, untied the mare, walked back, and offered the warrior the lead rope.

He tucked the scalp under his belt and accepted the gift.

What was she thinking? Wasn't she a captive now? Wouldn't they just take anything they wanted?

Excited yells caught their attention. One of the braves had found Maggie's favorite maroon dress. Another discovered the remaining trinkets and ribbons and other trade items she'd bought at the sutler's store at Fort Larned. He pranced with joy, holding a handful of fabrics high above his head.

Scar Chest shouted something to the others and then walked toward Traveler. Maggie followed. He reached for the horse. Traveler reared and struck out with its front legs. He stumbled back from flailing hooves.

She brushed Scar Chest aside and put her hand on the horse's neck. Traveler whinnied and calmed down, which caused Scar Chest to look at her with raised eyebrows.

Maggie pointed to Traveler and at her chest, claiming the horse.

Scar Chest shook his head and untied Traveler's lead rope from the picket line and walked away with him.

Maggie followed. "You can't take Traveler!"

He ignored her as the other braves unhitched Sonny and saddled the mare with George's saddle and bridle. They behaved as if she wasn't there. They packed loot on another horse and put the pack-saddle on Sonny, who fought from letting them pack anything else on top. They finally gave up.

Scar Chest mounted his horse, holding Traveler's lead rope.

She reached for her pistol but knew that it was an impossible fight to win. Instead, she ran to the brave, touched his leg, pointed at Traveler and then at her chest, and tried to wrest away the lead rope.

Scar Chest shook his head, bent down, and gently pushed Maggie away. He shouted something, and a brave dropped the mare's reins. Maggie ran to the horse and held the lead rope tight. Scar Chest rode off, leading his band of thieves.

Sonny stopped and dug in his hooves. The brave who lead Sonny fell backward off his horse. The others laughed, while he dusted himself off, he grabbed Sonny's lead rope and pulled, stretching out its neck. The mule hee-hawed. The brave dropped the line, ran back to his horse, and vaulted on top of its back. The others laughed as they rode off.

Maggie watched them ride up the slope until they disappeared over the ridge top and then turned around to look at the carnage.

She was in the wilderness, alone, with a horse she didn't know how to ride, an ornery mule, and a dead man.

Chapter 35

Maggie's chest and left shoulder ached from the bullet's impact, so she leaned against the rough bark of a cottonwood tree. Her left arm felt numb as her fingers gently explored her chest. She touched the cupped gold coin. The bullet had struck dead center. Had it hit a fraction of an inch differently, it would have slipped between the coins sewn into her corset. She would have died.

She surveyed the scene: a sunlit meadow in the afternoon, with shade trees casting shadows across lush grass, a soft breeze rustling the leaves, a spring bubbling cold water, and the bloody corpse of a scalped murderer staring at her with glazed dead eyes.

That *bastard*! And yet, she had shot him dead and watched without lifting a finger while the warrior scalped him. Was she now a savage, no better than Bobby? Or had she achieved a small measure of justice?

And why hadn't she taken Kit Carson's advice to put the gun to her head and pull the trigger when the band of warriors swooped down upon her?

More questions spun in her mind, around and around and around: Why hadn't she shot Scar Chest, who offered her Red's scalp?

Why did she put her pistol away? Why didn't the braves take her as a prisoner or as a hostage?

Questions made her dizzy. She slid down the tree trunk and slumped on the grass, in pain, confusion, and exhaustion.

Sometime later, she heard buzzing and felt something on her face. She slapped a fat, squishy fly. Hundreds of flies swarmed around the dead body. It would bloat. She looked at her ransacked wagon. She'd lost Traveler. Again.

"Goddamnit!" she shouted, surprising herself with her language. But Juan had been right. She had a tongue, and some words expressed feelings better than others.

Thinking about her feelings had to wait. She needed to concentrate on surviving. First: what to do with Bobby's body? Give him a Christian burial, or let maggots consume him where he lay?

If she stayed at the meadow for several days waiting to ambush Red, the twisted-mouth man's partner, maggots would be feasting on Bobby's flesh. The smell would draw predators. Burying him would be the Christian thing to do, even though she doubted he was a Christian.

She found the shovel in her ransacked wagon. Other objects lay scattered on the ground. The warriors had left anything they couldn't carry or use.

She needed to go through his pockets to find a better clue to where Red might have gone, or to find greenbacks or anything valuable. She stood over him, trying to ignore his glassy eyes, scalped skull, and bloody shirt. Flies buzzed around her face, landing on her nose, and corners of her eyes. She swatted them away.

Feeling like a robber, she bent over to slip her hand into his pocket and gasped at the smell. He'd shat himself. She tried to cover her nose with her left hand, but her hand didn't rise, still paralyzed from the impact of Bobby's bullet. She held her breath and turned his pockets inside out. There was nothing of value. She stripped off his belt and took his Green River knife with its long curved blade.

She began shoveling one-handed, cradling the handle under her right armpit and using her foot for pressure. Once through the top layer of grass, the ground here was soft dirt, without rocks or gravel. There were many fat earthworms that, she imagined, would enjoy Bobby.

Digging proved to be easy going and, after an hour, she used the shovel to pry the killer's body into a shallow grave. She stood at the head of the grave, wiped the sweat off her forehead, and looked down at him.

His head was black and crusty from the bloody scalping. A crooked front tooth made his grimace look almost comical. Glassy eyes gazed up at her as if asking, "why?" Why, indeed! She shoveled a scoop of dirt on his face and then stopped. She should say a prayer for his soul.

After sticking the shovel into the dirt, she folded her hands in prayer.

"Go straight to hell, you bastard! Amen." That was as Christian as she could be.

"He deserved to die."

Maggie dropped the shovel at the sound of Jenny's voice. Her daughter, forever fifteen, forever beautiful, forever wearing the blood-stained dress and missing the silver cross, stared at Bobby's corpse.

"Thank you, Mother."

"I brought one of your killers to justice."

"There's still the red-headed man."

Maggie wanted to hug her daughter, but that was impossible. "Which one violated you?"

"They wounded father and then took turns with me. Red forced Father to watch."

Maggie's eyes moistened. Her hand felt for her pistol, but she fought the impulse to shoot Bobby's dead body again. "I'm so sorry, Jenny."

"How will you find the red-headed man?"

"He said Red would return, so I'll wait here."

"You don't have any way out of here. You can't take the wagon."

Maggie looked at the cliffs surrounding the meadow. "I'll figure out something."

"You don't even know how to ride that horse," Jenny scolded. "You should have listened to Daddy."

"I told him ladies don't ride horses; they ride in buggies."

"That's old fashioned, Mother. Besides, Betty Notingham rode horses."

Maggie clenched her fist. "That's what your father used to tell me, but let me assure you, Betty Notingham was not a lady!"

"Good luck, Mother." Jenny faded.

Maggie watched her daughter dissolve, and she felt as if a part of her heart vanished with Jenny.

Later, Maggie covered the killer's body with dirt and rocks. He didn't deserve a cross or any other marker. Hopefully, after she left the meadow, the wolves would dig him up, eat his carcass, and shit him out.

She looked at callused hands and laughed.

Turning toward the wagon, she picked up Bobby's wide-brimmed felt hat. It had been custom made with a high crown with a leather band inside. She took off her calico bonnet and put on Bobby's hat that settled above the braids curled around her ears.

The hat was a bit too big, but she tore off a handful of long grass and folded down the inside band. Three one-hundred-dollar greenbacks fell out. Bobby's hiding place! She replaced the money before stuffing the headband with grass until it fit; its wide brim was better than her bonnet for keeping off the sun.

She climbed into the wagon and rummaged through what the Kiowa warriors had left. They'd taken everything they could carry and load on Bobby's packhorse: most of her food, the sheepskins, and blankets. They'd missed the hidden drawer under the driver's seat, which held her parasol, Ephraim's compass, swan-handled scissors, a sewing awl, needles, thread, black powder, bullets, percussion caps, all wrapped in a blanket.

At least she had something to keep her warm at night. There was also a ball of pemmican wrapped in leather, so she had enough food for several days. She replaced the attorney's letter in the drawer.

Her trunk lid was open. Her chemise was gone, now covering one of the brave's bodies. Just like at *White Haven* when a bushwhacker, wearing her chemise, had danced around the parlor while they forced her to play the piano.

She looked at the nearby spring. Its gushing clear water formed the headwater for a small creek. Animals must use the spring to drink and come into the meadow to feed.

Stepping down from the tilting wagon, she decided to look for anything the braves had overlooked. She remembered Bobby had leaned his rifle against a tree, but when she found the place, the gun was gone.

She walked to where his tent had been before the braves took it down. The tent stakes were still in the ground surrounding matted grass that marked the tent's interior. Near the fire pit, she discovered a tin bowl and dented plate and a fork with one tine missing. There were three cans of beans scattered about in the grass, as well as a small sack of flour. She poked through the ashes and charred wood in the pit. Other than several crushed tin cans, there was nothing she could use.

Nearby, there was a pole tied high between two trees. Bones and bits of deer hair lay scattered below. This game pole is where Bobby hung the animals he killed to be butchered. She'd soon be out of food. Too bad there wasn't a deer hanging there now.

There was something hidden in the tall grass several yards away. Maggie found a coil of thin cord that would be perfect for making small game snares if she could learn how to build one. A few yards further, she discovered something else the braves had overlooked – a horse lead rope and headstall.

She gathered her loot and took it back to the wounded wagon, where she took inventory. She would survive, at least for a while, but she would soon need more food.

She held her painful arm tight to her side as she walked to the spring. Sitting on the edge of its pool, she dipped her hand in the water. It was frigid. Maybe the cold would help her bruised body. She removed the revolver and derringer and placed them on the bank within easy reach. She struggled to get her blouse, chemise, and the corset with her gold coins over her shoulder and arm.

The ice-cold water took away her breath. She hesitated, thinking she'd enough pain for one day, but finally surrendered into its wintery arms. Goosebumps dimpled her body. She shivered uncontrollably. Still, the cold had to help heal her injury. She tried to flex the fingers of her left hand. They moved a tiny bit, but that could have been her imagination. She stayed in the water until she could no longer stand the cold, climbed out, and stood in the afternoon sunlight to let the warm air-dry her body.

She sat on the blank next to the pool and thought about killing Bobby.

She'd expected strong emotions: the joy of revenge, relief, satisfaction, sadness, or sorrow. She simply felt numb.

She was so exhausted, she couldn't even think about what to do next. It could wait; she had to sleep. But first, she should make certain Sonny and the mare didn't run away. She doubted if they'd stray; this was the first good grass they'd eaten in weeks.

The mare grazed next to Bobby's grave. Maggie unsaddled her and popped the saddle on its pommel next to the trunk of a cottonwood. After covering the leather with the saddle blanket, she looped the reins and placed them on top.

She hoped she'd remember how to saddle the horse again.

After haltering the mare, she tied the end of the picket rope around the trunk of a small tree. The horse could feed, but not drift off. Sonny wouldn't leave without the mare.

Too exhausted to eat, she staggered to the broken wagon, crawled under its bed to sleep dry on level ground. She wrapped herself in the blanket in spite of the warm afternoon sun. Tomorrow was another day; a better day to make plans.

Images of Scar Chest and his band grew vivid. She wondered if they would change their minds about capturing her. Would they return in the middle of the night? She imagined Red returning, riding in silently as she slept.

She nodded off, then startled awake, listening for the sound of hooves swishing through the tall grass. She pulled out her Colt Pocket .31, half-cocked the hammer so she could fire quickly, and then placed the gun close to her head where she could reach it before it was too late.

Chapter 36

Maggie spent the night trying to find a comfortable position so she could sleep. Lightning bolts of pain shot through her body each time she moved. She tossed, turned, and moaned, and begged for sleep.

Her anger rose.

Why?

Because she hadn't cleared her pistol from her waist sash before the bastard shot her? That killing Bobby wouldn't bring back her loved ones? That she had been naïve? That all the others who had warned her against seeking justice had been right? Had she undertaken a fool's journey?

Sleep was useless. Maggie rolled to her right side and, moaning, crawled out from under the wagon. It was cold. Shivering, she wrapped the blanket over her head and held it tight around her shoulders. Tree trunks appeared as black smudges of shadow against the night shy. A black spider web of branches outlined a star-filled heaven. Finally, a pencil line of red appeared outlining the ridges in the east.

She found several dead branches. Soon she sat in front of a small fire and cupped the blanket to capture its warmth. The mare, or maybe the mule, their bodies appearing as hazy gray forms, stomped a hoof. Ghostly steam rose from their backs.

The warmth of the fire felt good as she thought about yesterday's events.

When she set out from *White Haven* in Boonville to revenge her loved one's deaths, she didn't care if she lived or died. She would have welcomed joining George and Jenny.

Now? After her time with Henry, she wasn't sure she'd welcome death. Maybe there was something to live for after all.

The rising sun flooded the meadow, steam rose from the grass, and the mare stomped her hoof several times. Maggie shook her head and looked at the horse. During the night, the mare had grazed, circling the tree, winding the halter rope, so her head pinned against the tree trunk.

Maggie walked to the animal and unbuckled the halter. The mare rubbed its head against her before it walked close to the grave. Nose smelling the ground, she circled, folded her front legs, and flopped on her side. The horse rolled on her back and kicked her feet into the air, while Sonny looked on with approval. The mare rose with a heave, walked to Sonny, and they began to graze next to each other. Maggie decided not to picket them. They wouldn't leave the lush meadow during the day.

After eating a piece of pemmican, Maggie drank from the spring and then splashed cold water on her face. She decided she'd wait until the afternoon warmth to soak her shoulder and arm that felt better now that she moved around. She turned her face to the sun and closed her eyes.

"What now?"

She probably shouldn't talk out loud in case Red appeared, but the sound of her voice made her feel less lonely.

"What are my choices?"

She walked to the wagon and inspected the broken rear wheel, with its fractured spokes and the iron tire fallen off the wooden rim. She counted the damaged spokes and counted the spares in the bed of the wagon. There weren't enough to fix the wheel.

She had tools, but not the skill or materials to make it usable for travel. She looked under the wagon. The tallow bucket was still there. Using her forefinger, she dabbed a bit of grease over the scar on her cheek. Couldn't hurt.

She needed to finish her quest for justice. Bobby had told her Red might return soon, but what did that mean? A day? A week? A month? She didn't have enough food to stay long. Besides, with the broken wagon and Bobby's missing tent, there was no way to ambush Red.

She'd have to use the same strategy she'd used with Bobby – Red could reclaim his plantation. Hadn't worked too well on Bobby, but since it was Red's estate, perhaps she could fool him, and get him to Santa Fe.

Tracking him down was her second choice. If he didn't show up, she'd have to follow him. If he'd continued down the trail, perhaps people at Fort Union would have noticed a red-haired man with a squaw.

But how would she get to the fort? Walk? Ride? She couldn't carry enough water if she walked, so she'd have to ride and use Sonny to pack water. But she didn't know how to ride.

"Hope you're happy, George. I'm going to learn how to ride just like your Betty Notingham."

She laughed and then looked over her shoulder to see if George was listening. She was alone. She hadn't seen him since Council Grove.

Her third choice was to follow the Kiowa braves' tracks, negotiate for supplies, and try to get Traveler back. Kit Carson had told her to avoid contact.

On the other hand, she'd had two meetings with the Kiowa warriors, and they hadn't harmed her. Each time she thought the same scar chested brave argued against the others about taking her prisoner. Thank God, the men listened to him, or her fate would be sealed.

Fate. Had it been fate or freedom of choice that delivered her to this wilderness?

Why hadn't the Kiowa warriors taken her prisoner? Did the scar chested man think she was ugly? Did the scar across her cheek make her unworthy? Did he think she was too old to be useful?

It didn't matter. But, still.

Going after Traveler would be crazy. She'd be putting her life in the hands of savages with a reputation for ravaging white women.

Her logical choice was to stay near the spring, learn how to ride, hunt and gather food, and wait for Red.

The mare remained calm as she slipped the halter over her head and led it to the saddle. Rodents after the taste of salt chewed the leather reins. From now on, she'd hang the bridle and reins from a tree branch.

Maggie slid the saddle blanket on the mare's back. She hooked the offside stirrup over the horn so it wouldn't fold under the seat, and then strained to lift the saddle while balancing its weight with the still-numb left arm.

She didn't have the strength to lift the saddle high to drop it down on the mare's back, but slid it up and over. The saddle blanket fell off the other side, and the horse skittered forward. The saddle slipped and tumbled to the ground.

"Dammit!"

The mare turned her head and looked at her with what Maggie imagined were laughing eyes.

She stroked the mare's forehead and started the process again. She was successful on her third attempt. Now that the saddle was square on the blanket, she reached under the horse's belly, grabbed the latigo, threaded it through the keeper, and began tightening the strap.

The mare breathed in, inflating her stomach. Maggie pulled the latigo as tight as possible and then buckled it. She tied the flank strap and finally the breast collar. Finally, she slipped the bridle over the mare's head and, after a fight, slid the bit between her lips.

She stood back and admired her work. Now came the hard part.

Gathering her skirt, she reached for the saddle horn, raised her foot into the stirrup, and began to lift herself into the saddle. The mare stepped sideways. Maggie's foot slipped, and she stumbled against the side of the horse. It turned its head and looked at her in amusement.

She gathered her skirt again, pushing the material over her useless left arm, pulled the offside rein tight so the horse couldn't step sideways, lifted her foot into the stirrup, grabbed the saddle horn, and swung up toward the saddle.

The seat abruptly slid to the side of the mare, dumping Maggie on her back in the grass; her foot caught in the stirrup. Thank God the horse didn't panic. She opened her eyes. Sonny stood above her, his muzzle inches from her face, dark eyes staring at her. His lips quivered, spraying her with spit.

Maggie twisted her body until her foot slipped from the stirrup. She wiped her face on her sleeve, stood up, and looked at the two animals. It could have been worse; they could have spooked and dragged her across the meadow under flailing hooves.

"You want me to quit. I'm not going to stop until I ride you."

She loosened the latigo, waited for the mare to bloat, and kneed her sharply in the belly. The mare's ears flattened, and it exhaled, and Maggie jerked the strap tight, pulling the cinch snug before buckling the latigo.

She mounted the mare and used the reins to settle it down, and then tried to deal with the fabric bunched between her lap and saddle horn.

"What a nuisance."

She smoothed the skirt and then nudged the mare into a slow walk. Sonny hee-hawed. He followed close behind, his nose to her tail. Maggie rode around the meadow, learning how to weave through the cottonwoods, rein left and right, turn circles, trot and stop. She rode the mare to the creek below the spring for a drink. Sonny moved next to her, rubbing his head against Maggie's leg while the horse drank.

After unsaddling, Maggie watched them graze. Now Henry would be proud of her. Now she was just like George's Betty Notingham.

Chapter 37

Maggie knelt to drink from the spring. A fish dashed to a rocky hiding place.

"What will I use for a hook?" She'd ponder that.

In the meantime, the sun felt warm enough for her to soak her bruised shoulder and arm, so she plunged into the frigid water.

The fingers of her left hand flexed now without as much pain. She stayed underwater as long as she could stand the cold and then crawled to the grassy bank to allow the sun to dry her body. The heat helped her body relax, and soon her head nodded toward sleep.

A few minutes later, she was startled awake by a sound, a tumbling rock, or a snapping branch. It was a sharp sound, something out-of-place. Red approaching? Her right hand sought her Colt Pocket revolver while she covered her breasts with her bruised arm.

She listened.

A raven cawed from the direction the Kiowa braves had ridden into the meadow. A shadow skimmed across her. A red-tailed hawk soared above.

She imagined someone hidden watched her.

She thought about getting dressed but, if someone were close, slipping the dress over her head would make her vulnerable. She would be momentarily blind, unable to defend herself. If she ran to hide behind a tree, someone could spot her motion.

Better stay put.

She thumbed the revolver's hammer back, waited, and listened. Water tumbled over rocks, a soft breeze fluttered tree leaves, birds chirped, and a red squirrel chattered. Something moved. Two rabbits nibbled grass near the edge of the creek.

She waited, praying Red hadn't come back to catch her like this.

It dawned upon her that she hadn't concentrated on sounds she'd heard but hadn't considered: a nickered greeting from the mare, Sonny's hee-haw, or a nervous stomp of hoofs. Her animals had better senses than she; they would have heard or smelled something approaching.

Wouldn't they?

She watched and listened until she felt there was no danger. After dressing and, holding the gun to her side, she explored the area, looking and listening for anything unusual. The mare and Sonny looked up at her and then continued to graze. She remembered how that twisted-mouth killer, Bobby, had hidden behind the trunk of a tree, so she made a slow, cautious circle of the area.

Finally convinced no one was hiding to ambush her, she started a small fire, mixed a little water with flour in her frying pan, and placed it over hot coals to cook flatbread. She took a bite from the pemmican ball. She would soon have to find more food.

That afternoon, her shoulder and arm felt better, so she decided to ride again. She saddled the mare once more, remembering to knee its stomach before tightening the latigo, so the rig wouldn't slip and toss her off like the first time. She mounted up and, after spreading out the bundle of skirt fabric, set off to explore the series of hills from where the Kiowa braves had appeared. Sonny trailed close behind.

To her surprise, once she crested each ridge, every bench contained lush grass that would make excellent pasture. She nudged the mare into a trot across level places, and, after bouncing uncomfortably against the seat, she remembered watching George use his legs to raise and lower his butt in time with the horse's movements. 'Posting' was the term she thought he'd used. It was much more comfortable, yet her skirt again bunched under her legs, forcing her to pull at the fabric.

She reined the mare to a halt at the edge of a shallow, narrow ditch. She gripped the saddle horn and urged the horse forward. The mare balked, then gathered itself and jumped across, flinging Maggie's upper body back. Upon landing on the other side, the horse stopped, and threw her forward over the saddle to roll like a bowling ball down the animal's neck onto her back in the grass.

She still held the reins tight while she looked up at the mare's quivering moist nostrils. The mule walked up, looked down, and scrutinized her before raising its head to hee-haw as if that was the funniest thing it had ever witnessed.

"Ok, mister, if you think that's funny, you're next."

She saddled Sonny, surprised he didn't complain. The mule remained calm as she finished saddling him. Sonny stood still when she slipped her foot into the stirrup and swung her leg over his back. She settled in the saddle with a thump. Sonny didn't move. She adjusted her skirt; surprised the rustling sound didn't spook him.

"Huh."

Certain the mule would balk, she kicked his ribs with her heels. Sonny walked out at a comfortable pace, looking back once to make sure the mare followed.

Pleased by the mule's comfortable gait, she reined him back to the same place they'd crossed the ditch and held on for dear life. Sonny plodded through the ditch as if it wasn't there. Soon she had him in a smooth trot and, later, a gallop.

She spotted the old tracks made by the Kiowa braves and George's shod horse and followed up and over the hills. The tracks climbed a steep elk trail that switch-backed to the lip of the vast prairie.

They stopped at the top. Sonny wheezed, body covered in white foam, and the sweating mare came alongside and coughed. Maggie took off her wide-brimmed felt hat and wiped the sweat off her forehead. She'd forgotten the temperature of the plains. The prairie was an anvil upon which the sun hammered out one's soul.

The tracks headed east and became a mirage in rising waves of heat.

A mirage appeared on the horizon, a fuzzy, dark image rippling inches above the earth. The shape moved sinuously, like sea waves. Soon she made outriders, and horse's hooves striking the air, just like when the braves had approached for the trading session. Were these natives or whites?

She stopped and pulled out her Colt revolver, checked the chambers and primers, and waited.

The image became apparent; the mirage was a column of U.S. Army Cavalry. She slipped the gun back into her belt as two officers rode toward her. The rest of the troop trotted on. She nodded as they reined in close.

"Thought you was an Indian," the Captain said.

"You have bad eyes. I'm a lady."

The Lieutenant asked, "What are you doing out here?"

"I'm camped in the canyon. Headed to Santa Fe to find my brother."

"A woman, out here, alone? Why ain't you with a wagon train?" the Captain asked.

"I was, but my husband thought the wagon train was too slow and insisted we come ahead. Two white murderers killed him and my son."

"How'd you get away?"

"I was in the brush on private business when they rode into camp. I hid."

"Sorry. You're lucky Indians haven't gotten ahold of you."

"None of us have been lucky in this war," she said.

"Where you from?" the Lieutenant asked.

"We had a plantation in Missouri."

"She must be a Sesch, Captain."

The Captain rolled his eyes, "The war's over, Lieutenant,"

"Really? Is the war over? That's wonderful news," she said. "But for your information, I didn't pick sides. A pox on Jeff Davis, a pox on Abe Lincoln, and a pox on all politicians. Their war turned civilized folks into savages."

The Captain said, "You have strong opinions for a woman."

She laughed. "Wait until women can vote."

Sonny smelled the Captain's horse and bit its neck. The horse reared, and the officer jerked his left rein and spun his horse around.

"Ya got a mean mule there, lady."

"Sorry. Sonny doesn't like horses."

"Huh."

"What're you doing out here?" she asked.

"Punishing Indians for attacking wagon trains."

Maggie took off her hat, wiped the inside band, and put it back on. "My brother has red hair and beard; hard to miss. Might have a young squaw with him. Remember seeing them?"

The Captain said, "Saw a red-headed man at the Fort. He had a squaw with him. They left after we rode out."

"Where was he headed?"

"Don't rightly know, but they had two pack horses."

"I appreciate your help, gentlemen." Maggie nodded and reined Sonny around the officers, nudged him in the ribs, and trotted away. She had made the right decision to stay. Red probably rode to Fort Union for supplies. Sooner or later, he'd be back to check on Bobby.

She rode back toward the canyon. At the edge, she got off and led Sonny and the mare down the elk trail to her valley. Sonny's hoofs kicked small rocks that careened past her, bouncing ahead until lodging against a bigger rock or log.

They returned to camp. Maggie took the saddle off the mule and rubbed its ears.

"Well, Sonny, you were a pleasant surprise."

She remembered the fish she'd seen this morning in the spring. Returning to the wagon, she found a safety pin and tied it to string pulled from the coil she'd earlier discovered. She carried the shovel to Bobby's gravesite and, after rolling off several rocks, dug and found fat, squirmy worms.

Staying back from the edge of the pool, she threaded a worm on the safety pin and tossed it where she'd seen the fish. The line tugged, and she rushed to the banks while hauling in the line hand over hand. The large trout flopped on the grass. The pin slipped from its mouth.

Maggie fell to her knees and grabbed the squirming fish. Its slippery body wriggled from her hands, fell into the grass, flopping just out of reach until it slipped over the bank into the water.

She wiped her hands on the grass and then tossed another hooked worm into the pool. Maggie waited and waited until she became convinced there were no more fish.

The line jerked.

She hauled in a slightly smaller trout, but big enough for supper.

After eating, she stared at the glowing coals of her fire. It had been a good day. She was learning how to survive.

She thought of Henry's bright smile. The first time she saw him on the *Cora II*, his smile had seemed disingenuous. Later, she realized his expression revealed his inner warmth.

He might be a card shark, but he was honest. He didn't have to tell Maggie about his mission to protect her. He had ethical values. He'd loved his family and missed family life. She'd loved laughing at his gentle sense of humor. And it didn't hurt that she found him attractive. She loved to run her tongue across the scar on his cheek.

Maggie touched her scar. She smeared a bit more tallow on it.

Crawling under the wagon, she wrapped herself in the blanket and fell asleep.

Very late that moonlit night, sometime before the stars began to fade, a noise startled her awake.

She listened.

She half-cocked the revolver.

Listened.

Nothing.

Whatever had awakened her must have been a dream.

She placed her gun on the ground near her head and drifted back into troubled dreams.

Maggie's breath caught in her throat as someone dragged her kicking and writhing from under the wagon. Her fingertips brushed the revolver handle, but it was too late; she couldn't snatch the gun. The blanket slid over her head. Her back scrapped against the ground, forcing her dress and petticoat up over her waist.

She kicked again to free herself, but the grip on her ankles was too firm. She reached for her derringer. A rough hand gripped her fingers and squeezed until she screamed. Her hand came free, but the derringer was gone.

The shadow of a huge man loomed over her. She rolled over to crawl back under the wagon for her revolver. He grasped her ankles again and dragged her next to the fire pit.

He flipped her on her back and straddled her, sitting on her hips. She rose to strike him. He slammed his hands against her chest, leaned forward and pinned her hard against the ground. His left hand explored her chest.

"What are you hiding in there?"

The man held her to the ground with one hand and used the other reach into his shirt pocket. His thumbnail struck a match. The Lucifer flared, lighting his face.

He had a long red beard and hair. His eyes were wide, pupils dilated, and his lips curled back, baring his teeth.

"Well, lookee what I caught."

Chapter 38

The stench of rotten breath washed over her. Helpless, she forced her body to go limp, hoping Red would loosen his grip.

He released her and put one hand on the ground to rise.

She kicked, aiming between his legs.

"You bitch!" He grunted. His fist slammed into the side of her face. Everything went black.

When she woke, she discovered he had flipped her onto her stomach and tied her hands behind her back with a rope. Her ankles were bound as well.

"After I build a fire, we're gonna have us a little talk."

The eastern sky had turned the color of molten lead. Maggie watched him gather firewood. Soon flames rose from the fire pit, painting the scene in flickering light and black shadows.

He rolled her to her side, facing the fire. The front of her body felt the warmth of the flames, her back chilled.

"Where's your coffee?" he asked.

"Don't have any."

"Jesus Christ."

"Don't swear in front of a lady!"

"Huh?"

"Never mind."

He sat cross-legged next to the fire and studied her. Firelight lit the left side of his face. The right side was a shadow.

She said, "You're the man I'm looking for."

He frowned. "Where's Bobby?"

"Kiowas killed him."

"Why didn't they take you?"

"I'd gone into the bushes for personal business. I hid."

"Huh." He pulled a bag of tobacco and paper from his shirt pocket and rolled a cigarette before picking up a burning stick from the fire. He held the flame close to his roll-up, studied her for a moment, and then lit the end. He inhaled deeply before blowing out smoke that veiled his head before rising.

"I buried him." She pulled up her knees to ease the pressure on her shoulders and hips.

"Seen the mound. Been watching you nigh on a day."

Her intuition had been right yesterday when she thought someone watched her naked in the spring. Should have paid more attention to her instincts.

Red watched her and smoked down his cigarette. It was now light enough for her to see his yellow-stained fingers.

He pointed the roll-up toward her. "Wanna drag?"

"Don't smoke."

"Yeah, I forgot, you're a lady. Ladies like to fuck?"

She stared unblinking disgust.

He glanced at the eastern sky and shielded his eyes from the rising sun. He stood up, flicked the cigarette into the dying fire, and stretched.

"Time for me to head out."

"You're not going to leave me here like this?"

"You won't care." He reached into his front pant pocket, pulled out her derringer, cocked it, and pointed the muzzle at her head.

She closed her eyes and waited for the shot.

"This little thing all you had to protect yourself?"

She exhaled, not knowing she'd been holding her breath. "Indians stole my pistol and rifle."

"Red-skins ain't nothing but trouble. I know. Got me an uppity squaw."

She watched Red walk down the creek path until he disappeared out of sight. A far off raven cawed. A toad hopped inches from her face. It squatted and studied her with orange eyes, as if waiting for her to explain why she was invading his space.

Had Red left her to die, bound hand and foot, alone and defenseless next to a dying fire? She turned and could see the silver strap of her revolver handle deep under the wagon, reflecting the rising sun, but there was no way she could reach it.

Chapter 39

Several hours later, Red rode into Maggie's camp. A Kiowa girl about Jenny's age, wearing a buckskin dress, leather leggings, and moccasins, rode a small paint horse close behind.

Maggie gasped. Jenny's silver cross adored her neck.

Red held the end of a chain attached to an iron collar that encircled the girl's neck. Maggie remembered crying when she saw a neckband like that on a man at a slave auction.

The girl led two packhorses and gave Maggie a furtive nod as she passed. They stopped where Bobby's tent had been.

Maggie shouted, "Will you untie me? I'm cramping."

Red ignored her as he lifted off the packs from the horses. He wrapped the chain around the girl's waist and then pointed to their canvas tent and to the spot where Bobby's shelter had been. He walked to Maggie.

He untied the rope around her ankles and helped her up. She wobbled, and he held her arm to keep her from falling.

"I need water," she said.

He led her to the spring. "Drink your fill."

"Untie my hands."

He laughed and pushed her to her knees. She tried to lean over to drink but fell face forward into the water. He waited, watching her struggle. Just when she thought she would drown, he pulled her out. The next time, he held her arms while she drank her fill, then he led her back to the camp. They stopped near a huge cottonwood.

"You said you were looking for me?" he asked, as he watched the Kiowa girl struggle to raise the tent.

"Untie me, and I'll tell you."

He walked to the Kiowa girl, who struggled with the tent and shouted at her.

She said something in her native language.

He slapped her so hard she lost her balance and fell.

He pointed at the tent, walked back toward Maggie, and shouted over his shoulder, "Get the goddamned thing up."

"Do you understand her language?"

"Hell, no."

"Why did you hit her?"

"Didn't like her tone."

"Please untie me."

"Why should I?"

"I can't harm you. You have a gun and a knife and could easily kill me. Besides, you'd lose a lot of money if you hurt me."

"Money?"

"Untie me, and I'll tell you."

"Tell me now."

"I can help you get rich, but I'm not going to say another word until my hands are free."

"Jesus Christ!" He held up his hands. "I know, I know, you're a goddamned lady." He spun her around and wrestled with the knot until she was free.

She rubbed her wrists to get circulation into her hands.

He spun her to face him and pointed his revolver at her. He felt her chest. "Take off your blouse and corset."

"Absolutely not!" She crossed her arms over her chest.

The slap across her cheek knocked her down. Her nose dripped blood. She used her sleeve to wipe it off.

"Get up and give me your corset, or I'll take it off your dead body."

The Kiowa girl had stopped staking down the tent and watched. She nodded at Maggie as if she understood what he'd said.

Maggie struggled to her feet, took off her blouse, untied the corset strings, and handed the undergarment to him. He felt its weight, stepped back, and pulled out a gold coin.

"Looks like you already made me rich." He hung her corset on a nearby tree limb.

"You'll give that back to me after you hear my story."

"If I won't like your story, you won't need your money." He touched his growling stomach and hurried over to the girl, unwrapped her chain, and led her back to the tree, wrapped the links around the trunk and locked it. He hurried off toward the bushes close to the creek.

The Kiowa girl said, "I know your words. He does not know."

Maggie blinked. "How did you learn?"

"My mother was a white captive. He'll kill you."

"I have to get free to get a gun. We'll both be free. Can you help?"

"How?"

"Untie me."

The girl nodded and began working on the knot in Maggie's rope. "He can't catch me doing this."

"I'll watch and let you know when he starts back."

"My name is Angeni."

"I am Maggie." She felt the girl twist the knot for a better grip.

Several minutes later, Maggie saw the top of a brush move. "Stop. He's coming."

Angeni turned away.

Red returned, unchained Angeni, and put her back to work on the tent and then returned to Maggie.

"You are Patrick Doyne."

"How do you know that?"

"My name is Maggie. I represent Thomas F. Billings, Esq., Attorney at Law," and I carry an urgent letter to you regarding your father's estate."

"He ain't got no estate!"

"Your father owned a plantation that was illegally taken by a banker's foreclosure and sheriff sale. After the war was over . . ."

"The war's over?"

"Yankees won."

"Shit."

"The courts overthrew all the foreclosures and sales as unconstitutional. The plantations will revert to their owners or their heirs if they come forward before the deadline. After that, the properties go to the federal government."

"I don't believe it! What proof you got?"

I carry a letter from Thomas F. Billings, Attorney at Law, to Mr. Patrick Doyne."

"So, what's the catch?"

"Catch?"

"Somebody's got to pay the lawyer and you."

"You're right. The government pays the attorney for each property owner found. I get a percentage of the lawyer's fee. That's why there's a deadline. There will be no payment after the deadline."

"Show me the letter."

"It's in a compartment under the seat of my wagon. I'll show it to you."

He untied her and held her arm tightly as they walked to the wagon. The sun, higher now, cast a black shadow on the ground under the wagon bed where her revolver lay hidden.

Chapter 40

Red dragged her to the wagon.

Maggie said, "The letter is in a drawer under the front seat. I'll get it."

"You think I'm stupid? You've probably got a gun hidden in there." He laughed and shoved her hard against the wagon. He stood on tiptoes and opened the compartment.

She stepped back to dive under the wagon for her gun.

Spotting her movement, he grabbed the back of her hair and slammed her into the wooden side of the wagon. He twisted her shoulders around to face him and choked her neck with one hand.

"Trying to run on me?" he asked, pushing his body against her, pressing her hard against the wagon.

"Tripped," she managed to choke out.

He held her hair while he rummaged through the drawer and found the envelope. He held it out arm's length to read its address lines. "That's my name."

"Told you. Now let me go."

He forced her arm behind her back and pushed her back to the camp. He forced her down and tied her again to the trunk of the cottonwood tree. He shouted at the Kiowa girl and pointed instructions for her to make a fire.

"Read the letter to me."

The rope around her waist bound Maggie tight against the tree. While the knot was on the far side of the trunk, her arms were free. She opened the envelope, took out the letter, and pointed to his name at the top of the page. "See, this letter is to you." She offered it to him.

"You read it."

She didn't know if he couldn't read or wanted her to read it to him to see if she was accurate. Using her most formal voice, she slowly read the letter aloud.

"Pipe!" He yelled at the Kiowa girl. She ran into the tent and returned with a pipe and packed it with tobacco. She held a flaming stick from the fire over the bowl while he sucked in and lit it. He blew out smoke and dismissed her with a wave of his hand.

"So what'd we gotta do to get back my plantation?"

"We need to get to Santa Fe before the deadline, where an attorney will certify you are Patrick Doyne. You'll get your family's plantation back. You'll be richer than finding gold out here. You can go back to Missouri to claim the plantation and live like a king."

"Huh."

"We'll have to leave today to beat the deadline."

"You seem mighty anxious."

"I want my share of the money," she said.

"You say the Yankees won the war?"

"That's what I heard from a cavalry officer."

"Damned Yankees burned down the house and barns. Daddy killed himself. Momma died of a heart attack."

"Sorry about your folks. You can rebuild a house. Can't make good land."

"Yankees will free the slaves. Land's no good if there ain't nobody to work the fields."

Maggie didn't have an answer to that.

"I'm gonna nap on it." He placed his pipe on the ground, called the Kiowa girl, and chained her against the tree.

"I can't stand like this all day, let me sit down," Maggie said.

He nodded and tied her in a sitting position next to the girl. He inspected his knot and disappeared inside the tent.

Maggie looked at Angeni. "Untie my knot."

The girl reached behind the tree trunk. "I can't reach it."

We're going to have to do something," Maggie whispered.

Angeni nodded and lowered her head as if she were napping. She suddenly reached down and captured a toad. She raised it and showed it to Maggie.

The animal looked like the same toad that had watched her when Red left her tied near the fire pit, but there might be hundreds of toads here.

Angeni smiled at her. "Hold my cross flat."

Maggie raised the silver cross over the girl's neck and held it flat.

The Kiowa girl stroked the area near the glands behind the toad's head. The animal excreted a milky-looking fluid. She turned the toad over and scrapped the liquid off on the flat surface of the cross. Angeni gently placed the toad back on the ground. After a moment, it hopped away.

"What are you doing?" Maggie asked.

"You'll see." Angeni held the cross flat and watched the sun's rays dry the fluid. After it had dried, she picked up Red's pipe and scrapped the flakes into the bowel.

A few minutes later, Red pushed open the tent flap, stepped out, yawned, and stretched. He unchained Angeni and demanded she fill his pipe. He used his thumbnail to strike a match, held the flame over the pipe bowel, and sucked in, and then raised his head and blew a stream of smoke and watched it rise.

He sat in front of Maggie and took another puff from his pipe. "I don't believe you. You're lying. So what am I going to do with you?"

"Don't you want to get rich?" Maggie said, thinking of nothing better at the moment. She didn't like the direction of the conversation.

"Well, you see, Aunt Flow visited that little squaw, and I'm a man who needs a woman."

Maggie exhaled. There would be no unwanted child born of Red or Bobby. No visible, squalling, daily reminder of the trauma the Angeni had survived.

"You're a little old for my liking, but any port in a storm. Besides, you must have more experience." He laughed and sucked on his pipe.

"Tell me about the young girl you raped in Missouri while Bobby forced her wounded father to watch."

"What are you talking about?" He took a long suck on his pipe. His eyes suddenly dilated, and he shook his head. The pipe fell out of his mouth, and he began laughing.

Maggie looked on, astonished. Angeni walked toward them.

"The stars. Oh, the stars." He reached up to gather in the stars. Cupping them in his hands, he put them in his mouth and swallowed them. Laughing, he stood up and staggered around and around, filling his mouth with stars until he stumbled into the tent.

Angeni cracked open the tent flap to look at Red, and then ran to Maggie to untie the rope binding her to the tree.

Maggie listened for Red moving in the tent but heard only loud snoring.

"Hurry, Angeni, before he comes back."

The rope loosened, and Angeni helped Maggie up.

"Watch Red. I'll be back," Maggie whispered. She ran to the wagon and dove underneath to retrieve her revolver, scrabbling on her hands and knees, frantically feeling until she touched it.

She backed out from underneath the wagon and heard Angeni scream.

Maggie ran toward the tent.

Red's fist knocked Angeni to the ground. He pulled his knife and grabbed the girl's hair and jerked her to her feet.

He shouted, "You let her go! Were is she?"

"Right behind you!" Maggie said, even if she was thirty feet away.

Red spun, forearm around the girl's neck, and he dropped the knife on the ground. He pulled his revolver from his holster and swung it toward Maggie. He used Angeni as a shield, peeking around her head to aim.

Maggie could see only a part of the right side of his head. Like barking a squirrel out of a tree, she raised her Colt revolver and pulled the trigger. Red crumpled, pulling Angeni down on top of him.

Maggie ran to them, pulled the girl off and pointed her gun at his head. A thin stream of blood pumped from the side of his head. She didn't need a second shot.

Red was dead.

Chapter 41

Maggie stood over the killer's body, pointing the revolver at his head, and she felt the adrenaline rush from her body, leaving her empty and weak. She'd made Jenny a vow that she'd bring the murderers to justice.

Leaving the plantation, Maggie imagined she would locate them and have the local sheriff arrest them. She'd never dreamed that she'd be the judge, jury, and executioner. Now it was over, yet Maggie felt no joy or even a sense of satisfaction. She simply felt hollow.

Angeni touched her shoulder. "Are you all right?"

Maggie nodded and she turned toward the tent and took two steps. Seized by a thought Red was not dead, she spun, walked back, and touched his glazed eye with the muzzle of her pistol. He did not blink. He truly was dead.

She stood next to the tent.

Jenny appeared in front of her. "Thank you, Mother."

"It's over, Jenny. They will never rape or kill anyone else. Ever."

"I knew you would bring them to justice."

"It was hard."

"Daddy will be happy."

"I hope so," Maggie said. She knew she'd never again see George. "You've given me peace. I love you." Jenny faded away.

"Wait!" Maggie reached for Jenny, overcome by the feeling she would never again see her daughter. "You can't leave me like this. Not after all we've been through. I need to talk with you. You can't just disappear from my life." Maggie covered her face and cried.

It wasn't fair for Jenny to just say thanks and disappear.

She'd promised her daughter justice, and if killing the murderers had achieved any meaningful justice, surely there was more to say than a simple 'thanks.' But maybe that was all there was to be said. Perhaps that word said it all and there was nothing else to be said.

Words would not bring Jenny back.

She walked into the tent to compose her emotions. A few minutes later, Angeni pushed open the tent flap and walked in. She held the knife in her right hand. Her bloody left hand raised Red's scalp high, and the girl screamed a curse of revenge. Maggie watched and remembered the Kiowa warrior, Scar Chest, scalping Bobby. She couldn't blame Angeni.

"Let's take off that neck collar," Maggie said.

After finding a Bastard Cut half-round file with the wagon's tools, she led Angeni to the spring. The girl washed Red's blood off her hands before Maggie wet a cloth with the freezing water and tucked it between Angeni's neck and collar so the heat of filing the head off the rivet wouldn't burn her neck.

Maggie got a solid grip on the collar before she began. She soon turned the collar to the soft part of the girl's neck and pushed out the rivet. The collar opened. Angeni was free.

Angeni wrapped her arms around Maggie, and they held each other.

Maggie held the girl at arm's length. "We need to get you back home. Army patrols want to punish Kiowas. If they catch you, they will send you to a reservation. You will live with strangers, and never again see your family. I'll protect you and ride with you to your village."

Angeni saddled horses and packed what they needed for the trip, while Maggie took her gold-filled corset from the tree limb and laced it on, and covered it with her blouse. She found the serape in the back of the wagon bed and slipped it over her head. She left the Bible in the drawer under the diver's seat and took the poetry book.

Maggie led them on the trail the Kiowa warriors had taken after Bobby's death. When they climbed to the top of the prairie, Angeni reined her horse next to Maggie.

The girl pointed. "That way home." She handed Maggie the halter rope for the packhorses, rode off, and motioned for Maggie to follow.

Maggie sat upon the mare, leading the packhorses, following a young Kiowa girl in the middle of the wilderness, amazed at how their situation had changed.

Did she want to follow the girl into a hostile village? Take the risk that she would become a prisoner? She should say goodbye, turn around, and leave. But an army patrol might find Angeni before she reached safety. What would she do if this girl were Jenny?

Two days later, Angeni led Maggie into a vast rocky area along the rim of a deep canyon. They wove through tumbled house-sized boulders; walking on rocks so loose Maggie feared one of the horses would break a leg. There was no trail or evidence others had ever been there.

The slope grew steeper and she worried they would slide off into space. She would fall in a tumbling mass of horses and ropes and packs and falling rocks, trying to stay in the saddle as she spun over and over, then pushing away so the horse wouldn't crush her when they smashed upon the canyon floor. Yet, she realized it didn't make any difference, because they'd all die when they hit bottom.

And then she spotted a pile of dry horse dung on the rocks. Others had been here. She exhaled.

Angeni rode straight for a rock cliff as high as a cottonwood tree. It looked like a dead end. At the last moment, the girl turned left, guiding her horse through a crack barely wide enough to slip through. She found an indistinct trail and led them down through the rocks to the floor of a barren-looking canyon.

Angeni turned right and led them close to the steep wall of the valley, so anyone watching from above would be unable to spot their tracks. The canyon veered left and soon fell toward an immense, fertile valley.

A stream carved lazy curves through riparian pastureland filled with cottonwoods. Tall grass swayed in the morning breeze. Several miles later, Angeni pointed to a tendril of smoke that rose into a cloudless sky.

They followed the creek through a bottom full of lush grass and trees, walking on a faint trail that soon became wider, and heavily used. The path skirted a bend in the creek, and Maggie saw horses and natives downstream. There must have been thirty or forty tepees in the village.

Angeni called out to a scout hiding on the side of the trail. He sprinted ahead. Soon they rode through a corridor of men and women staring, pointing and talking in excited tones. Maggie marveled at their buckskin clothes, beaded moccasins, and dresses adorned with rows of elk teeth.

Several men wore wool shirts and broad-brimmed felt hats, for which they must have traded. One man wore a stovepipe hat like

President Lincoln's. The men carried bows, lances, and war clubs, but no one made a move to threaten her.

She saw a woman wearing the chemise stolen from her trunk. Another wore her best dress. Maggie squeezed her fist tight. Maroon was her favorite color, and she had not worn the dress during the trip, saving it for a special event. The skirt was too long for the woman; the hem dragged on the ground, making it filthy. Maggie pretended not to notice.

An acid taste lined her mouth, and she sweated with fear, but she dared not show emotion. She was simply out for a Sunday afternoon ride with a friend.

Chapter 42

Dogs barked, and children scurried. A group of boys took turns running toward Maggie, trying to touch her leg, missing, and running back to their friends, all shrieking with laughter.

They rode through a wall of men and women that separated before them, creating a tunnel that curved gently to the left toward the biggest tepee covered with buffalo hides sewn together in a conical shape. A painting of bison adorned the side. A shield, hanging from a pole at the entrance carried the same design. A scalp also hung from the pole, Bobby's long black hair gently blew in the wind.

A Kiowa couple stood in front of the tepee. Angeni reined in front of them, sprang from her saddle, and ran into their embrace. Laughing and crying, they enfolded her with their arms, the family spinning in a joyful circle.

Villagers cheered and cried and laughed and talked over each other. Angeni's father held her close, pointed to Maggie, still mounted atop the mare, and asked a question.

Angeni babbled, gesturing to her neck with her hands, and then ran to the mare, motioned for Maggie to dismount and held her hand as they walked toward her parents.

Her father wore moccasins, fringed leather tube-like leggings, and a breechclout. A white scar replaced his nipple.

Scar Chest.

His eyes were wet with tears, and he wrapped his arms around Maggie. He lifted her off the ground and spun her around, saying something over and over again. He smelled fresh, like juniper trees. When he stopped, his wife hugged Maggie and said, 'thanks' in English.

Curious men and women crowded behind her. Children giggled and laughed. An almost naked little boy, bald with glistening black eyes, elbowed his way through the crowd to stand next to her. He leaned against the side of her leg. She rubbed his head.

Angeni's mother wore a long buckskin dress adorned with rows of elk teeth and porcupine quills. Green and yellow-painted tribal designs embellished the dress. She was tall and pretty, with curious blue eyes and loose blonde hair.

Maggie smiled and introduced herself.

"I am Chenoa. My husband is Enyeto."

"I know, Enyeto. We met when I killed the twisted-mouth man."

"He told me. Calls you Can-Not-Be-Killed-Woman."

"I wish that was true."

Enyeto walked to the mare Angeni had ridden, looked at Red's scalp tied to the bridal, and said something to his daughter. After she answered, he took it off, and ordered a brave to take the horses away. He tied Red's scalp on the pole under Bobby's.

Enyeto sat on the ground in front of the tepee and motioned for Maggie to sit facing him. Chenoa sat to his right, Angeni to the left, while Maggie adjusted the pistol in her belt and sat. The little boy sat behind her.

A woman appeared, holding two bowls of soup. She handed a bowl to Enyeto and then bent to give Maggie one. The woman then retrieved two more dishes, gave one to Chenoa, the other to Angeni. People crowded to watch. She felt the little boy's hand on the small of her back.

The soup looked - and smelled - like beans and corn. Enyeto raised his bowl to her and drank, and Maggie raised her bowl toward him and sipped a delicious broth. She smiled and nodded and smacked her lips.

"Is the little boy yours?" Maggie asked Chenoa.

"He is the son of the tribe. His parents died of the sickness three years ago. Everyone takes care of him."

"How long have you lived here?"

"I was fourteen when Enyeto captured me." Chenoa's words carried the lilting melody of the Kiowa language, forcing Maggie's full concentration.

"Have you tried to escape?"

"Why?"

"To return to your family."

"Enyeto is kind. I love him. Our people are good. Life is good here."

Maggie couldn't believe a white woman could be happy living with natives.

Enyeto said something Maggie didn't understand, and Chenoa translated.

"He said Angeni's friend saw these two men take her away. We tracked them to Fort Union. We could not reach them without the Army killing us. Later, we tracked one man to the meadow. You shot him before we could kill him."

Maggie nodded. "That's when you took my husband's spotted horse."

Chenoa translated. Enyeto grinned.

Maggie waited for more of a response and then said, "The twisted-mouth man and his partner, the Red-headed man, raped and killed my daughter and killed my husband. They stole my husband's horse and my daughter's silver cross. I had to bring them to justice."

Enyeto nodded and said something to Chenoa before standing and walking away.

Chenoa said, "He said you are a good warrior. You are welcome here as long as you like."

"Thank him for me."

Chenoa showed her a tepee. Someone had spread out her blanket and placed her other packs. "You will stay here as our guest."

Later that afternoon, the great Kiowa war chief, Satanta, led twenty braves into the camp to be welcomed by Enyeto. Tall and muscular, Satanta's hair flowed from a high forehead. A prominent Roman nose split a handsome face.

That night, after a feast, Satanta rose and spoke. Maggie listened to Chenoa's translation as he told about his role in defeating Kit Carson at the Battle of Adobe Walls.

"Each time Carson blew the bugle to give the troops instructions, I blew counter-commands on my horn. When Carson blew 'go forward,' I blew 'retreat.' He blew 'go left.' I blew 'go right.' His troops were thrown into confusion until we allowed them to retreat."

She thought Carson and Bridger had either omitted those details, or didn't know that part of the story. But of course, Carson would have known. He was there.

Satanta's speech went on and on and on.

"When the leaves turn color, I will sit with the Comanche, the Plains Apache, the Southern Cheyenne, and the Southern Arapaho and meet with white representatives on the Little Arkansas River.

"I will demand reparation for the Sand Creek Massacre, plus demand unrestricted hunting grounds. The whites want peace, safe traffic on the Santa Fe Trail, and a limitation of our Territory."

He added, with a certain amount of pride, that his old enemy Kit Carson would be one of the representatives for the whites.

"In the meantime, the Army wants to punish us because of our raids against wagon trains. So keep watch and be careful. Be very careful."

Chapter 43

Enyeto ordered a Buffalo Dance to honor the great Satanta. Men painted their faces and wore headdresses with buffalo horns, and they danced to the rhythmic beat of drums, gourd rattles, and songs, while the women sang and danced in counterpoint, stomping feet in time to the music.

Chenoa broke out of the dance circle, grabbed Maggie's hands, and pulled her into the dance. Maggie shuffled to the music's rhythm. She danced and recalled the New Year's Eve Masked Ball at Boonville's Thespian Hall. Like Missourians, this tribe used dance to express happiness, gratitude, and celebration. She recalled joyous times with Jenny and George.

Later, Maggie couldn't sleep and listened to night sounds. This was a new place, different than being on the Santa Fe Trail with the wagon train, or in the quiet meadow.

The village had new rhythms, new sounds: the gurgling of the river, neighing horses, a laugh, muted words, a dog's bark, a cough, the call of a hoot owl, an answer from another owl from the trees downriver.

Maggie told herself to get to sleep, but she reviewed her day in the village with Chenoa, Enyeto, and Angeni. These so-called savages were human beings, outwardly different but not different than her friends in Boonville. They, too, were humans, struggling to survive and make meaning of their lives.

She would leave in the morning. But where would she go? To Denver City, hoping Henry would be waiting, greeting her with his smile and wrapping her in his arms?

The sensible thing would be to return to Boonville and *White Haven*. That was her fate. That was her responsibility. She had to return to oversee whatever transition was needed to keep the plantation productive.

But how could she do that if there was no labor to plant the fields and harvest the crops? How could she make sure there would be enough revenue to prevent the government from foreclosing because *White Haven* could not pay its real estate taxes?

George would have said that returning to Boonville was her fate.

The next morning, before Satanta and his warriors returned to their camp on the upper Canadian River, Enyeto introduced Maggie to the war chief.

"She rescued Angeni from the whites who captured her. She is our friend."

Satanta said to Maggie, "Then you are the friend of the Kiowa. You will be welcome in my camp. I will spread the word that you are one of us."

They watched Satanta lead his warriors from the village, and soon returned to their normal life.

She was in her tepee when Chenoa called to her. She bent through the entrance and saw Enyeto holding Traveler's reins. The horse wore George's saddle.

"You saved our daughter. Enyeto wants to give you this spotted horse."

Maggie threw her arms around Enyeto and kissed his cheek. He touched his face, and Chenoa smiled and nodded.

Angeni stepped forward and offered Maggie the silver cross. "Mother says this was your daughter's."

"Yes, but you are now my daughter as well. Wear it and think good thoughts about me." Maggie slipped the cross over the girl's head and tears flooded Angeni's eyes.

Several hours later, after she'd packed, Maggie rode Traveler and led a packhorse to the front of Enyeto's tepee. Chenoa, Enyeto, and Angeni came out.

Maggie tipped the wide brim of her felt hat low and took a deep breath to avoid crying. She didn't want to look weak and lose face in front of the villagers.

Angeni and Chenoa cried, and even Enyeto's eyes were moist.

Enyeto held his right arm skyward and folded his fingers into a fist. "The Great Spirit rides with you. Return to us."

She glanced at Bobby and Red's scalps on the pole, hair waving in the breeze, and then wheeled Traveler and rode through a gauntlet of Indian men, women, children, and barking dogs.

People reached out to touch her legs as she passed. Was this their custom when a guest left camp, or was touching something more? Perhaps a good luck sign? Maybe it was a gesture that said she was part of them? Whatever it meant, she felt grateful.

The sun was bright and the leaves fluttered – a gentle breeze on her back carried the scent of village campfires. Traveler stopped in the middle of the stream and lowered his head to drink. She leaned on the saddle horn and watched the current sweep around his legs and thought life is like a river: flowing, weaving, and forever changing, the same, but never the same.

She rode to the crest of the canyon and looked at the vast prairie. When she left Boonville, she'd been an empty shell, confused by the Bible's dogma, and her soul filled with revenge. Today, looking across the desert, she felt at peace and understood how small and precious we are in our short time on this spinning globe.

If God did not exist, as she now believed, she still needed to have faith in a higher power, and she was comforted by her belief that Enyeto's Great Spirit would become her guide.

Traveler nickered, impatient to continue.

It was time to choose.

She could travel back east to Boonville and *White Haven*, and attempt to recreate her life before the war.

But Boonville would not be the same without George and Jenny, without trustworthy friends, and without her role as a community social leader. The Civil War had taken from her every sense of being – her marriage, motherhood, friendships, her concept of civilization, and even her dreams for the future. She had been a cultured, proper lady. But now?

Now she was a different woman – self-reliant, emotionally and physically hardened, grounded in a new understanding of humanity and faith, and the realization that love of oneself and others is the only way to live her one and only life.

Ephraim would do his best to keep the plantation going. She might have to sell it, but she could return anytime to retrieve the remainder of her buried gold and greenbacks.

Perhaps, after his recovery, Henry had returned to Missouri. But he had also talked about heading west to Denver City to make his fortune.

Her choices boiled down to these: she could turn east toward civilization, or further explore the West.

She reached into her possibles bag, pulled out dear old Ephraim's compass, and opened it. The needle swung to the north. If she rode north-by-northwest, she'd hit the upper Canadian River, where Chief Satanta usually camped.

Farther north still, she could visit Kit Carson at Fort Garland. He'd enjoy swapping stories.

And after that?

Henry had talked about Denver City. He said he loved her, and he missed children and family.

Henry was right:

Life is for the living.

Maggie reined Traveler north-by-northwest.

~ The End ~

What happened to them?

Jim Bridger

In 1865, Bridger served as a guide and U.S. Army scout during the first Powder River Expedition against the Sioux and Cheyenne that were blocking the Bozeman Trail (Red Cloud's War). He was discharged from the Army at Fort Laramie later that year. Suffering from goiter, arthritis, rheumatism, and other health problems, Bridger returned to Westport, Missouri, in 1868. He died on his farm near Kansas on July 17, 1881, at the age of 77.

Kit Carson

Carson was appointed brevet brigadier general and appointed commandant of Fort Garland, Colorado, in the heart of Ute country. Carson had many Ute friends in the area and assisted in government relations, including negotiating with Satanta and other representatives at the Little Arkansas Treaty. He was not present eighteen months later at the Medicine Lodge Treaty when the United States government ignored the Little Arkansas Treaty and took away 90% of Native American lands.

After being mustered out of the Army, Carson took up ranching, eventually settling at Boggsville in Bent County, Colorado. In 1868, at the urging of Washington and the Commissioner of Indian Affairs,

Carson journeyed to Washington, D.C., where he escorted several Ute chiefs to meet with U.S. President Grant, to plead for assistance to their tribe.

Soon after his return, his wife Josefa died after giving birth to their eighth child. Her death was a crushing blow to Carson. He died a month later at age 58 on May 23, 1868, in the presence of Dr. Tilton and his friend Thomas Boggs in the surgeon's quarters at Fort Lyon, Colorado. His last words were, "Goodbye, friends. Adios, compadres." The cause of death was an abdominal aortic aneurysm. His resting place is in Taos, New Mexico.

Samuel Poteet

Samuel Poteet was born in 1820, in Alabama, and spent his boyhood days on a farm. He went west, and in 1848 settled in Jackson County, Missouri. He joined Alexander Majors as a teamster across the plains and became master of a train.

Majors, Russell & Waddell carried government freight to western forts and for many years employed as many as 4,000 men, and the mules and oxen in their trains numbered over 10,000.

After Majors, Russell & Waddell took bankruptcy because of their investment in the disastrous Pony Express, Samuel continued with his own wagon train freighting business. He spent fifteen years at this business and then turned his attention to farming his 600 acres of exceptional land, well improved.

Samuel married Majors' daughter, Rebecca, and had nine children.

Captain Joseph Kinney

Captain Kinney's profits as a "riverboat baron" enabled him to build "Rivercene", a grand mansion and 500-acre estate across the river from

Boonville in New Franklin, Missouri, an architectural gem enshrined in the National Register of Historic Places today. However, after serving as a bed and breakfast inn, the house appears to have been abandoned as of October 2018.

From 1869, Kinney left the river and took up residence at Rivercene, where he concentrated on his steamboat business and other merchandising up and down the river from Boonville. He died in 1892.

Captain A.J. (Bud) Spahr

Captain Bud Spahr was employed as a pilot on the Missouri River for fifty years, first using Captain Kinney's boats and later with the Star Line. He made regular trips from St. Louis to Kansas City, and, for a time, to Fort Benton in Montana, the head of navigation on the Missouri River. It usually required two to three months to make the trip to Fort Benton, and, depending on the current, and the return trip took between eight to ten days.

As a pilot, Captain Spahr received between $600 to $700 per month. The last 25 years of his work on the river were for the government to improve the Missouri River. In 1868, his crew had a skirmish with the Indians in Montana, and again at Fort Peck, where one of his numbers died.

Spahr, who was 6'6" tall, was fond of telling the story of how he brought Sitting Bull and 250 Sioux Indians down the river from Fort Buford to Fort Yates after Sitting Bull's surrender in 1868.

Satanta (White Bear)

On October 14 and 18, 1865, the United States and all of the major Plains Indians tribes, including Satanta, negotiated with representatives of the U.S. government, including his old enemy Kit Carson, and signed the Little Arkansas Treaty.

The white representatives wanted peace, unmolested traffic on the Santa Fe Trail, and limitation of Indian Territory. The Indians demanded unrestricted hunting grounds and reparations for Chivington's massacre of Black Kettle's band at Sand Creek. Treaties made here gave the Indians reservations south of the Arkansas River, excluded them north to the Platte, and proclaimed peace.

The Little Arkansas Treaty is one of the shortest treaties in history. The agreement lasted less than two years, the reservations it created for the Plains Indians were never created at all, and existing reservations were reduced by 90% eighteen months later, in the Medicine Lodge Treaty. By that time, Kit Carson was dead.

Satanta was later arrested, imprisoned, escaped, and recaptured. After he was returned to the state prison in Huntsville, Texas, in 1874, he saw no hope of escape. For a while, he worked on the chain gang that helped to build the M.K. & T. Railway. He became sullen and broken in spirit and gazed through his prison bars for hours, towards the hunting grounds of his people.

Satanta killed himself on October 11, 1878, by diving headlong from a high window of the prison hospital.

Captain Joseph A. Eppstein

Joseph A. Eppstein was born in Germany on January 1, 1824, and was 14 years old when the family came to America. In 1843, he went to St. Louis and, after serving in the 1848 Mexican War, engaged in the Boonville mercantile business with his brother Viet Eppstein until 1860, when he purchased his brother's interest.

The 1860 Cooper County Census revealed that he owned one un-named slave.

When the Civil War broke out in 1861, he organized a company for the Union, every one of whom, with a single exception, was of German birth or ancestry. This company was known as the "Boonville Corps." He then organized a battalion and a company of cavalry, but these were only for local service. He later organized the 6th Battalion Missouri State Guards and, after that, several companies, both cavalry, and infantry.

In 1867, he was elected to the legislature, then served several terms as treasurer of Boonville. He was appointed postmaster, which he held until he died peacefully on March 4, 1886.

Reverend N. M. Painter

Reverend N.M. Painter, from Vicksburg, Mississippi, was installed as the pastor of the Boonville Presbyterian Church in March 1855. Reverend Painter delivered the sermon "The Duty of the Southern Patriot and Christian in the Present Crisis" on Friday, January 4, 1861, a day of national fasting declared by President James Buchanan.

Painter believed that God directed the rise and fall of nations, and attributed the increasing sectional strife to God's punishment for the nation's moral decline. He cited Sabbath-breaking and profanity as examples of the nation's wicked behavior. Painter thought the South, purged of the sinful North, would enjoy God's favor.

He led the national Presbyterian Church split into Confederate and Northern. Reunification did not occur until 1988, using the Boonville's church chalice, the wine cup used in the Christian Eucharist.

Reverend Painter was arrested near the end of the Civil War as a prominent Southern sympathizer, and banished by the Union to Massachusetts.

Mayor Henry E. W. McDearmon

McDearmon was a carpenter and contractor. During the 1850s, he was a partner in Homan & McDearmon. One of their projects, Boonville's Thespian Hall, was considered the "finest home of the theater in mid-Missouri."

Henry served eight terms as mayor of Boonville between 1858 and 1865. He also served as county treasurer from August 3, 1863, through February 7, 1865, and was the town marshal.

Shot about a month before the first battle of Boonville by a friend and Confederate sympathizer, McDearmon's right arm hung limp. After his recovery, he again served as Boonville's mayor and town marshal.

In January 1865, he shot a drunk Union soldier while defending Mary Beck in her confectionary store. The soldier's comrades obtained an arrest warrant. McDearmon fled west for the Rocky Mountains. However, several years later, after being exonerated, he returned to Boonville, where he lived another fifteen years with his son before dying a widower and invalid in 1882.

George Caleb Bingham

Bingham's paintings of American life along the Missouri River exemplify the Luminist style, which soon went out of style. Left to languish in obscurity, Bingham's work was rediscovered in the 1930s. By the time of his bicentennial in 2011, he was considered one of the greatest American painters of the 19th century.

Bingham was a captain in the United States Volunteer Corps, which formed to guard Kansas City. In September 1861, Confederate General Sterling Price marched his troops to Lexington, Missouri, just thirty miles east of Kansas City. Bingham's company engaged in the battle but surrendered. The terms of surrender "included an oath that the Union men never would fight again against the Confederacy," so Bingham was once again a private citizen.

Mr. Bingham's family life was tragic: his first two wives died, several of his children died in infancy, and a surviving son was lost while in his early 20s on a trip to Colorado. Bingham spent many months and much money trying to determine the fate of his son, but never could.

He was appointed state treasurer in January 1862. His salary was $1,750 per year but was raised to $3,000 in 1864, at which time $1,000 per year was appropriated for the pay of bookkeepers and clerks in the treasurer's office.

During the last two years of his life, he taught at the University of Missouri in Columbia. He died of cholera in Kansas City on July 7, 1879, Union Cemetery.

Acknowledgments

It's impossible to create a novel like *Maggie's Revenge* without help, for which I'm grateful.

My good friend professor Russ McGoodwin, provided editorial feedback and spotted elements that I overlooked.

A man of the mountains and dear friend, Nic Patrick, advised about nature scenes.

Nic Borst educated me about various natural poisons found in the southwest, from mushrooms to the excretions of a toad.

Thanks to my "beta" readers, who pointed out that the story began in a different place, thus cutting over 137 pages of a bloated first draft. They were Susan Borst, Jane Butcher, Jerri Hurd, Russ McGoodwin, Tish Winsor, and Nancy Wittemyer.

Joyce Patrick, Melody Conway, and Mike Malloy helped define the story. John Ulmer educated me about mules.

Kelly Smith at *Friends of Historic Boonville* introduced me to archivist Kathleen Conway, who helped identify and locate 1860s homes that Maggie visited, but which no longer exist.

Tish and I spent a delightful day in Boonville with historians Jim Higbie and Pat Hanna. They identified where Union General Lyons debarked with his troops from his steamship on the Missouri River, the road they marched, the battleground, Tracy's Old School House, fortifications, and more. They also shared terrific stories during our delightful time together.

David Brown, my editor at DarlingAxe.com, helped me structure and edit the story. His insights and suggestions were valuable, and he was a great help. Once again, Nick Zelinger of NZ Graphics applied his creativity to the cover and interior design.

And special thanks to Caroline Borst for drawing the maps outlining Maggie's journey from Boonville to Independence, and on her crossing the Santa Fe Trail to the killer's camp.

And my eagle-eyed friend, Dave Downey, caught the very last (I hope) typos in the manuscript.

I value my conversations about writing with Ron Stewart, my friend, and author, who writes under the name *R.J. Stewart*. His novel, *Then Comes a Wind*, is a family saga set in the Sand Hills of Nebraska. His latest work, *Errors of Night*, is a delightful historical novel set in Italy.

Sources

Several of the sources used as background for Maggie's story.

Diaries/Letters

Lizzie Thompson letter, Nov 1, 1864
   Cooper County Historical Society

Letters by Nancy Chapman Jones to her daughter Mary
   Ibid.

Elvira Scott Diary
   State Historical Society of Missouri

General Lyon Letter 1861
   The Mississippi Valley Historical Review
   Vol. 9, No.2 (Sept. 1922), pp. 139-144

Memoirs of Marian Russell Along the Santa Fe Trail
   Land of Enchantment: University of New Mexico Press

Elizabeth Earl letter, Sept 22, 1863
   Quantrill's Raid Lawrence KS
   Civil War on the Western Border
   Kansas City Public Library

The Memoir & Diary of Rebecca Mayer on Her 1852 Honeymoon
   Along the Santa Fe Trail
   Joy Pool, Nation Park Service/SFTA

Diary of a Journey from Boonslick, Missouri to Santa Fe
   Major Alphonse Wetmore
   Missouri Historical Review, Vol. 8
   State Historical Society of Missouri, 1914

Civil War on the Western Border
General Sterling Price
Kansas City Public Library

History of Cooper County, MO
W.F. Johnson
https://archive.org/stream/historyofcooperc00john/historyof-cooperc00john_djvu.txt

Melton's History of Cooper, Missouri
http://thomafamily.org/Mainfile%20Histories/History%20of%20Cooper%20County%2C%20Missouri%20by%20EJ%20Melton.pdf

The Boonville McDearmons, the Civil War Mayor
http://mogenweb.org/cooper/Biographical/HEW_McDearmon/pdf

History of Cooper County, Missouri
Henry C. Levens and Nathaniel M. Drake
From the first visit by White Men, in February, 1804, to the 5th day of July, 1876
Leven & Drake 1876
Perrin & Smith, Steam Book and Job Printers, St. Louis, 1876

Boonville – An Illustrated History
Robert L. Dyer
Pekitanoui Publications, Boonville, Missouri, 1987

Books/Articles/Other

Bereavement hallucinations
"Between 50% and 80% of widows heard voices of the deceased, saw their images, felt their touch, and sometime felt their presence unspecified in any of the senses."
   Rees, 1971 and Weiner et al.
"61% of the widows reported hallucinatory experiences of their deceased spouse."
   Olson, Suddeth, Peterson, Egelhoff, 1985
      Journal of the American Geriatrics Society/ Volume 33, issue 8

The Thin Light of Freedom
   Edward L. Ayers

First Battle of Boonville
   Daily Constitution, Chillicothe, MO

Hiram Young: Black Entrepreneur on the Santa Fe Trail
   William P. O'Brien

The Kiowa Collection: Selections from the Papers of Hugh Lenox Scott
   Library of Congress, World Digital Library

Melton's History of Cooper County, Missouri
   Transcribed by Dorothy Harlan

Civil War on the Western Border
      The Missouri-Kansas Conflict 1854-1865
   Kansas City Public Library

Centralia Massacre, Bloody Bill Anderson
   Ibid.

1860 Cooper County Votes, Missouri's 1860 Election Results
Missouri Division, SCV

Ride Around Missouri: Shelby's Great Raid 1863
Sean McLachlan

Seventy Years on the Frontier
Alexander Majors

The Santa Fe Trail in Missouri
Missouri Heritage Readers, Mary Collins Barile

The Santa Fe Trail: Its History, Legends, and Love
David Dary

The Way to Rainy Mountain
N. Scott Momaday

Wildwood Boys
James Carlos Blake

The Captured
Scott Zesch

Stories of the Old Santa Fe Trail
Col. Henry Inman

Sign Talker, Hugh Lenox Scott Remembers Indian Country
R. Eli Paul

Travel Guide to the Plains Indian Wars
Stan Hoig

Blood and Thunder
Hampton Sides

Over the Santa Fe Trail 1857
William Barclay Napton

Jesse James, Last Rebel of the Civil War
T.J. Stiles

James Bridger
http://historytogo.utah.gov/people/jamesbridger.html

Mountain Man Jim Bridger
http:xroads.virginia.edu/~HYPER/HNS/Mtmen/jimbrid.html

Jim Bridger – United States American History
https://www.u-s-history.com/pages/h316.

War Drums and Wagon Wheels – The story of Russell, Majors and Waddell
Raymond W. and Mary Lund Settle

Arabia Steamboat Museum
400 Grand Boulevard
Kansas City, MO 64106

CPSIA information can be obtained
at www.ICGtesting.com
Printed in the USA
FSHW020822230420
69465FS